VALERIYA SALT is a multi-g
She studied history and earned ai
Petersburg University of Culture
she'd lived for many years in different corners of Eastern
Europe before settling down in the north of England.

Follow Valeriya on Twitter: @LSalt1

DIVE BEYOND ETERNITY

VALERIYA SALT

NORTHODOX PRESS

Northodox Press Ltd
Maiden Greve, Malton,
North Yorkshire, YO17 7BE

This edition 2023

1
First published in Great Britain by
Northodox Press Ltd 2023

ISBN: 9781915179210

This book is set in Caslon Pro Std

This Novel is entirely a work of fiction. The names,
characters and incidents portrayed in it are the work of the
author's imagination. Any resemblance to actual persons,
living or dead, events or localities is entirely coincidental.

In memory of my grandfather,
who fought for his country in the Second World War.

Chapter One
Zara

Boston, U.K.
Present day

The small research vessel rolled and pitched wildly on the storm swell of the North Sea, the horizon disappearing beneath the dull waters. An armada of heavily pregnant clouds advanced from the west, readying their attack, giving no ground to the eternal blue sky, or permitting the sun to penetrate their thick grey armour.

Zara never felt seasick. In fact, the long drive from Portsmouth to Boston, to reach the wreck, exhausted her more than a few hours in the pre-storm sea. She daydreamed that in a previous life, she could've been a mermaid, or a pirate, or maybe a submarine captain.

She squinted, tasting the salty spray on her lips as she observed the mission's progress. The gusting wind punched the small boat, jerking it to and fro in a maddening waltz.

'The dive is taking much longer than I expected.' Anita Patel, the team's sonar specialist, interrupted Zara's thoughts. 'I informed Professor Milne we've never worked with such a large object before, but he insisted.'

'Looks like the storm is approaching much faster than we planned,' Zara mumbled in reply. 'The sea is too rough.'

She also wondered about Professor Milne's strange choice of divers. Instead of summoning the university's usual contractors, he

1

had employed a random company they knew little about.

Perhaps he wanted to keep the mission low profile. Discovering this dark underwater shape, mysteriously buried in a sandbank, sounded like science fiction. And yet the professor had agreed with North Waters Offshore that it could be of interest to the university and had sent Zara to investigate.

'What do you want me to do?' Ms Patel stared at Zara, waiting. 'Do you want me to call off the operation right now or-?'

'How much time do we have?'

'About an hour's worth of oxygen in the divers' tanks.'

Zara fixed her eyes on two monitors, watching the remotely operated vehicle - ROV -transmitting underwater video from the darkness.

For the last hour, the two divers had been trying to clean the layers of sand away from the wreck, using a specialised pressurised air hose. The sonar monitored the location of the wreck over a hundred-foot radius, and there was no mistaking in distinguishing shape of the U-boat. Her three-bladed propeller, small conning tower, periscope, antennae, snorkel, and hydroplanes.

'There's one thing we know for sure - this is a U-boat.' Zara exclaimed shifting her gaze from the sonar to the camera screens and back. 'U-4713/A,' she read the number on the conning tower aloud. 'This is a rather unusual number. 4713/A? Where did you come from?'

'She looks like she left port yesterday,' Anita said. 'Look, the hull's rubber coating is undamaged. No signs of sea life's interference. There's no debris around her either.'

'No signs of torpedo impact or a strike by a mine.' Zara nodded. 'Nor implosion from within.'

'Pete, Ivor... can you get closer to the rock?' the supervisor asked the divers, turning to the screen. 'We need to see the surface where it meets the hull.'

Ivor gave a thumbs-up signal, dragging the pressurised air hose to the rock where it met the submarine.

'Can you see this?' Ivor's slightly accented voice sounded from the radio. His camera moved closer to the hull.

Even in the murky water, Zara and Anita could distinguish no damage to the U-boat.

'It looks like she's growing straight out of the rock! How on earth?' Anita shot an anxious look at her colleague.

'I have no idea, but…' Zara trailed off in thought. 'The only way to know is to glimpse inside,' she said finally. It sounded like a huge favour to ask, far too dangerous, far too risky, and outside of the company's regulations, but it seemed like the only way to clarify her theory.

'I'm sorry, Miss Rose, but I can't put my people at risk,' Anita said. 'Professor Milne agreed that only-'

Zara exhaled. 'I understand. Safety first.'

Anita had made it crystal clear she wasn't ready to sacrifice her divers and the company's equipment for the sake of her crude scientific guess.

The wind whipped Zara's hair over her face, thunder rolled in the distance. 'The storm's approaching. We have to leave.'

Anita nodded and commanded the divers, 'Guys, return to the boat. We're leaving.'

'Give us a minute,' Pete's low voice crackled from the radio. 'I just want to film the conning tower's hatch a bit closer.'

'Can we have a clear image of the propeller, please?' Zara asked the second diver, before turning to Anita. 'Markings on the blades can indicate where the propeller was manufactured and which shipyard assembled the vessel.'

Ivor acknowledged, 'Copy that.'

The two women watched the diver cleared sand from the hatch's handle. The screen blinked into complete darkness.

'Pete?' Anita bellowed. 'Pete, what's going on? Your camera's offline.' She squeezed the radio but heard nothing.

The second camera seemed to have frozen as well.

'A technical issue?' Zara shifted on her feet.

'Pete? Ivor? What's going on? Where's Pete?' Anita almost screamed.

Zara grabbed Anita's shoulder and stared at the screens.

'Ivor? Pete?' Anita repeated, turning the radio's volume to maximum.

'I'm not sure.' Even through the radio's interference, Zara could hear Ivor's panic. 'Pete was right here a second ago-'

The second screen blinked into darkness. The radio fell silent. Only the sound of the approaching storm howled around them.

Chapter Two

Zara

Winchester, U.K.
One week earlier

It was a dream, not Professor Milne's email, that woke her so early. A dreadful vision which had made her cry and groan in bed. She was drowning. The murky, ice-cold water filled her lungs, burning every choked breath. She had seen her father. His strong, muscular arms had pulled her from the chill towards the laser-blue sky. Her father hadn't visited her dreams for a few years, since… The nightmare had been so vivid, so frightening and unsettling that she couldn't return to sleep.

She turned back to her desk, continuing her examination of the unknown object, observing the long, dark shape sticking out of a seafloor.

'Whatever it is, it shouldn't be there,' Zara mumbled to herself. 'The waters are shallow in these fairways. They're far too narrow and dangerous for… anything, actually.'

She continued to search through the images on her laptop screen, zooming in, poring over every picture down to the last detail. The old-fashioned clock in the living room chimed seven. Distracted, Zara shot a tired glance outside, forgetting her investigation.

As expected in late March, Winchester was dull and rainy on that chilly Saturday morning.

At least the professor's email would make for entertaining reading. She poured more coffee into her mug with a chuckle.

The vibration of her phone made her jump and turn away from the screen.

'Hello. Morning,' she mumbled, picking up the call.

'Ah, Zara, I'm sorry if I woke you, but this can't wait,' the familiar, excited voice of Professor Karl Milne sounded in her ear. 'I'm sure you'll be as interested in this as I am. The photos I sent you yesterday? Have you seen them?'

'Yes, I'm going through them right now.'

'I didn't know you were such an early bird.'

'Never mind. I struggle with insomnia sometimes,' she said, switching the subject. 'You surprised me, sending them to my personal email. Shouldn't they go through the university's official inquiry first?'

Professor Milne paused for a second. 'Well, not at the moment. At least, not until we're one hundred per cent sure what it is. That's why I want to hear your opinion before I contact anybody else from our faculty.'

Zara poured more coffee from a glass jar. 'Okay.'

'The pictures aren't the best quality, but the company promised to send me more, and a video filmed by their divers,' he continued. 'The recent storm broke one of their wind turbines, and the company wanted to recover a blade from the water, but-'

'There's something there.'

'North Waters Offshore contacted our faculty because they believe it's a shipwreck. However, I wanted to talk to you first before summoning our team.'

Zara laughed. 'A shipwreck? There? You know better than I, the waters in this area of the North Sea are so shallow and treacherous that only small vessels can navigate safely. This looks enormous.'

'I know, I know, and yet…' The professor took a meaningful pause. 'I'd be extremely grateful if you could check the navigational charts for me.'

'I can do it on Monday, but I can tell you right now that there shouldn't be any ships there. Not World War Two era.' Zara shrugged.

'Thank you, dear.' His smile carried through the phone. 'I'll let you know if NWO sends any more information. I think it could be an interesting addition to your research. If it is, I'd love to see you again in Portsmouth.'

'Ah, that's what it's all about.' Zara beamed. 'The whole shipwreck story is just baiting me back to Portsmouth. You know you're always welcome here if you want to see me.'

'Thank you. I know we can always rely on each other.'

They talked about the weather and the never-ending storms, which had already caused so much damage. Then the conversation turned to Zara's dissertation and other insignificant things, before finally saying a warm goodbye.

'Bizarre!' Zara released a deep sigh, switching off her laptop and heading to the kitchen for breakfast. Milne sounded impatient but excited about the findings, like a child with a new toy. Zara chuckled to herself as the caffeine kicked in. He often romanticised the myth over the facts.

Chapter Three

Zara

Portsmouth, U.K.
One Week Later

'Whatever it is, I've never seen it before.' Zara set her laptop down and reclined in her office chair. 'The water is so murky. I can hardly distinguish anything from these photos. They're no better than the first bunch you sent me a few days ago.' She shrugged, turning to a tall, grey-haired man in his late sixties.

Professor Milne nodded. 'The story with this wind turbine breaking down and losing its blade in the sea doesn't sound unusual, but then the specialists from NWO called. When I talked to them previously, their divers swore to God they saw half a submarine's hull sticking out of the seafloor and covered by a thick deposit of sand. My first thought was about you and your dissertation. That's why I rushed to forward these photos on Saturday morning.'

'I agree, it looks like a part of a hull.' Zara returned to her laptop. Going through the blurry photos, she zoomed in on one of them.

'Looks like a number.' Milne pushed his chair to her desk, taking a seat next to Zara. 'We've studied the class XXIII U-boats to death, all extensively catalogued, including those destroyed during or straight after the war. U-4713 was ordered for commission in 1944, but wasn't ready when the war ended. But I've never heard of U-4713/A.

'What an exciting mystery for you to solve, and an opportunity to enhance your academic portfolio.' He patted her shoulder. 'Imagine if we're right? If the guys from NWO have accidentally found an uncatalogued XXIII-type U-boat and not a half-decayed trade vessel while they were searching for a turbine blade?' His pale grey eyes shone with excitement.

Zara rubbed her chin and shot a concerned look at the photos. The idea still sounded insane. What did they have to prove the professor's theory, apart from these poor-quality photos and the words of some divers who had probably never seen a U-boat in their lives? She checked and rechecked the navigational charts from the war. And, as expected, found nothing.

'I wouldn't jump to conclusions, but if your assumption is correct, where's the rest of the hull?' She pointed to the photo of a dark, elongated mass sticking out of the bedrock. 'It looks as if… half of the object has disappeared inside the rock.'

'Strange.' The professor agreed.

'We need more information.' She sighed. 'I'd need to go there with special equipment and investigate further.'

'March isn't the best season to dive in the North Sea, you know. You're not planning to dive, are you? I don't question your abilities, but the conditions are far too stormy and the sea too murky-'

'In that case, I hope the university will assist me with manpower.' She winked, knowing Milne long enough to predict his reaction. He could use his influence of a dean to help her with everything she required.

'Of course. Just tell me when you're ready to go.' Milne smiled charmingly.

Zara exited the arched doors of the University of Portsmouth's Park Building. It was a sunny day, but the air still held a chill. It seemed like spring was going to be late, with strong winds fetched from the Atlantic. Zara pulled her velvety trench coat tighter and, instead of going back to her car, strolled down King Henry Street. Turning a few times, she reached the greenery of Victoria Park and took a seat on a bench, needing some time to clear her mind.

Despite the cold weather, spring teased the park with its first flowers. Golden streams of daffodils spread in all directions, accompanied by dark purple and creamy-white hellebores. Zara's thoughts were far away from the spring blooms. She'd known Professor Milne for a long time. He'd been an enormous help with her dissertation over the last three years. Closing her eyes, she leaned back against the solid bench, not believing that he would involve his past in the investigation.

'You'd like it, Zara. I'm sure,' Milne's enthusiastic voice sounded in her mind, recalling his last phone call. 'Don't worry about your accommodation. I'll organise something for you near to the university and the city centre. What? Why you? Of course, I have specialists, but none have conducted research on World War Two German naval tactics. I've been studying underwater warfare for the last thirty years, but never had such a chance. It's a once-in-a-lifetime opportunity. I wouldn't miss it if I were you.'

Her mentor was right. Her expertise and interest in the Kriegsmarine, in U-boats, and their so-called "Wolfpacks" – a mass-attack strategy against convoys – could've assisted both with her dissertation and the entire scientific community. Such an unexpected invitation was an honour; she couldn't miss the opportunity to answer all those questions. Could the wreck be of the type-XXIII U-boats? What was her destiny and what was she doing in shallow waters, so close to enemy shores? How had this gone undocumented?

Chapter Four

Zara

Boston, U.K.
Present day

The darkness of the evening coalesced with the seething storm, completely obscuring the harbour. After almost an hour of waiting, the coastguard's rescue mission had brought no results. The police had questioned Zara and Anita about the two missing divers. Zara had spent less than a day there, but it seemed like she'd already traversed the seven circles of hell.

Following a quick shower and her first meal since their pre-dawn breakfast, she could finally rest in her hotel room. She pieced her thoughts together while waiting for Milne's call. She opened her laptop and watched the first video from the ROV that Anita had salvaged before the police arrived. Anita was in deep shit. Zara drew in a long breath before releasing it. She needed to explain to her bosses and the divers' families what had happened. If only they knew the truth.

It was a type-XXIII U-boat, there was no doubt about it. A so-called Elektroboat, a new class of small U-boats, built late in the war and operated from April 1944 until the end. The innovative design of their hull made them ideal for the shallow waters of the North Sea and inspired submarine design for the next two decades. Zara knew them all and could recognise the model with her eyes closed. The same slim-looking hull carried only two torpedoes and no anti-aircraft machine guns on the deck. They had a relatively small conning towers with an uncluttered upper deck and a maximum crew of eighteen. Zara couldn't be mistaken. The strange number: U-4713/A? They'd only built sixty-one vessels of this type in total. So where did this beauty come from? Could it have been some kind of experimental sub? A prototype? The more of the video Zara watched, the more questions it raised.

If it was a prototype, then why had she been out in the open sea and where was her bow? Not to mention the fate of her crew. Throughout her dissertation's research, Zara had become acquainted with the names of all the German U-boat captains who had operated during that period, but she was sure none of them ever commanded the mysterious vessel.

The crew. She swallowed her emotions, imagining almost two dozen young men suffocating or drowning in the icy darkness, trapped in the claustrophobic, cramped U-boat. She probably shouldn't have taken it so close to heart, should've just waved her hand and though "Well deserved, you Nazi bastards!" And yet she couldn't. Germans, British, Russians, Americans. The years of her study and research had made her compassionate and respectful towards these men, regardless of their allegiance. Just sailors following orders. The lives of the crew weren't enough, though. Some seventy years later, U-4713/A required more sacrifice. The two divers had vanished without a trace in the bleak waters of the bay, but Zara would bet their disappearance was no coincidence.

The loud quaking of an incoming video call made her jump on her bed. She stopped the video to answer before Professor Milne's worried face appeared on the screen.

'Sorry, I couldn't call earlier. This damn meeting with the chancellor lasted forever. I didn't even have time to look through the videos you sent me. Now, tell me all the details. What happened, exactly?'

'If only I knew.' She sighed, recalling the events from the very beginning. 'Now, I'm stuck here. If they can't find the divers in the next twelve hours, I'm sure they'll call me and Anita for questioning again. I'm glad the police haven't sent us for a drug and alcohol test after we told them everything, considering how unbelievable it is.'

'Indeed. It's a bizarre sounding story,' the professor said. 'I feel awful. I dragged you into this mess and I should've come with you, but this upcoming external audit at the university…'

Zara shrugged. 'No, it's not your fault. Who could have known? As for the vessel, I need to go there myself. We have no other option but to investigate further.'

'Jesus! Do you want to dive yourself? That's a suicide mission.' Milne arched his bushy eyebrows. 'I won't allow you to risk-'

'I'm afraid it's too late now.'

'Don't go there on your own, at least. You need some help. I know you're not a fan of involving foreign specialists at this stage, however-'

Zara frowned. 'Foreign specialists?'

'Dr Stefan Krause, a naval historian from Kiel. He works for the German Naval Association.'

'Krause, Krause… sounds familiar.'

'It would surprise me if it didn't. Dr Krause specialises in German U-boat technologies. He's written numerous articles on the subject.'

'I think I remember reading a couple of his articles,' Zara said. 'I didn't take them seriously, though. All speculation, nothing more.'

'Some of them sound more like fiction than science, but his latest research on the Elektroboats' prototypes prompted me to contact him regarding our discovery.'

'I'm sure if we manage to recover the sub, or the remaining half, Dr Krause will be the first to put his claim on her and take the vessel to Germany.'

'I know, I know.' Professor Milne waved. 'However, he's a specialist in this field who can shed some light.'

'Is he going to come here?'

'He replied to my email yesterday and sounded rather excited when I called him before I met with the chancellor. He's on holiday now, but he's ready to sacrifice it.'

'Must be desperate for this U-boat.'

'Perhaps he knows something we don't?'

Chapter Five

Zara

All Zara could do was wait. She sat in her hotel for two days, watching the storm pelt her window, waiting for news from the police or Milne's German guest. She didn't waste time, digging deeply into Dr Krause's research.

The doctor had arrived in Portsmouth from Germany the day prior, and after a short meeting with Milne, had rushed straight to Boston. Milne kept Zara posted about their guest's whereabouts and provided Dr Krause with her phone number.

There were no messages from the doctor. She checked her phone for the tenth time and chuckled to herself. Everything was going according to Milne's plan.

On the third morning, she readied herself for the historian in the hotel lobby. Professor Milne had arranged it all, keen for them to collaborate.

Zara enjoyed her late morning coffee, staring out the panoramic window at the raging sea. Spread about the low horizon, she could see a few scattered bands of dark grey clouds, bloated with rain. Another patch approached from the west, hanging almost black, consuming the sky above the hotel.

A large white Volkswagen pulled into the hotel car park. Zara watched the male figure, dressed in a coal-grey coat, exit the car, and make his way to the lobby. He looked exactly as Milne had described him. Tall, in his late thirties, he wore a pair of black-rimmed spectacles.

'Dr Krause?' Zara said, rising from her chair as he entered the lobby. The man nodded with a broad smile. 'Nice to meet you. Welcome to England. I wish the weather and circumstances could've been brighter.'

'Nice to meet you too, Miss Rose.' Dr Krause stretched out a pale hand.

They ordered coffee, and he took his coat off. 'Professor Milne briefly explained what has happened here,' he started. 'I believe I can help you with this investigation.' His laser-blue eyes fixed on her. His accented voice sounded quiet but confident. 'If you read at least one of my latest articles.'

'Well, I must admit your statement about these previously undiscovered prototypes...' Zara couldn't resist a sarcastic remark, recalling a series of articles which claimed that they built two prototypes of XXIII-class U-boats in Hamburg at the end of the war: U-4713/A and U-4713/B. According to the article, they never completed the last boat, but... 'What happened to the first vessel of this new sub-class? What about the captain and the crew?' she inquired. 'I'm sorry, Doctor, it's either me or the article's translator, but the theory has nothing to do with actual history.'

'I understand your doubts.' Dr Krause didn't sound offended, much to her relief. 'As mentioned in the article, U-4713/A went on a secret mission to the North Sea in April 1945, following which contact ceased. She carried only a skeleton crew of six people under the command of Captain Ulrich Schultz. It looks like you've found her some seventy years later.'

'I read the article, but I've never heard of this Captain Schultz. Where did he come from? An officer promoted late in the war? It's highly unlikely, taking into consideration the nature of the mission. What about the other crewmembers? Not a word about them, either.'

'My research is still in progress. That's why I've dropped everything, including my holiday, to come here.' Dr Krause held his ground. He took a large sip of his Americano and continued. 'I've spent almost three years digging into the archives in Kiel, Hamburg, and Berlin, and I couldn't find anything on the crew or their secret mission. As for the name of the captain, I suspect he may have gone under a false identity.'

'But why?'

'Possibly the secrecy of the mission and the project in general.'

'I'm sure Professor Milne has shown you the photos of the U-boat. At the moment, we can only speculate what could cause such damage. Do you think it's somehow connected to her last mission?'

'I'm not a hundred per cent sure it is.' The doctor's eyes shone in the half-light of the lobby. 'Have you ever heard of the Philadelphia Experiment?'

'Of course, but they proved it to be a hoax.' Zara couldn't hold a chuckle.

There was nothing in common between their U-boat and the famous "legend" from the early forties. The U.S. Navy destroyer escort USS Eldridge claimed to have become rendered invisible to the enemy's devices. Based on Albert Einstein's theory of unified electromagnetic and gravitational fields, some self-proclaimed "researchers" declared that such fields would enable the refraction of light around an object so that the object became completely invisible.

'Yes, the Philadelphia Experiment was a hoax, but after everything I've discovered about U-4713/A and after watching the videos and listening to the story about the two divers – I believe this "experiment" had a decent scientific basis, the roots of which stretched as far as Hamburg's U-boat shipyard.' Dr Krause lowered his voice. 'There should be something on this vessel which could confirm my theory.'

Zara swallowed the rest of her lukewarm coffee and stared outside. 'I'd love to show you around the town, but Boston is a rather dull place, especially in this weather,' she said. 'I bet you feel exhausted after such a long trip.'

'I do.' He nodded with a tired half-smile. 'I arrived late in the evening yesterday and was very grateful when Professor Milne agreed to meet me at his office. I could hardly sleep the entire night and had too much disturbing information to digest. An early start from Portsmouth this morning didn't help the matter either.'

'I suggest you check in and get some well-earned rest.' Zara rose from her chair, ready to return to her room. 'We could meet for dinner later and discuss all the arrangements for tomorrow.'

Dr Krause was right. There was too much information for her to think over.

* * *

Back in her room, Zara tried to continue her work, but a gloomy mood had settled on her, supported by the dull weather outside and consecutive nights with poor sleep.

The best thing she could do was follow Dr Krause's example and take a nap for a couple of hours. She switched her laptop off, but the blip of an incoming message on her phone caused her to postpone her plan.

Morning, Zara. Hope your meeting with Dr Krause went well.

Have you watched the latest news? If not, it's worth having a look.

She read Milne's message twice and frowned. Following his advice, she switched the TV on, but as expected, the program was about to finish. Zara opened the local news on her phone. The very first line stated:

A diver, declared missing two days ago off the coast of Lincolnshire, found unconscious on a Cornish beach.

A diver, thought to have died in an accident during a routine dive in the North Sea earlier this week, was found alive on a deserted beach in Cornwall. The diver was one of two missing following the accident, which occurred while attempting to recover a damaged wind turbine. A Cornish fisherman discovered Ivor Kazinski in the early hours of this morning on a deserted beach in Port Isaac. They brought the man to a Port Isaac hospital, who remains in a comatose state. Despite no signs of injury other than a few minor scratches, seawater was present in his lungs during the examination.

Cornwall? How on earth could he reappear hundreds of miles away, on the opposite side of the country? And where was the second diver, Pete? Her first impulse was to share this news with her German counterpart, to admit that his theory might not be as fictional as she had previously considered, but she decided against it. He needed rest. They couldn't do much now. Sooner or later, the U-boat would give up her secrets.

* * *

'I hope you're well rested and ready for tomorrow's dive,' Zara addressed as Dr Krause came into the lobby. 'I suggest we have something to eat and discuss our next steps.'

It was a fresh evening, though the humid air sat like a purring cat on her chest.

'Did you hear the latest news about the missing diver?'

'Yes, Professor Milne sent me the article. Nothing we can do now but wait. Even if Ivor comes out of his coma tomorrow, we won't have our answers for at least a few weeks.'

'We can only rely on ourselves now.'

They walked along the busy high street to the town centre. Despite the storm calming down, the grey clouds promised nothing but bad weather and an early twilight. The icy wind ruffled Dr Krause's black hair, revealing greying temples. Zara wrapped her woollen coat tighter around herself. They settled on a traditional pub off the town square.

'I've heard they do an amazing fish and chips here, if you fancy something authentic,' she said, taking a seat at a long wooden table in the far corner of the pub. 'I'll opt out in favour of a healthier option, though.'

'I quite understand. I've been to England a couple of times before, but could never understand the dish. Fish and potatoes fried in oil. All I can say is yuck!' He chuckled.

Zara couldn't hold back a smirk. 'We'll need our calories for tomorrow's mission.'

'Professor Milne tells me you're an experienced diver. I don't think you need to worry about tomorrow,' Dr Krause said. 'In fact, Milne talked about you with great admiration.'

'I've known him a long time, well before I started my research and dissertation,' she replied carefully.

'So, there's some personal interest there as well?'

'Sort of.' She nodded. 'He has assisted with a lot of my

work. He also found me a placement at the University of Winchester to finish my doctoral dissertation, so he's not only my counterpart and mentor. So, in agreeing to manage this project, I've also agreed to assist an old friend.'

Dr Krause smiled, but asked no further questions.

A waiter brought their meal, and they kept silent for a few minutes, enjoying the local food.

'What brought you into this area of history?' Dr Krause broke the long pause. 'World War Two, submarines, U-boats. It's such a specific topic…'

Zara beamed. 'Exactly. Specific, unusual, and strange. Submarines differ from any other weapon. They're slender, stealthy, deadly ghosts of the sea. Completely untraceable and undetectable; the most elegant hunters of all.'

'Sounds like poetry.' His eyes glinted behind his spectacles. 'However, in reality, they're floating metal coffins, packed with twenty to fifty desperate, sweaty, and agitated men who need to fight for survival every hour, and where the price for a tiny mistake is far too high, not romantic at all. Submarines aren't a chivalrous type of warfare, either. Lurking in the dark waters, hiding somewhere below, crawling along convoys, following an unsuspecting ship and suddenly… boom! "Hello. Here we are!"' He waved in a mocking gesture.

'And yet I prefer the romantic touch.' Zara reclined in her chair. 'My father brought me up like that, always a dreamer. I could've joined the Navy, but I was too indecisive. My mother was against the idea and by then my dad wasn't with us anymore. Unfortunately, I had nobody to support my dream.'

'Sorry to hear that.' Dr Krause bowed his head. 'Was he a submariner?'

His charming smile and deep blue eyes had no effect on her.

The U-boat and all the credit for her discovery belonged to Zara.

'He was a Chief Engineer on a trade container ship, but because of some health issues, he retired much earlier than expected. He went all around Europe and the Atlantic. And from one of his trips, he brought home my mum. She worked for a shipping magnate and was born and raised in Alsace.'

'Oh, you should've said that straight away? Do you speak German? If so, please don't torture me with English,' Dr Krause joked.

'Don't make excuses, Doctor, your English is perfect. I understand a few German phrases, but I prefer English and French. My Mum's half German, she and her relatives always speak French or English.'

'I'm sorry. It was a stupid joke. I didn't mean to offend you.'

Zara just waved. 'Don't apologise. German occupation of Alsace happened seventy-five years ago. My maternal grandfather was an ethnic German, like most people in his town, but he didn't support the regime. He helped the resistance. Now it's your turn? What brought you to the science of submarines?'

'My story is nowhere near as exciting as yours. I dreamt of the Navy and have always been interested in history, but my health issues – asthma and myopia – have left me ashore. Marrying young didn't help matters either.'

'Asthma? Damn! I hope you know what you're doing. Diving with asthma is not a joke, Doctor.' Zara half-jested. She didn't need another half-dead body in a coma. 'I bet your wife wasn't happy when you cancelled your holiday to come here.'

'We divorced many years ago. Our marriage lasted just a few months.' He bit his lips, avoiding direct eye contact. 'As for my asthma, please, don't worry. It doesn't control me.'

Zara shrank down in her wide leather chair. 'I'm… I'm sorry,

Doctor. It looks like it's my turn to apologise,' she started. 'I should've thought before asking such personal questions.'

'It's okay. You didn't know, and I started this conversation. I'll forgive you, but please, call me Stefan.' He winked, his broad smile easing the awkward moment. 'It's much shorter and quicker. Tomorrow, we'll need to communicate at a high pace.'

'You'll have to call me Zara, then.'

Chapter Six

Zara

They set off before the sunrise. Zara had hired a small private vessel moored at a pier on their arrival.

The rescue mission had been called off following Ivor's mysterious reappearance in Cornwall, but Zara still didn't want to attract attention from either the coastguard or the police. And so, they had opted for a smaller boat that Zara could pilot herself. She kept wondering how strange that the wreck had been left unoccupied despite the ongoing police investigation.

The sun shone high in the quiet azure sky, and she thanked God for the bright and clear weather after a week of severe storms.

They loaded the boat with air tanks, diving suits, and other equipment. Zara revved the engine, and the vessel glided through the smooth, murky waters. She had brought her own diving suit, and the doctor had travelled with his gear from Germany. Yet, they would only be able to hire basic cameras and equipment for the mission. Their air tanks wouldn't last more than an hour or so, and the cameras were nowhere near as advanced as the ones Anita Patel had provided for her divers. They had realised they couldn't risk attracting more attention to their research, so had to work with whatever was available.

Zara navigated the boat, shooting Dr Krause worried looks. He had been quiet the entire journey to the dock, hardly saying a word, and replied at random.

'I'm sorry about yesterday's inappropriate questions,' she started after another long pause, sensing the doctor's discomfort after their prior discussion. 'I should've been less intrusive, more tactful.'

'If you mean your questions about my wife and divorce, it means nothing. It doesn't bother me at all. I've left it far behind and want it to stay there.'

Zara felt his stare as she focused on the sea ahead.

'I married in my early twenties,' he continued. 'We were both young and rushed into things, confusing love for attraction and passion. We made mistakes and without love or mutual respect, relationships can't last, at least in my experience.'

Zara glanced at him sympathetically. He wasn't wearing his black-rimmed spectacles today, probably changing them for contact lenses. He looked younger; only his grey temples and sad eyes hinted at his age.

As they reached the spot, Zara cut the engine, and Dr Krause dropped the anchor.

'I'm going to get changed,' Stefan said, picking up his bag and descending into a tiny enclosed cabin.

'I don't want to leave the boat empty. I can go first on my own,' she suggested. 'If I need any help-'

'I appreciate your concern, but I can manage. I won't leave you alone there. As for the boat, the weather is clear. What's the worst that could happen?'

* * *

Ten, fifteen, twenty… Zara counted, descending into the cold and murky infinity of the sea. She could only rely on her watch to gauge the depth. Another couple of meters and finally, the dark mass lurked under her feet, growing from the rock. She hadn't dived often in these waters, preferring the warm, clean currents of the Adriatic or majestic coral beds of the Red Sea, full of colourful flora and fauna, but for an occasion like this, she would suffer any inconvenience.

Stefan seemed determined. His dark, elongated silhouette blurred below.

She caught up as he started to film, moving along the length of the vessel from the propeller to the dark rubber-covered hull, and then up to the conning tower and hatch.

'She's amazingly preserved!' The doctor's excited voice sounded in Zara's headset. 'I can't believe she's lain here for over seventy years.'

'Professor Milne and I couldn't believe our eyes either when we saw the first photos,' she replied. 'She looks even more impressive in real life.' She swam to meet him at the hatch. 'Wait a minute. What's that?' She pointed at the long tube next to the antennae.

'A periscope?'

'I know what it is.' Zara swam around the periscope, couldn't believe her eyes. 'It wasn't here when the divers disappeared. Don't you remember the video? It wasn't here when we filmed it.'

'I don't remember the details, but…' Stefan faltered. 'It's odd. Why would they raise the periscope on this depth?'

'They didn't,' Zara almost yelled. 'The periscope was down.'

'Alright,' Stefan voice's sounded reconciling. 'Now what?'

Zara kept on examining the periscope's column. 'Bizarre as it may sound, but I suspect that the hull is still pressurised.'

'Then, we need special equipment to get inside.'

Zara didn't listen, focusing on the sealed periscope's basement. Her gloved hand ran around the black rubber. 'We may have a chance.' She gave him a thumbs-up. 'The seal is broken.' She pointed at a tiny stream of bubbles, raising from the seal.

'The moment of truth.' Stefan nodded, grabbing the metal valve lacking any signs of corrosion. 'Let's try to open it and look inside.' He clenched the opening valve and attempted to turn it. Zara rushed to assist him, but there was no need as the valve turned freely. The dark throat of the hatch opened to them, releasing a massive cloud of bubbles.

Zara shot a questioning look at the doctor, then peered inside the conning tower. 'Another, internal hatch? Meaning that-'

Stefan shrugged. 'We might be lucky. The conning tower is depressurised now, but there's no water in the hull.'

Without a second thought, he pulled his air tank from his shoulders. Trying to keep his balance, he took a first, uneasy step on the metal ladder, which disappeared to somewhere in the unknown confines of the vessel. Zara followed, squeezing into the hatch with her air tank in hand. Squeezing inside, she shut the first hatch. The tiny dark space between two hatches seemed claustrophobic even to one slim person with an air tank. Stefan opened the second hatch which led him directly to the control room, and he almost slid down the steps with a loud splash of water.

The ultimate darkness and silence swallowed them. Stefan hurried to switch on his torch, and Zara followed his example. The two cold, whitish beams crisscrossed the space.

'Not a hint of water, apart from the water that followed us through the hatch.' Stefan shared his observation. 'How on earth is it possible after all these years?'

'The air is humid, but…' Zara replied, checking her devices. 'The scales confirm oxygen levels are within the norm-'

'Well, there's only one way to check.' Stefan interrupted, and before she had time to protest, he had pulled his diving mask off. 'It's stuffy, smells metallic, of machine oil, damp food, but breathable.' He smiled, inviting her to follow his example.

'No respect for health and safety,' she mumbled, but the idea of breathing through the plastic pipe and wasting the precious air in her tank wasn't attractive either.

They looked around – machines almost filled the entire compartment or hung from the low ceiling. Valves, gauges, and scales of all sizes and colours. The control room looked as if the crew had abandoned it just a few hours ago. A wide periscope column without a hint of rust descended from the ceiling.

'The crew?' Zara exclaimed. 'Where're the bodies?'

'Sou'westers, boots, leather coats.' Stefan nodded to the

weatherproof gear racked in the dark corner of the room. 'Still wet.' He touched the coats.

Zara shrugged. 'Condensation?'

'Let's check the rest of the sub.'

'I can't believe for a moment the main compartment is empty.' The possibility that the entire crew had left the brain of the vessel for a moment was mad and didn't match Zara's understanding of Kriegsmarine policy.

They took a couple of clumsy steps to the connecting compartment, trying not to trip on their fins. A loud bleep of the apparatus made them both jump and turn around. A dim, erubescent light illuminated the U-boat. They could both distinguish the narrow corridor from the engine room on the stern to the crew compartment on the bow where the vessel had met the rock on the seabed.

Stefan swore in German. 'Damn! The emergency light.'

'Should we… eh… go back to the surface?' Zara faltered in the dead silence of the room, surprised by the desperation in her voice.

Stefan took a single shy step into the next compartment. 'No. We'll proceed.'

A tiny room with a sliding door on one side of the aisle represented the radio and communications room. Zara slid the door open. It was empty as expected and only the old-fashioned abandoned equipment identified its purpose.

Stefan touched the narrow wooden desk and the radio headset. His black eyebrows arched. Even in the dim light of the sub, Zara could see sudden sadness in his eyes.

She frowned. 'What's wrong?'

'I'm fine, fine. Just wondering why there's no dust.'

'Please, tell me we're both hallucinating.'

'We'll see.' Stefan nodded to his camera, still filming their every step.

Built into the walls were two rows of slim bunks; too small, even for a skinny teenager. And yet these were the only place where the crewmembers could rest between watches, normally sharing one bunk between two sailors. The crew quarters preceded an even more cramped galley with minimal appliances. They passed the mess and reached the only onboard "luxury" of the captain's quarters: a separate space with a bunk, a folding working desk, locker, and a single chair, screwed to the floor. The setup of this U-boat wasn't much different from the numerous U-boats Zara had investigated, and yet the bizarre feeling of a presence didn't leave her.

She stepped into the claustrophobic galley. 'God! There's barely any space here to make a cup of tea, let alone cook a proper meal for eighteen or twenty men three times a day,' she mumbled, picking up a lemon from the floor. 'Look. It's still fresh.' She showed it to her confused peer.

He pointed to the rectangular loafs in the far corner. 'Bread looks pretty fresh as well. No mould on it at all.'

'I haven't noticed food storage anywhere else aboard,' Zara said. 'The provisions here aren't enough to feed an entire crew for months.'

Stefan shrugged. 'Or they didn't indent for a long journey.'

'How long did it take to get to the North Sea, even for an extremely fast U-boat, do you think?'

Stefan bit his lower lip, 'Maybe they relied on supply U-boats?'

Leaving the galley, the two proceeded further down the dim corridor, stretching into dark infinity.

'How on earth..?' Stefan's trembling voice sounded from the next room.

Zara came closer, peeping past Stefan's shoulder, and froze on the spot. The bow of the vessel, where the two loading torpedo tubes should have been, had disappeared completely. Instead, the dark, rugged mass of the bedrock stared back at them.

'Look here,' he continued. 'It's incredible.' His gloved hand ran slowly across the metal surface, where it seemed to turn to stone. 'It looks as if the rock has tried to swallow the vessel, but choked on her.'

'There's no damage to the metal, not a scratch. As if the walls of the boat were gradually turning into stone,' Zara agreed, touching the place where the wall galvanized with the rock.

Stefan stepped back, allowing his camera to catch the surreal bizarreness of the picture.

'Let's go to the stern. I need a better look at the engines,' he suggested after a pause.

The two made their way to the stern, back through the mess, the captain's quarters, and the control room, passing the same compartments again.

'Ah, I didn't notice it at first. The toilet.' Zara chuckled, nodding to the tiny facility.

'Better known amongst sailors as a head or a shithouse.' Stefan smirked. 'Wait. What is this smell?' He sniffed the air and opened the toilet's door wider.

'Dirty pi… ehm… people!' Zara covered her nose with her palm, shooting a glance at the metal toilet's pot. 'This is a proper chemical weapon here. Weren't they taught to flush after themselves?' She pointed at the detailed instruction displayed on the wall beside the toilet.

'I regret opening it now. The whole sub will stink.' Stefan slammed the door shut. 'Wait a second.' He stared at her. 'How could they have abandoned her here over seventy years ago-?'

'It's fresh, it has to be.'

'It must be a joke. There must be some logical explanation for it. Are you sure nobody has entered the sub before us?'

'And why would somebody do that? Risk their lives just to use a seventy-year-old U-boat's toilet?'

'I don't know,' Stefan almost shouted. 'Do you prefer to believe a German crewmember did it here seventy years ago?'

Zara didn't reply and proceeded to the next compartment.

The engine room was a narrow cave where the mighty engine

filled cramped space from floor to rounded ceiling. It crouched like a giant caged animal, leaving no corner unused. Cold-water pumps, lubrication and fuel pumps, pressed-air cylinders with manometers, thermometers, gauges, and scales in an array of colours and sizes, presenting every likely kind of indication. At first glance, everything looked normal and intact. The noisy giant had been asleep for three-quarters of a century.

'What's that?' Stefan attracted her attention to a smaller machine she hadn't noticed at first. 'Auxiliary engine? Why did they need it here?'

Zara took a few steps closer, examining the unknown piece of machinery. The idea of Elektroboats was lightweight and high velocity, guaranteed by a minimal arsenal of weaponry and a smaller engine compared to conventional U-boats. The same question was circling in her mind. Why did this U-boat need a smaller secondary engine?

'What are these pipes and scales?' Stefan continued to muse aloud, examining his new finding more closely. 'Wait a minute, it's a…'

He pulled something which looked like a small door handle, and half of the metal panel swung open, revealing the engine's entrails. Something in the bowls of the engine split the light like a prism.

'Jesus! I've not seen anything like it before,' he exhaled.

Zara had to admit she felt lost in the nest of pipes and wires which filled the body of the engine. But one element, in particular, stood out straight away. A foot-long glass cylinder sealed with metal disks at either end. Multicoloured wires connected the disk to the rest of the engine. Inspecting, she noticed some scales engraved on both disks, something which looked like an axis with coordinates. The content of the cylinder was truly mesmerizing. It was full of a strange, multicoloured liquid. A tiny black sphere, a barely visible dot, fluctuated in the centre, suspended between two silvery spirals.

Stefan mumbled something in German, staring at the mysterious device.

'Stefan?' Zara touched his arm. 'Are you okay?'

'Yes. I just need to tell you something.' He squeezed her shoulders, his bright eyes shining in the red light of the room. 'This device confirms my theory. This is the last piece of a puzzle I've been trying to solve for the last few years.'

'Puzzle?' she asked, taking a step away from him. What was he hiding?

He opened his mouth, ready to reply, but before he could, the red light flickered and darkness flooded her sight.

'What's that?' Zara whispered in shock. 'What's going-?' The last words stuck in her throat as she glanced at the device.

The rainbow-coloured liquid turned almost black. The black dot grew larger between two spirals, filling the entire cylinder.

'Stefan!' She shouted, pointing to the device.

Intense white light dazzled her. Zara levitated, suspended in the electrified air. Squinting between the flickering lights. When she opened her eyes, Stefan was gone. The room was unrecognisable. It looked more like a control room than an engine compartment now. A thick, white smoke surrounded her. The smoke was as dense as looking through the murky waters of the North Sea. Unable to focus on anything, yet, she could observe the entire compartment in three-hundred and sixty degrees, without needing to turn. The muted hum of the engine resonated through the dim light.

A tall male figure materialised from another compartment. His face blurred and yet Zara recognised his Kriegsmarine officer's uniform without difficulty. His voice sounded silent and unnaturally slow, as if somebody had turned down the speed of the recording, but she distinguished a couple of words in German.

'Schneller, schneller! Alle Männer zu den Kampfstationen.'

The man was approaching Zara, and she realised he didn't see her. She opened her mouth in a soundless scream as the officer passed through her like she wasn't even there. The painfully bright light made her close her eyes again. When she opened them, the light was dim, but this time, the image was in focus. Her normal vision had returned. Sounds, previously muted and distorted, now seemed too loud.

Glancing around, Zara realised she stood in the middle of a concrete tunnel some fifty to sixty feet high. Its dark walls were almost invisible behind the lines of arm-thick cables, wires, and pipes. The thudding noise of some heavy machinery, the clang of tools, metal on metal, the high-pitched buzzing of high-voltage electricity running through the cables.

What was this place? An underground factory? A dry dock? She noticed a narrow miniature railway track, leading deeper into the tunnel's throat, used by miners to transport coal and other minerals.

She was walking along the track when a shadow materialised from the darkness ahead of her. The light blinked, crackling and ready to extinguish. A cold draft of air ran along the tunnel, fetching the smell of strong chemicals, forced Zara to cough. The light subsided, and for a few seconds, she couldn't see a thing.

With a bright flash, a male figure morphed in front of her. Dressed in greasy overalls and a high-visibility jacket, the man looked painfully familiar.

'Father?!' Zara screamed, recognising his deep, dark eyes and neatly trimmed beard in the dimly lit space.

He looked some twenty, twenty-five years younger than she remembered him, but the similarity was unmistakable.

The man dropped the wrench he held in his hand and ran.

Zara screamed again, following him into the depth of the tunnel. 'Dad? Dad! Stop! Please… Where are you going? Why are you running? Please, wait.' She screamed. Tears ran down her cheeks, stinging her eyes.

The tunnel seemed like it had no end. The humming and

other colliding sounds made her almost deaf. She tripped a couple of times but kept running. The quicker she ran, the farther the figure moved away from her.

The air became unbearably hot. It sounded as if some gigantic beast inhaled and exhaled heavily.

The figure had disappeared behind the next turn, and Zara found herself in front of a crossroad with a wide square pillar of concrete in its centre. Wrapped in thick cables and wires, the pillar glowed with an electrical current passing through it.

Where had he gone? And what was she supposed to do now? Zara panicked, noticing another shadow form the silhouette of a man in a black SS tunic with an officer's cap.

He appeared from nowhere, materialising from the darkness of the tunnel. She tried to distinguish his features, but it was too dark. She stared at him unblinking, but his features seemed ever-shifting. Was he young or old? Large or slim? She couldn't say. Just a ghostly spirit in an abandoned industrial purgatory.

'Who are you?' She finally asked, wiping her tears, surprised how loud her voice sounded, reverberating all across the tunnel.

The shadow grinned. His dazzling, disturbing white smile was so out of place with the grey-brown surrounding. His black cap sat low on his head; his eyes undiscernible.

'Der Meister.' He grinned even wider.

With a metallic clang, a sliding door opened in the centre of the pillar. Der Meister made an inviting gesture.

'What's there?' Zara frowned. 'Behind this door?'

'Schmerz und Wiedergeburt.'

'Pain and rebirth?' Zara mumbled.

The man just kept on grinning, gesturing to the door.

What if her dad was there? Zara took a step closer but saw only pitch-black oblivion behind.

Der Meister's smile never rested. His face warping into a motionless, featureless mask.

Zara took a step inside, an unknown force pulling her

farther in. The metal door slammed shut behind her. A minute of complete darkness followed by another. Only the familiar monotonous humming of a six-cylinder diesel engine surrounded her. The thought came from nowhere.

The white light flashed again, and an immense hall with a vaulted ceiling revealed itself to her. She twisted around, taking in the vista. Human-size glass pods stretched along the walls, spanning from floor to ceiling as far as she could see. A system of wires, cables, and metal pipes gurgled and hissed.

Zara moved closer to the nearest pod. A disembodied scream rippled through her like a shockwave. Through the thick glass, she could see a creature: half-human, half-machine. Its pale grey naked body looked fossilised. The spine protruded through its paper-like skin so much that Zara could distinguish every single vertebra and joint of cartilage.

She was unable to perceive whether the creature was a male or a female, nor did its fetus-like position in the pod reveal any clues to Zara. Long, thick needles protruded out of its bald head, connected to pipes in its nose, a snout-like maw grafted on into a pipe. Or was the creature wearing some kind of mask? Despite its closed eyes, the scene left no doubt the creature was alive. Deformed and deteriorated, it looked like a surreal, psychotic, and nightmarish H. R. Giger painting.

She moved from one pod to another in silent horror. The sound of the engines resonated louder and louder.

She swallowed a surge of nausea. Were they charging the engine or did the engine keep them alive?

Some twenty paces in front of her, she noticed a concrete pad in the centre of the walkway. A black amorphous sack hung from the ceiling above it. She could have sworn it wasn't there when she entered the hall. Coming closer, the sack revealed itself to be covered in pulsating veins and yellowish slime, beating like a phantom organ.

The engines stopped abruptly, and the sack burst. With a loud wet splash and a slap of disgorged flesh, the naked body of a man hit the concrete pad. His fetal form was nubile yet athletic, covered in a placental slime. Its skin vibrated a halogen-white glow, highlighting his platinum-blond hair.

Zara couldn't help but compare this creature to an angel descending into this biomechanical hell.

With a supersonic bang, the hall submerged into darkness.

* * *

Zara landed on the metal floor of the engine room. Next to her, Stefan crouched, squeezing his shoulder.

'God! What's happened?' Zara screamed.

'I have no idea,' he yelled, still pressing his hand to his injured shoulder. 'Christ! I banged my arm when I landed.'

'Did you experience something? The dazzling light, the milky air around, all sounds muted. Did you see the officer? The tunnel and the SS officer? The pods? Is it connected to the cylindrical device somehow?'

Stefan rose from the floor, summoning the strength to say something, but a sudden thud made them both jump. The entire structure of the U-boat vibrated erratically. The engine awoke, gauges flickering back to life, and in a second, the whole compartment filled with a deafening noise.

'What is that?!' Zara shrieked.

'It seems like we're surfacing,' Stefan mumbled, nodding to a pressure gauge.

With a sharp hissing and gurgling, the compressed air streamed in.

'The tanks are blown. It's not a dream. We're emerging.' Stefan yelled, but Zara didn't need further explanation.

'The air compressors. This valve here!' Stefan continued, trying to shut down the deafening hammering of the engine. 'The bow. Look, it's back.' He pointed into the dim interior of the vessel, where Zara could distinguish the rows of bunks and torpedo tubes.

She clutched the valve. 'Damn! Go to the control room. Somebody needs to guide her. Otherwise, we'll crash into the rock or worse, flip on our bow.' He wanted to protest, but she pushed him in the back. 'I'll be fine here. Just go.'

Taking off his fins, Stefan rushed to the control room.

The metal floor plates jerked and yawned, the boat reclining some thirty degrees forward.

'She's bow-heavy.' Zara swallowed her shock, staring at the surrounding pipes and buoyancy cells. 'Blow them all,' she shouted to Stefan over the intercom. 'Hell! It should be at least three crewmembers here. Three strong men, working in the engine room. I'm slaving on my own.' She gritted her teeth, squeezing the valve and turning it until her knuckles went white. Salty sweat covered her forehead.

Slowly, the floor leveled. The vessel stabilised on her keel. The diesel exhaust gases forced the water out of the buoyancy cells.

'All blown. Engine full stop.' She could hear Stefan's voice again, this time screaming in exultation. 'Great job, Chief Engineer Rose.'

The gauge arrows were jerking, crawling backwards, but the engine had slowed to a stop.

'Has she stopped completely?' Zara stared at the scales.

The roaring, oily giant stood quiet now. All sounds subsiding.

'It looks that way. Your father would be proud of you, I'm sure.' Stefan nodded with a wink, emerging from the dark depths of the compartment. 'Let's look outside.'

They threw the hatch open and emerged from the bowels of the U-boat.

'What?! What time is it?' Zara glanced at her watch, which seemed to have stopped.

The sun hung low above the horizon, the last rays of daylight painted the sky pink and pale orange. The dusk was about to cover the smooth, dark waters. A few heavy cumulus clouds with fluffy tops and flat bellies covered half of the sky, shadowing the slim body and the dark conning tower of the submarine.

'My watch has stopped. We can't have spent more than thirty minutes onboard.' Stefan sounded confused.

'But it's late evening now. It looks like we've spent over eight hours there.' Zara's head was spinning, and not only on account of the stuffy air of the vessel. 'Doctor… Stefan, please! Tell me what the hell happened to you?' She clutched his shoulders, staring into his eyes, but he carefully took her hand.

'Please, Zara, try to calm down.' His soft voice relaxed her. 'I don't have all the explanations right now, and I'm as scared as you. The first thing we need to do is to get to our boat and call for help. We can't leave the vessel in the middle of the sea. The coastguard needs to organise a tug and moor her in Boston for the time being. Ideally, we need her in a dry dock, but I don't think they have one here.'

'The nearest dry dock would be in Hull, about two hours' drive north.' She loosened her grip on Stefan and let him go. 'I don't like the idea of calling the coastguard. You know exactly what will happen next, don't you?'

'The Navy's involvement-'

'Involvement?' Zara repeated with a wry smirk. 'They'll tug her to the port and organise twenty-four-hour security, guarding her against everybody, including us. Until the Navy's thorough search is done, nobody will have access to her, trust me.'

'I'm afraid we have no choice. Eventually, the Navy will search her. The question is: how much can we learn before the Navy confiscates her?'

'The captain's log,' Zara suggested. 'The onboard journals and war logs should document their last journey. What about the navigation charts? They should shine some light on what happened to the boat and how she ended up here.'

'You're right, we haven't checked them,' Stefan agreed. Before she could object, he opened the hatch and disappeared into the reddish interior.

Zara hesitated for a second. The last thing she wanted was to go back inside. Before she could decide, Stefan reappeared on the conning tower.

'Nothing,' he proclaimed, disappointment on his pale face. 'The captain's locker is empty, and so is the chart chest. No documents or belongings, everything's gone.'

'Strange. I didn't notice any personal items of the crew at all. What about a code book? They would've recorded all communication between U-boats on patrol and orders from the Headquarters there.'

'Nowhere to be seen.' Stefan shook his head. 'I've checked a couple of officers' lockers. They're empty as well. All their possessions vanished.'

'What about the escape gear? We haven't inspected it?'

'Untouched. The crew wasn't in a hurry. It looks as if-'

'As if the men were well-prepared for their departure.'

'Let's reach our boat and call the coastguard.' Stefan sighed. 'Nothing much we can do here now.'

After the coastguard had picked them from the sea and the U-boat had been towed to the shore under Naval supervision, Zara and Stefan finally returned to the hotel, struggling to digest the situation they had been landed.

Chapter Seven

Zara

Zara and Stefan spent the rest of the evening in the hotel lobby. Zara, still shaking, ordered coffee. They kept silent, submerged too deeply into their thoughts.

'Tomorrow, this place will be crawling with reporters and national television, hungry for a story.' Stefan broke the silence. 'We can't allow it to happen. We need permission from the Naval High Command, from the Harbour Master Office, maybe even the Prime Minister… from whomever to access the vessel again.'

'That's why I've contacted Professor Milne. He'll pull a few strings and quell the media storm, at least for the time being. I hope he'll be able to help us with access to the boat as well.' Zara sighed, staring into the darkness of the night where a fresh storm front was brewing. 'He should be here any minute, said he'd been visiting his friends in Lincoln. It should take him about an hour.'

'It's Saturday today. Far too late, he won't be able to help us. I don't think it was the right thing to call him.'

Zara shrugged. 'The mission was his idea.'

'Zara, this device… it's extremely dangerous.' Stefan touched her sleeve slightly as she turned to him. 'The more people know about it, the higher the risk. Let's hope the Navy's disarming unit doesn't begin their investigation until tomorrow morning, or in the best-case scenario, until she's secured in the dry dock. The device… I wanted to tell you something, but all this happened so quickly,' he struggled, voice lowered.

'Yes, you said something about the device, about the puzzle, and then that blackout…'

'I know it sounds crazy and you won't believe me, yet what happened to us today proves the rest of my theory.' He faltered before continuing, 'the cylindrical object attached to the engine is a part of the project Die Fledermaus or The Bat. Simply abbreviated to DF. Another example of the Nazi Wunderwaffe.'

'Why have I never heard of this project?'

She was well aware of the Wunderwaffe, a Nazi idea of a so-called "Miracle Weapon," which could've helped Germany win the war: from the notorious V2, the first ballistic missile, to the mysterious Bell, a flying object that could theoretically change gravitational fields and take off vertically. World War Two historians had rigorously studied these projects in all their details, but Die Fledermaus was something new.

'I discovered it by chance in one of Berlin's archives, researching the 4713 prototypes of U-boats. Remember when we discussed the Philadelphia Experiment? In the thirties and early forties, the German scientists were working on a nuclear weapon, producing so-called heavy water – one of the key ingredients for a nuclear reactor.'

'I know about German factories in Norway and the Allies' attempts to sabotage them during the war, but-'

'Yes, but heavy water was just a part of the story.' The doctor didn't let her finish. 'Experimenting with different nuclear fuel, the scientists discovered something else, significantly more powerful than any bomb. They called it black matter. A highly unstable, weightless, and undecaying particle which could change its charge.'

'I've heard about anti-matter and dark matter, but black matter…' Zara glanced at him in disbelief. 'How does it connect to our U-boat?'

'The scientists knew little about its properties. They couldn't even sustain it to study any further, so at first, it seemed to me they lost their interest in it. Not for long, though. In an archive in Hamburg, I discovered some documents, some correspondence, just a few letters going back and forth between SS-Oberführer Dr Gerhard Stromm and Admiral Karl Dönitz. The letters purported Dr Stromm, a prominent physicist, tried to persuade the Admiralty to use an experimental device on some of his Elektroboats.

'The device required a lot of energy to gain momentum, so the auxiliary engine served this purpose. Although the scientist didn't go into technical detail or the characteristics of the object, I believe it was Die Fledermaus. That's why the 4713/A prototype appeared. They needed a slightly modified version of the XXIII class.'

'If so, how does black matter fit in with all this?'

'I believe it's a key ingredient,' Stefan replied. 'What happened to the U-boat's crew, the divers, and us results from Die Fledermaus' black matter device.'

Zara listened, unable to say a word. Had the stress of the day influenced his common sense? What's next? Abduction by aliens?

'So, what exactly happened to all of us?' she asked.

He sighed. 'I'm not sure. Based on what I researched and what we both experienced aboard, I believe the black matter is comparable to a photon, a particle of light. It's massless, it doesn't decay, and time doesn't exist for it,' he continued.

Zara shifted in her wide chair, but didn't interrupt.

'Because it has no mass, but emits an enormous amount of energy, black matter can easily exceed the speed of light.'

'Is it possible?' Her brain desperately tried to scramble any knowledge and half-remembered lectures of Einstein's theory of relativity, but her long-forgotten school lessons helped little. 'Wouldn't it create a black hole?'

'No. For a black hole, we need a huge amount of mass in an infinitely small space, which would constantly increase, and then would become infinite. The black matter is massless, but because its velocity exceeds the speed of light, it's capable of creating a singularity – a point where time becomes infinite.'

'What? So, you're saying the U-boat travelled through time? Like in Star Trek or something?'

'No. Not like in Star Trek or any other sci-fi film.' Stefan smiled a warm, reassuring smile. 'Though the idea of teleportation is pretty similar to DF. According to the archive's files, black matter turns any matter it interacts with into black matter. However, this process is reversible. No object or living being would've survived such a speed, so black matter splits all particles, turning them into black matter, then reassembles them.'

'Wait a minute. Does it mean that the U-boat looks so well-preserved because… time has stopped for her? Her hull was growing out of the rock, because-?'

'Most likely, because DF malfunctioned, and the part of the hull became embedded into the rock,' Stefan continued. 'However, time hasn't stopped. It became infinite. Black matter interacts with the space-time continuum in a way that allows it to detach time from space, creating the time singularity where the past and the future don't exist or, better to say, they're equal and intertwined.'

'I suppose it explains my vision of two crewmen and…' she sighed. 'My father.'

'Exactly,' he agreed. 'That moment, the moment of blackout. The device switched on again. You saw the past, but it wasn't time travel, because roughly speaking, at that moment, time ceased.'

'But the tunnel? The underground factory? The bodies in the pods? What was all that about?'

'Who knows?' Stefan shrugged. 'I know very little about the device, even less about black matter and its interpretation of time. Maybe it was one of the pasts which, in fact, never happened? I can only speculate.'

'If you're right, and the device doesn't work properly, it means that the crewmembers and our diver, they… what?'

'It has permanently suspended the crew in time.' Stefan finished her thought. 'Ivor was lucky to return, and so were we.'

Zara shivered. She kept silent for a couple of minutes, staring at the stormy darkness outside.

'U-4713/A's secret mission was to test DF.' The doctor paused. 'They retrofitted the Elektroboat for this new type of weapon. Their closed-circuit engine, which required no air intake and could run when submerged, provided not only higher speed but also-'

Zara nodded. 'Yes, an opportunity to charge the device when submerged, without involving batteries.'

'They were stealthy,' Stefan continued. 'Powerful enough to agitate black matter. And carried fewer people as a ship or even a conventional U-boat, so if something went terribly wrong-'

'Nobody would've noticed. Admiral Dönitz was obsessed with his "Wolfpacks". He believed Germany would have won the war if they hadn't spent so much money, time, effort, and people building all those massive mega-ships like Tirpitz or Bismarck.'

'He wasn't far from the truth, though. The "Wolfpacks" became the Allies' worst nightmare at the beginning of the war. Now, imagine if DF had succeeded? There would've been no Allied fleet left. All U-boat crews wouldn't have needed to know the routes of enemies' ships or Allied U-boats. They wouldn't have needed the Enigma machine to send and receive encrypted messages.'

'Then, the Nazis could've used the same technology to transport weaponry, vehicles, troops, supplies, and pretty much everything to any part of the world. I presume these scales are at the top and the bottom of the cylinder to set coordinates, to direct the black matter how, when, and where to reassemble,' Zara mused.

'Probably.' Stefan shrugged. 'You understand now how dangerous this device is. It's even more dangerous because it's faulty, and we don't know how to stop it. We need to gather a symposium of physicists, chemists, and engineers; specialists who're savvier in this subject than you and I. And we need to do it fast.'

Zara tried to add something, but saw the lobby doors open. A familiar tall figure in a beige coat walked towards her.

'Zara, Dr Krause.' Professor Milne greeted his colleagues. 'God! I'm glad you're safe. Sorry for the lateness. I left Lincoln as soon as I got your message.' He touched Zara's shoulder slightly. 'But this damn road accident slowed the traffic. Now, I want to hear everything, all the details.'

After a firm handshake with Stefan, the professor took his coat off and perched in the vacant chair.

'Coffee, Professor?' Stefan suggested. 'Although I'm sure you'll need something stronger after listening to our adventures,' he added with a crooked smile.

'No, no. I'm fine. Let's move straight to business.'

Supporting and adding to their stories, Zara and Stefan relayed what had happened. Professor Milne listened without interruption, and only arched his eyebrows from time to time in surprise.

'I need to see it myself,' he concluded.

'Now? It's almost eleven o'clock,' Zara gestured to a round, minimalist-looking clock on the wall. 'Besides, the Navy and the coastguard have the boat. I'm afraid they won't allow you anywhere near her.'

'You're right.' He nodded, hand tapping on the armrest. 'It's too late, and the weather isn't great for a stroll along the sea. We'll go first thing in the morning, but I can tell you now, this device is some kind of adjustment to the auxiliary engine to increase productivity and reduce the fuel intake.'

'I know our evidence sounds bizarre, Professor.' Stefan shook his head. 'How do you explain our blackout? What about the crew? The still missing diver?'

'My digital watch has stopped, and so has Dr Krause's mechanical watch. And some unknown force had freed the submarine from the rock,' Zara said, supporting Stefan.

'Surely, I haven't been there with you, and of course, I don't have all the answers right now. Most likely, what has happened to you is some kind of pressure and temperature-induced stroke. It has affected your consciousness and perception of time. As for your watch, you might've broken it when you tried to break into the sub.'

'What about the emerging U-boat, her pristine condition, and the crew?' Stefan held his ground.

'You told me you were filming the whole dive on your camera. Instead of arguing, shall we have a look at it?'

Chapter Eight

Zara

'I don't understand.' Stefan shifted his gaze from the professor to Zara and back. 'The camera battery is completely dead,' he continued, examining his camera.

The tiny screen was black, and the feed connected to his laptop showed nothing but an empty file.

'Well, the empty battery explains why there wasn't any video.' Milne shrugged. 'Most likely, you forgot to charge it last night.'

'No. The camera worked. I saw it filming.' Zara shook her head. 'I can't believe our evidence has just vanished.' She squeezed her head with her hands, gathering the mass of amber-brown hair in a high ponytail.

'Dear colleagues, please.' The professor made a wide gesture. 'We're serious scientists, not conspiracy theorists chasing some Flying Dutchman. We need to build our research on real, concrete historical data. I understand you both went through a lot today. Tomorrow, we'll inspect the vessel together. I'm sure we'll find out that all your stories about ghosts, time travel, and the secret super weapon have a less exciting but more realistic explanation. Now, we all need to rest.' With that said, he wished Stefan a good night and left the room.

Stefan and Zara exchanged looks.

'I'll try to talk to him.' She touched his sleeve. 'Professor Milne is right about one thing. We'll need to stay focused tomorrow. Please, try to get some sleep.'

Zara caught up with Milne in the long hotel corridor.

'Professor, I need to talk to you.'

'Please, Zara, can it wait until morning? I can imagine how stressed you feel right now, but all you can do is go to your room and relax.'

'Why don't you believe us? Why did you invite me and Dr Krause to investigate this case if you don't trust our expertise?'

'I'm really worried about you. If you feel unwell again, if you notice something strange, if you see unknown people in your room, speaking in German, let me know, and I'll drive you to the nearest hospital.'

She swallowed her frustration at the harsh dismissal, but clearly, Milne wouldn't spend more time arguing. He turned around and disappeared around the corner.

* * *

Zara washed her face with hot water and stared in the bathroom mirror. An exhausted, pale reflection stared back. She desperately needed a rest. She sighed, about to step into the shower cubicle, when the light dimmed in the bathroom, flashing a couple of times as if a candle going out.

The cold mirror steamed up, turning Zara's reflection into a misty shadow. The light flickered back to life.

She heard a dreamy bleep, bleep, bleep... the ambient sound of a submarine's sonar pulse.

Zara turned, shooting a look in the mirror. Those eyes... those bottomless, ice-blue eyes bore into her through the fog. She screamed, and the vision vanished.

'What the hell is going on with me?' she mumbled, backing away from the mirror.

Her first instinct was to call Stefan and Professor Milne, but what could they do? Besides, the professor was sceptical about their experience. This time, he would have her put on psychiatric watch.

'I'm just stressed. Nothing more. After our adventure, it's no wonder I'm seeing things,' she mumbled, turning on the shower to maximum, drown out the intrusive thoughts. Milne was right. She was a scientist, not a paranormal investigator. She needed to pull herself together.

After a hot shower and a change into her cosy pyjamas, her body relaxed, and she snuggled on her king-size hotel bed with a book. The soppy romance she'd been reading for a while should've made her sleepy. She opened the book, but struggled to focus. She tried to analyse the events of the day again and again. What if the low oxygen level and constant change of pressure had caused..?

A light knock at the door made her jump and put aside the book. She got up and glanced through the peephole.

'Stefan, can I help you?' She opened the door, wrapped in her dressing gown.

'Oh, I'm sorry if I woke you. I know I'm a bit too late,' he mumbled, closing the door behind him. 'I just need to ask you something.'

Dressed in a plain white T-shirt, navy-blue hoodie, and velvety trousers, the doctor looked like he was ready for bed as well, but something had made him change his mind at the last minute.

'I was going to read a bit before bed, but… please, come in, take a seat. Can I offer you a drink?' She fussed around the coffee table with a kettle and a tray of assorted teas and coffees.

'Thank you, I'm fine.' He sank into a wide chair in the corner. 'I know my question will sound strange and perhaps even out of place. I remember you told me about your great relationship with Professor Milne, however…' He sighed, visibly struggling. 'Can you trust him?'

'What makes you think otherwise?'

'It was Professor Milne who first called me. He asked me to take part in this research, but now-'

'Oh, I see. You're upset because Milne dismissed your story, our story. To be honest, I feel a little disheartened, too. Tomorrow, I hope we'll have the chance to prove we're right.'

'Tomorrow. If only we had so much time.' Stefan stared into space. 'The volume of black matter in that device is more than enough to send the whole of Lincolnshire to hell, not just the U-boat.'

'You mean that little, fiddly black dot in the middle of the cylinder?'

'Yes, if we can see it with our bare eyes, it emits a huge amount of energy.'

'Is it dangerous?'

'No. At least while it doesn't interact with the normal matter,' He chuckled nervously. 'But the power of black matter is devastating, and we have no means of controlling it. At the moment, it seems to be suspended between the two metal spirals. There's some strong gravitational or electromagnetic field which keeps it in place, but who knows how long it'll be there?'

'How this field works?' she asked.

'If only I knew.' Stefan released a deep sigh. 'I don't want to stir the pot or break your friendship with Professor Milne, but it seems to me he knows more than he's telling us. What I have to figure out now is where he got this information.'

Zara didn't know what to answer. The professor's reaction had hit her hard, so how could she trust Dr Krause, whom she'd only met two days prior?

'I'd better go.' He rose from the chair and rushed to the door. 'Ah, good choice.' He nodded to her book on the bedside table. 'I'm sure handsome knights and hot-headed princesses will guarantee a good, deep sleep.'

She shrugged, too tired to argue. 'What did you expect me to read? U-boats' technical manuals or the memoirs of Admiral Dönitz? Life exists outside research, you know.'

'I hope we'll solve this mystery as soon as possible. I can't wait to return to normality. Good night. See you tomorrow.' Stefan opened the door, ready to leave, but turned slightly, their eyes meeting.

She saw confusion and hesitation in his eyes, as if they knew so much more than he was letting on. There was also deep warmth to them. Or was that just wishful-thinking?

'Stefan, if you have something to say, just say it, please. Say it now. I don't want to be caught unaware again.'

'Good night, Zara,' he said, stepping into the deserted corridor.

'I read the Admiral's memoirs,' Zara added from the doorway, Stefan's tall figure about to disappear around the corner. 'They had no mentions of Die Fledermaus.'

He nodded and continued his way.

Chapter Nine

Professor Milne

After check-in, Milne unpacked his case, thinking of everything his colleagues had told him. Careful of being spotted, he made his way downstairs and back to his car. To his relief, the reception and carpark were empty, except for a few deserted vehicles. The beastly storm raged, howling and smashing at his car's windows, but the professor only beamed his lopsided smile. Even the weather was on his side.

When he reached the gates of the port, he flashed ID to a security guard. He stopped the engine when a familiar short figure, dressed in a high-vis vest and helmet, approached, slouching under powerful punches of wind and rain.

'You're late.' The man was in his late-thirties with fine features and jet-black eyes.

'I'm sorry. I needed to deal with a few issues.' Milne didn't want to admit his delay was due to Zara. 'Have you brought them?'

The man nodded to a black case by his hip.

The professor frowned. 'That's it? Are you sure these batteries are powerful enough to hold black matter in place for long?'

'You can trust me with it. I've always been more technically savvy than you.' A broad smile illuminated his companion's face.

'I hope so, Captain.'

He knew it made no sense to quarrel with Ethan. Besides, they didn't have time for disputes.

'Let's have a look at your fancy device,' Ethan mumbled into the raging storm.

They rushed to a jetty where the silhouette of the U-boat towered above the dark waters. Ethan waved to a security guard and nodded to Milne. 'He's with me.'

The guard saluted absently and wrapped himself tighter in his waterproof military jacket, without looking at his captain's companion.

'Be careful on the hull. It's slippery.' Ethan warned Milne when the two ascended the U-boat.

Milne clutched the conning tower ladder while Ethan opened the hatch and gestured, inviting him inside. With Ethan's help, Milne slipped from the metal ladder to the control room.

'Amazing! Just like Zara and Stefan described her.' Milne held his breath for a second, mesmerised by the pristine condition of the compartment. 'Not a hint of rust. All machines and stations are as intact as they were over seventy years ago.' His torch glided across the room's rounded walls and ceiling.

'Come on. We haven't time to explore.' Ethan put his hand on Milne's shoulder. 'Let's go.'

They followed the dark corridor all the way through to the engine room.

'Here it is.' Milne nodded to the auxiliary engine and opened the little door protecting Die Fledermaus.

'That's it?' Ethan seemed unimpressed, but Milne just nodded. 'Let me deal with it.' The captain took a couple of steps closer, pulling on protective gloves. He opened his case, arranging his tools.

'Ah! Please, be careful. Remember what happened to the two poor divers? If my dear colleagues are right… well, I don't want to share their fate.'

'Please, be quiet for a second and let me detach your precious device?' Ethan said, unmoving, focusing on the multicoloured wires linking the glass cylinder to the engine. 'It's more complicated than it looks.'

Milne bit his tongue and watched the captain as he fussed over the device.

His thoughts turned to Stefan. Milne knew from the start it was risky to invite the German to assist the investigation, but Stefan was the most renowned subject's specialist, after all. He'd recognised the weapon straight away. Zara wouldn't have been able to do it on her own. But how had Stefan learned about the device? Well, it hardly mattered now. The main thing was that Stefan and Zara had found the U-boat, discovered the device, and identified them. The German would serve as a pleasant distraction for Zara, as easily lead as she was. Milne chuckled to himself. He could read her like a book.

'Here you go.' The captain pulled Milne out of his reverie, nodding at the glowing cylinder in the case. The cylinder remained attached to the two rectangular metal boxes. 'As I've already told you, these batteries are powerful enough to keep the fields stable for up to twenty-four hours. After that, you either need to change them or-'

'Don't worry. That's enough time for me and Die Fledermaus.'

'I still don't understand why you want to do it,' Ethan mumbled, closing the case, and heading out of the engine compartment. 'If this thing's as great as you told me, you could've used it yourself. After all-'

Milne put his hand on Ethan's shoulder. 'You have no idea what this tiny black dot can do. I've heard and read enough about it to understand that this is just the tip of the iceberg. What those two divers experienced, what Zara and Stefan experienced... It's just a fraction of what Die Fledermaus is capable of. It shouldn't belong to any individual or group, or country, and I'll ensure that it doesn't.'

'And if it makes you rich, even better, I suppose,' Ethan interrupted with a smirk.

'Do you want your cut or not?'

'Of course.'

'Then cease your questions, keep the case, and wait for further instructions.'

'What?! If this device is as hazardous as you claim, I don't want it anywhere near-'

Milne passed by without even looking at him, making his way back to the control room. 'Honestly, Ethan, sometimes I doubt that you're my son,' he called on the way to the ladder.

'You'd better ask Mother about it, but I'm sure she'll tell you to piss off,' Ethan snapped, following his father along the corridor. 'To be fair, I'll support her with this one.'

'I can't trust the people I'm dealing with.' Milne turned to him. 'If something happens to me and the deal fails, at least you and the device will be safe for the time being, and time is the most crucial thing right now.'

Ethan said nothing, only watched Milne ascend the ladder. On the surface, the rain had ceased, and the storm had abated. The two men kept a stubborn silence.

'Zara,' Ethan broke the prolonged pause. 'You said she was in danger.'

'Ah, don't worry. The girl is in excellent hands now.' Milne waved. 'She's getting along well with our German colleague.'

Ethan pursed his lips and, without a word, headed to the ladder.

Chapter Ten

Zara

How on earth, after such a stressful day, had she slept through the alarm? Her night had been dreamless, and she'd awoken exhausted. After a quick shower, she headed straight for breakfast in the hope her peers were still waiting. The breakfast service almost finished; the cafe was empty apart from the staff cleaning tables ahead of the lunch service. To her surprise, Stefan was still finishing his coffee, alone and staring out the window.

'Morning! I'm sorry I've overslept,' she started. 'Where's Professor Milne? I thought you might've had breakfast together?'

'Good morning.' Stefan nodded; a bit confused. 'I haven't seen him yet. I thought the same about you, or perhaps he's still in bed.'

'Strange. He's usually an early bird.'

'I'd advise you to have your breakfast first.' Stefan gestured to the half-empty trays of porridge, omelette, sausages, and other assorted morning specials, which waiters were about to carry back to the kitchen. 'We could visit Professor Milne after you finish. I'm sure he won't go anywhere without us.'

'Ah, I'll just grab coffee and a croissant.' She stood, heading to the coffee machine. 'It's almost nine. We can't waste time,' she added, returning with a plate of porridge and a cappuccino.

Stefan didn't object, just focused on his phone. Following his example, Zara scrolled through her emails and text messages. She had a missed call and a text from Milne at quarter to six.

'Everything okay?' Stefan frowned.

'Professor Milne tried to contact me early in the morning, but I was asleep. He left a message.'

'What does it say?'

She turned her phone to Stefan so that he could read:

Morning, Zara. Apologies for such an unexpected turn, but I've returned to Portsmouth on an urgent matter. My wife is in hospital. It looks like she had a stroke overnight. I'll let you know as soon as her condition stabilises.

Stefan nodded. 'Just when we needed him the most.'

'I don't want to disturb him with calls or messages. I hope his wife's better soon, and he'll rejoin us. We'll need to return to the U-boat alone. A second chance to film everything, and figure out how to detach the device from the engine safely,' Zara said. 'Though I doubt the Navy will grant us access so easily.'

'They won't. We'll need to persuade them to let us board, accompanied by a Navy representative. And when we do, we'll need to know with certainty how much time we have before the field holding black matter collapses.'

* * *

They drove to the Boston port where the Navy had quarantined the U-boat. The sun dazzling them from the endless Lincolnshire sky, but even the sun couldn't burn through Zara's gloom. Things had been slowly slipping out of her control from the first when she'd agreed to lead the bizarre investigation. Now, instead of solving this enigma, they were drowning deeper and deeper in the mystery. What if their visions had just been hallucinations, after all? Milne hadn't made their investigation easier with his absence. And perhaps Stefan was right not to trust him. Who could she trust?

Meanwhile, Stefan found a place to park and cut the engine. 'It's busier than it was yesterday. Surely, that can't be a good sign.' He frowned, stepping out of the car.

Zara followed, heading to the dock where the conning tower of the U-boat rose from the murky, smooth waters.

'The Navy's doubled their watch. They've turned the whole place into a temporary military base,' she said, noticing the military personnel fussing around the vessel.

She wanted to say something else, but a slim male figure stood out from the group of naval personnel, coming closer to the historians.

'Captain Ethan Milne.' The man in uniform nodded in greeting. 'Dr Krause, I suppose,' he continued, turning Stefan without acknowledging Zara.

'Well, yes. What's going on here?' Stefan mumbled.

Zara couldn't believe her eyes. 'Ethan? What are you doing here?' The last person she'd expected to see was a man from her past.

Stefan shifted a confused gaze from Zara to the captain and back. 'Ethan? Ehm. Do you know each other?'

'Please, Miss Rose, let's keep it professional.' Ethan's eyes shot her a strict look. 'I'm here on behalf of the Royal Navy High Command.' With that said, he unfolded a document and proffered it to the confused pair. 'As you probably know, the U-boat is the property of the Royal Navy now. I'm here to arrange her transportation to the nearest dry dock.'

'I understand that, Captain, but this vessel is of enormous historical and scientific value,' Stefan protested. 'Can we at least-?'

'This vessel carries a significant risk because of the weapons and torpedoes aboard. There may be remains of crewmembers too. If so, the weapons should be safely removed and disarmed. And any bodies, or whatever remains of them, returned to the German authorities. This is a task for the Navy, not for a museum.' His thin lips stretch in a mocking half-grin.

'You should know better than us, there're no torpedoes aboard,' Zara almost yelled. 'We're in the process of studying the sub. You can't take her from us now.'

'I'm afraid I can.' Ethan waved the folded document in front of her. 'If you want to challenge this decision, your university should write directly to my superiors. For the time being…' He turned to Stefan. 'She's mine.'

'Bullshit!' Zara hissed, but Ethan turned back to his crew and stevedores.

Zara and Stefan watched the two tugs approaching the sub, turning around, ready to pull the dark, slender structure from the port back to the open sea and then to Hull.

They kept silent on their way back to the town. Zara stared out the car window, in deep shock, unable to find the right words to break the silence. Stefan looked annoyed and unwilling to talk.

'I think I deserve some explanation.' He exhaled without looking at Zara. 'Captain Milne. A relative of Professor Milne, I'm guessing. Sorry, Zara, but I don't believe in coincidence. You have a past with him.'

Zara exhaled with a bitter smile. 'Unfortunately, I know him very well.'

Chapter Eleven

Stefan

'Captain Milne didn't look worried about his mother's health.' Stefan smirked, sitting in the armchair in Zara's hotel room.

She offered Stefan a drink to avoid any undue interest from hotel guests or the lobby staff.

'It seems like the only thing he was interested in was the U-boat,' Stefan added.

'This is where all the issues start,' Zara turned, shaking her head. She rose from her chair, approaching the coffee table and switched the kettle on. 'Professor Milne's wife isn't Ethan's mother. His parents divorced after his older sister died,' she continued, preparing the tea. 'Ethan blamed his father for everything wrong with his childhood. He thought Milne loved his sister more than him. And later, blamed his father for his parent's divorce and his career failures. But more pertinent to our conversation, he hasn't fully recovered from his father taking my side after our break-up.'

Stefan said nothing. What was there to say? These memories were clearly painful, but he needed to know the truth about Milne. Now, every insignificant detail could help. 'Ah.' He started finally, piecing things together. 'So that's why the professor continues to support you?'

'He's treated me like a daughter since Ethan introduced us.' A bitter smile crossed her face. 'Which explains Ethan's annoyance and jealousy. Imagining his father loves me more than him because Milne sees something of his daughter in me. Just one of Ethan's endless delusions.'

'That's why you separated?'

'Oh, there was more to it.' She waved. 'We'd been together for almost three years, but we were never ready for a serious relationship.' She sighed, taking a few steps closer to the window, avoiding direct eye contact with Stefan.

Stefan realised she needed some space. She needed an opportunity to share these painful moments of her past with somebody, somebody who was not too close to give advice or judge.

'Ethan has always blamed other people for his failures, but never accepted his responsibilities. Blaming Milne for his childhood, his commanders for their rigid hierarchy, his colleagues for impeding promotion, and me… well, probably, for building a successful career. At some point, we realised our feelings had faded. But Ethan seems to have gotten his long-expected promotion to captain.'

Listening to Zara, Stefan wondered what had attracted her to Ethan Milne. Ethan's long face and fine features, a series of slightly neurotic gestures, and abrupt manners reminded Stefan of a scavenger. Kapitän Frettchen. Captain Ferret.

'I wonder how quickly he and his crew arrived here,' Stefan commented instead. 'The coastguard said nothing about the Navy yesterday.'

'I know what you're going to say. But we can't call Professor Milne or disturb him now when he's with his wife. We need to take the risk and deal with Captain Milne and the Navy ourselves. Or follow the sub to Hull and somehow gain access.'

'You want to break through the cordon and deal with the device yourself?'

'We can't wait until the university and the Navy exchange angry official letters.' She shrugged, her normal confidence and composure resurfacing. 'When Professor Milne returns-'

'If only he does,' Stefan said sotto voce.

'Why are you so suspicious of him suddenly?'

Stefan swallowed his annoyance, knowing they didn't have

time for secrets. 'I have evidence which leads me to believe Professor Milne knew about Die Fledermaus long before our investigation started, showing the professor was in touch with one of the U-boat's crewmembers.'

Chapter Twelve

Stefan

Berlin, Germany
Two years earlier

Stefan shyly knocked the door.

'Come in,' a fragile voice responded, and he entered the room.

Small but tidy, the room had minimal furniture adjusted for the needs of its occupant. A traditional room in a care home, specifically designed to ease their residents into their final years.

'Guten Morgen, Herr Dix,' Stefan greeted an elderly wheelchair-bound gentleman. 'My name is Doctor Stefan Krause. I'm a historian. Your daughter has contacted me on your behalf.'

'Ah, Guten Morgen. Come in, Doctor.' Walter Dix bowed his balding head lower. 'Please, take a seat.'

Stefan took off his jacket and took the chair, ready to listen. The old man's faded, watery eyes challenged him for a few seconds. Stefan wondered whether Herr Dix remembered the reason he came to visit him.

'Your daughter informed me in her email that you served in the Kriegsmarine as a Junior Radio Officer in Hamburg in 1945.' He broke the prolonged pause.

'I read your recent articles, Doctor, about U-4713/A.' Herr Dix squinted slightly. 'I thought my experience of service on this type of submarine could be useful in your research.'

'Did you serve on U-4713/A at some point?' Stefan frowned, discerning whether the octogenarian was telling the truth or whether it was merely a product of the man's dementia, and he was wasting his time.

'I was there in April 1945 when she made her last journey to the North Sea. A crew of six.'

'Six? That wouldn't be enough, even for a skeleton crew. How did you manage the watch?'

'We were testing some top-secret weapon. The watch? With this device aboard, we didn't need to bother about it. The boat either ran submerged or…' His weak shoulders dropped. 'We "jumped".'

'Die Fledermaus…?' Stefan faltered.

'Ah. You know more about the boat than you've let on in your articles, don't you?' His host smiled a laboured smile. 'The words of an old man cost nothing for such a high-profile researcher like you. I understand that. However, I think this may confirm some of your theories.' With that said, Herr Dix opened his desk's top drawer and retrieved an old, thick journal. 'These are my memoirs, so to speak. They start with my transfer to Hamburg in 1944 until… well, my unexpected appearance in Berlin in 1946,' he continued, handing the journal to Stefan.

'Thank you. Any documents of this period have enormous value,' Stefan mumbled, still unable to understand what Herr Dix was hinting towards. 'What exactly happened to you and the rest of the crew? I presumed there were no survivors. What was the U-boat's last mission?'

'A better question would've been what was the mission of our Captain, Ulrich Schultz. The U-boat was still going through some tests, but our commanders blindly followed the insane orders of madmen in Berlin who foolishly believed in a miracle weapon. All except Captain Schultz.'

Dix closed his eyes for a second and released a deep sigh. Not wanting to rush his host, Stefan kept silent.

'He was a strict, secretive, ruthless commander in his late twenties. Those days, submariners rose quickly through the ranks. I'm sure you know it as well as I do.' Lips trembling, Herr Dix continued his story. 'I was only seventeen, so my appointment for such an important position surprised and excited me. But I wasn't ready to die. Only, I wanted to prove my worth to my captain and peers.'

'So, what was Schultz's plan?'

'He planned to escape using the device. As for the U-boat and her crew, he wanted to get rid of us to cover his tracks.'

'And how did you find out about his plan?'

'The night before our last patrol, I stayed on board later, trying to fix some minor issues with the radio. Despite the orders from the High Command to rush all U-boats back to sea as soon as possible, our captain was particular about any insignificant flaw in the equipment.

'I had almost finished and was about to leave when I realised I wasn't alone. I heard two low voices in deep discussion in the captain's quarters. I recognised them as the Captain and First Watch Officer, Hermann Thiel. I found it strange that the officers preferred to come aboard so late at night, but paid little attention to their conversation, being more interested in drinking with my friends and having a good sleep in a proper bed before the voyage.'

'How did they execute their plan? And what about the rest of the crew?' Stefan asked.

'I told you, Doctor, they planned on getting rid of us.' Tears shone in the man's pale eyes. 'Nothing would've stopped Captain Schultz and his henchman, Thiel. I knew the First Watch Officer for his cruelty. Rumours had spread about his criminal past, and yet he must've had serious support within the High Command, a close relative or a friend. He was my superior officer, and I had to obey his orders, so made no mind of rumours.

'The next day, the U-boat left the base, heading to British waters. I was in my radio room, listening for the Allied boats and ships, when two gunshots ripped through the monotonous humming of the slow-running engine. I jumped from my seat and rushed to the engine room.

'I saw our motorman, lying face down on the floor of the compartment, then the figure of the First Watch Officer emerged from behind the hatch. The black barrel of his gun pointed at my head.

'Acting on instinct, I kicked him between the legs and pushed him out of the engine room, hurrying to close the hatch. I avoided death, but sealed myself inside the engine room. The scene lasted about five seconds, but I remember it in vivid details.' The old sailor stopped, wrinkled hands clenched on the armrests of his wheelchair.

Stefan leant closer, touching the sailor's fragile shoulder. 'I'm sorry to revisit these painful memories. I think I'd better leave you to rest and read the end of the story from your journal.'

'I invited you here.' Herr Dix shook his head. 'You haven't heard the strangest part of the story yet. When I was alone in the locked engine room, I saw the body of our Chief Engineer in the corner, shot in the back of the head. I heard the angry voices of Thiel and Schultz from behind the hatch, struggling to open it. Back then, I didn't understand what was going on and why the two officers intended to kill the whole crew. Recalling the facts much later, I've realised it was a part of their plan.'

'How did you escape the locked engine room?'

'Die Fledermaus was my only option to escape.'

'I assumed only the superior officers knew how to operate the device.'

'Yes. Only the Captain, the First Watch Officer, and the Chief Engineer were trained in the machine's use. The Chief Engineer lay dead in front of me, and the remaining officers intended to break into the compartment to silence me. What was I supposed to do?' The old man made a wide gesture. 'I had to take the risk. I saw how the Chief Engineer used the device a couple of times, so I checked the auxiliary engine, turned the disks, and opened Pandora's box.' He stopped and reclined in his wheelchair.

'So, what happened next?'

'Time appeared to freeze. Schultz and Thiel broke into the engine room. All at once, I saw Thiel shoot the motorman and the chief engineer. Then I pictured myself in my radio room the day before and saw Schultz examining a Polish pilot's jacket. My past collided with my future and…' His lips trembled, tears running down his creased cheeks. 'Faces of people I'd never met, perhaps even yours, though I don't remember certainly now. I found myself in a hospital in the middle of the night. They told me I had appeared unconscious the previous day on the doorstep of a random house in Berlin. I awoke on April 10th… 1946.'

'You travelled through time.' Stefan shook his head. 'Die Fledermaus is a time machine?'

'I'm no scientist, Doctor. Just a simple radio operator.' Herr Dix wiped his tears with a pocket handkerchief and gained some composure. 'I don't think it was possible to use the device to traverse time, definitely not travel into the past. Or at least, not before they built Die Fledermaus.'

Stefan nodded. 'Otherwise, the Nazis would've travelled back and-'

'They didn't design the device for travel through time. They designed her to travel through space. What happened to me was some kind of malfunction. By the end of the day, I couldn't even use it.'

'But the Captain and the First Watch Officer knew. Who can say if their plan worked, and they escaped, disguised as… Polish pilots? And what happened to the sixth sailor?'

'Schultz got rid of the navigator in the control room, while his peer massacred the others in the engine compartment.' Herr Dix released a heavy sigh. 'Most likely, their initial plan worked, and the two murderers resurfaced in Britain.'

'Captain Schultz was in his late twenties in 1945, and Officer Thiel? About the same age? If so, they must be in their late nineties now,' Stefan mused, more to himself. 'Even if they survived, I can't see them–'

'For the last thirty-five years, I've been searching for the truth.' Herr Dix interrupted. 'All I want is to bring these two to justice for their crimes. I couldn't talk to anybody about my mission, as you might understand. Even my family, my wife and daughter, didn't believe me. They said my story was a mix of fearful imaginings and the drugs doctors gave to the soldiers and sailors during the war to keep them awake. My search for the two officers or, at least, somebody who could identify their whereabouts post-war has led nowhere.'

'Which is why you invited me here?'

'Yes. I want you to find if these people are still alive. Their crimes should never have gone unpunished. And, ultimately, I want you to find the U-boat or whatever remains of her and disarm Die Fledermaus.' He stared directly at Stefan. 'Trust me, son, this is the most dangerous weapon humanity has ever dealt with.'

Chapter Thirteen

Stefan

Boston, U.K.
Present day

'So? Did you follow Mr Dix's lead and approached the crews' relatives?' Zara asked when Stefan finished his story.

'I couldn't find anything about Captain Shultz. It seems like it was just one of the many aliases he assumed during and after the war.' Stefan shrugged, disguising his eyes from Zara. 'Besides, if the mission were top-secret, they would've destroyed all related documents, including the crew's identities, at the end of the war.'

'What about First Watch Officer Thiel? An officer with a criminal record aboard an experimental U-boat?' She shook her head. 'I doubt Admiral Dönitz would've allowed that to happen. Submariners had always been his crowning glory, the pride of the German fleet, knights of the sea.'

'It's 1945 we're talking about. The U-boat fleet suffered the highest rate of human causality. I don't think Dönitz had the luxury of picking his men anymore. Besides, if Walter Dix was right and Thiel had some powerful benefactors in the High Command or-'

'Thiel might've been acquainted with Die Fledermaus's creator, Dr Gerhard Stromm?'

'There's no mention of it anywhere. Maybe Thiel's criminal past was just a rumour. His service history isn't different from many other submariners. He started the war in a steamer and rose through the ranks. In 1943, after a short training period, he joined a U-boat crew. His records are unremarkable. Nothing to cling to.

'As for his family, the only relative whom I tracked down was his niece. She was about five or six in 1945. After the war, her family immigrated to Switzerland. Most likely, she married and changed her surname. Either way, I don't think she can shed any light on her uncle's business. After a few weeks of studying Walter Dix's journal, I asked to meet him again in case he recalled more details about the last voyage of U-4713/A. But unfortunately, Herr Dix died a week before my second visit.'

'What a shame.' Zara nodded. 'I hope he didn't suffer.'

'I hope so, too. I've sent a card with my condolences to his daughter. She said her father passed peacefully. She also gave me her permission to use his memoirs in my future publications.'

Zara said nothing, just stared at him for a few seconds, but Stefan couldn't bear her gaze.

'So, you're telling me not to trust Milne, and yet you were hiding something from me? How can I trust you?' she asked with resignation. 'How can we work together, if any time we struggle, you peel away another layer of the onion?'

'I'm sorry, Zara,' he started, but she interrupted him.

'How does Milne fit into all this? Do you care to say, if Captain Schultz or Officer Thiel or both of them had survived, he might've learned their version of the story and... God! It was never about the U-boat. It was all about the device. Why does he need it?'

'I don't know yet.' Stefan shook his head. 'Whoever has Die Fledermaus has full control over time and space.'

'Anything else I should know about the U-boat?' She made an annoyed gesture, clearly provoking him for another apology.

'I've told you everything I knew about her.' Stefan rose from his chair, heading to the door. 'I think we both need some time to digest what happened to us in the morning. It makes no sense to go to Hull right now.' She needed some time for herself. This meeting with her ex-boyfriend upset and unsettled her even more.

'I'm fine. I don't need a rest.'

An impatient knock at the door interrupted her. They exchanged worried looks.

He volunteered. 'I'll open it.'

'Good afternoon, Dr Krause.' A tall woman in her late fifties greeted him from the doorstep. 'I hope I didn't interrupt your meeting.'

Without invitation, the lady entered the room. Short brownish hair, a long black coat, and thin, stubborn lips without a hint of lipstick – Stefan recognised the newcomer straight away. She was the last person he wanted to see right now.

'Good afternoon, Miss Rose. May I...?' The woman gestured to a chair and took a seat, without waiting for Zara's reply.

'Who are you? How do you know our names?' Zara didn't react to the woman's greeting, shifting her confused look from Stefan to the stranger and back.

'My name is Patricia Cartwright,' the lady said, taking off her gloves and unwinding a wide monochrome scarf. 'I'm a Chief of Operations for the National Security Unit. My department is conducting a joined operation with MI5.' She waved her ID in front of the two.

'The National Crime Agency,' Zara read aloud. 'But why are you here? We've done nothing wrong?'

'Nothing wrong personally. At least, not yet,' Cartwright agreed. 'But your mentor, Professor Karl Milne, is a subject of interest.'

She stared at Zara for a few seconds, as if trying to understand what affect her words had produced. Stefan kept silent until his turn to answer.

'Professor Milne? It must be a mistake. He's a prominent

historian, respected in scientific circles. He works for one of the biggest universities in the country. I'm sure he has nothing to do with any crime. If you mean the missing diver-'

'Please, Zara, take a seat.' The woman gestured to another chair. 'Doctor.' She nodded to a still silent Stefan, inviting him to join their conversation. 'Our meeting is unofficial. That's why I came to you myself. I need your help with Milne and the device.'

'What?!' Zara demanded. 'Did you follow us all this time? What's the NCA's interest in the World War Two relic?'

'I think you know better. Die Fledermaus is much more than just an archaeological discovery. Professor Milne is well aware of it too. At the moment, he's at a hotel in central London, trying to sell the device. My team has been following his movements. With the help of Dr Krause, we attached a tracking device to the professor's car.' She nodded to Stefan. 'My IT team is tracking his mobile phone.'

'Are you..? God! How many lies have you told me?' Zara jumped from her chair, eyes burning into Stefan. 'Who even are you?'

'Please, Miss Rose, pull yourself together.' The woman made an impatient gesture. 'Dr Krause has nothing to do with the agency. He's simply agreed to advise my team during this investigation. I contacted him straight after he had a video call with Professor Milne. I explained to him the whole situation and asked for his help in identifying the device.'

'This is true,' Stefan replied with a nod.

'So, would you spend a couple of minutes of your precious time to explain the whole situation to me as well?' Zara snapped, retaking her seat.

'That's exactly what I'm trying to do.' Agent Cartwright didn't react. 'I must admit we've found out about Professor Milne's shady business accidentally tracking down some dodgy solicitor on the dark web. We had enough on this guy to put him behind bars for a long time. However, the agency will monitor him for the time being, aiming to catch a much bigger fish. The tactic worked. Professor Milne or, better to say, his solicitor contacted our subject about two weeks ago.'

'When North Waters Offshore informed us about their unusual finding,' Zara mumbled. 'What makes you think Professor Milne is involved in some dodgy deals on the dark web? Even if so, why would he use a third party, making a long chain even longer?'

'Well, because he's not technically savvy and afraid to be arrested the next minute he appears online. Perhaps he prefers an old-fashioned way of leading business. Or he doesn't want potential buyers to know his real identity.' The agent shrugged. 'Either way, the two solicitors have been discussing the details of the deal, payments, and the main thing, the device for the last few days, calling it just "the cloak".

'My worse suspicions have confirmed when the scientist contacted his German counterpart and asked for help, and then the news about the two missing divers went viral on TV and the Internet. I've conducted some research, digging deeply into the war years' classified files, and found out a few mentions of some mysterious cloaking device which Nazi Germany supposedly created at the end of the war. More speculations and hints, scattered across several sources. So, when I read Dr Krause's publications about a new type of U-boats and their top-secret mission, I asked him for a favour to be our eyes and ears in Boston. It seems like Professor Milne has taken a risky manoeuvre by sending his son for the U-boat and distracting you from the device, while he meets his customer's solicitor in London to sell Die Fledermaus and receive his money.'

Zara bit her lips. 'So, are you saying that Professor Milne visited the vessel last night and stole the device? The story with the Navy's involvement was just a hoax to make us chase the already empty submarine all over the coast?'

'The Navy's involvement is genuine. After all, the boat should remain under its jurisdiction until confirmed safe to step aboard,' the woman said. 'Here, Milne has killed not two, but three birds with one stone. After stealing the device from the U-boat, he gained some time to deliver it to London. He distracted you from his business, whereas your boyfriend took his revenge.'

'If you mean Captain Milne, he has nothing to do with me,' Zara snapped. 'Your intelligence isn't quite up-to-date.'

'Maybe so, but your romantic relationship is the last thing that bothers me right now.' Cartwright nodded. 'What I care about is the apprehension of Professor Milne, his solicitor, and his buyer.'

'And what do you want from me?'

'My team can't arrest Professor Milne straight away. The last thing we need is his and his buyer's disappearance together with the device,' Cartwright started. 'I need you to go to London. Your presence shouldn't raise any concerns. You'll try to distract the professor and prise out as much information on the device and its buyer as possible, while my team will try to find and confiscate it. It's a simple, follow-and-report task. Of course, my team will cover you.'

Zara shrugged. 'Even if I agree, how am I supposed to explain my trip to London and my stay in the same hotel? I think you underestimate Professor Milne.'

'After the Navy had confiscated the U-boat, you had nothing else to do but to leave Boston and…' She faltered. 'You might decide to show Dr Krause around London. Have you ever been to London, Doctor?' She turned to Stefan.

'More around airports and archives,' Stefan mumbled, but he knew it was too late to back down.

'Yes, see.' Cartwright grinned. 'Pretend you're on a date with Dr Krause and want to show him London.'

'What?!' Zara jumped from her chair.

'Don't like this idea? Fine. You can tell your mentor that after the Navy had taken over, you returned to London to continue your research at… oh, I don't know, the Imperial War Museum.

I think the hotel is close to the museum's archive.'

'Sorry, I won't take part in this circus.'

The door slammed behind Zara's back.

Stefan smirked. 'Now what?'

'It seems like you're getting along well with Miss Rose.' Cartwright's composed, calm tone was unflinching. 'I'm sure you'd be able to persuade her to assist us.'

'Us? I don't work for you. I agreed to work with your agency. A decision I'm already regretting. It's not in your power to give me orders, Officer. As for Miss Rose, I won't lie to her anymore and I won't deal with or leave her to deal with a criminal like Karl Milne.'

Agent Cartwright had held a pause for a few seconds. Her black eyes stared somewhere into space. She put on her gloves and scarf slowly.

'Let me remind you, Doctor, when you agreed to help us, one thousand pounds per day plus the full coverage of your travel expenses left aside all your regrets and concerns about your or anybody else's safety and wellbeing. I think your expertise is a bit too expensive for British taxpayers. In the NCA, we can't afford it.' She squinted. Her eyes, these two deep black coal pits, scrutinised him. 'I'll talk to Miss Rose again. I'll tell her you're out of business and try to persuade her to work with my team on her own. At the end of the day, she's the one who aided Milne from the beginning. The NCA can't turn a blind eye to the fact.'

Stefan gritted his teeth and repeated, 'I'm not leaving her. If she's going to London, I'll go with her.'

Chapter Fourteen

Professor Milne

Portsmouth, U. K.
Seventeen years earlier

'Good morning. I haven't seen you here for ages.' Milne stretched his hand for a handshake, putting his golf club aside and smiling at an elderly gentleman.

'Ah, damn arthritis. Nothing serious.' His acquaintance shook his grey head and unzipped a bag full of clubs of all shapes and sizes. 'The weather seems warmer today. I exercise while I have a chance,' he added, his accented voice sounding distant.

'Yes, the last sunny days of autumn. I come here every weekend now. Another week or two and that's it. Rain will turn this course into a swamp.' The professor nodded with a polite smile.

Mr Nowak didn't reply, just hit a ball with a vengeance.

'Oh, crap!' The eighty-something-year-old yelled when the ball hit the ground and disappeared into bushes on the opposite side of the golf course.

Despite his age and occasional health issues, Marek Nowak always looked agile and fit. Determination and confidence never left him. Playing golf together or going on a short hike, Milne always admired the old pilot and wondered whether his career in an RAF Polish squadron during the war tempered Mr Nowak's personality or was it his passion for such a competitive and exclusive sport like golf?

Alberich, Mr Nowak's German shepherd, pricked his ears and ran to the bushes in search of his owner's golf ball.

Well-disciplined, intelligent, and strict, Alberich was an ideal companion for his lonely owner. Milne smiled to himself, amused by how the dog helped to bring the lost balls back, releasing the elderly gentleman from a long wander around the course.

'It's Remembrance Day soon. Do you plan anything special with your Polish comrades-in-arms?' Milne made another attempt to revive their conversation.

'Eh? Oh, yes. The Remembrance Day.' Mr Nowak nodded. 'No. I'm not going anywhere. Not so many of us have remained, let's be honest,' he continued. 'Some boys are in wheelchairs, accompanied by their carers. Some barely can speak. Others don't even remember what they had for breakfast today, bless them. What a misery! I remember them being young and strong, flying Vickers.' He stopped and raised his faded eyes to the autumnal sky. Alberich's appearance from the bushes with the ball in his mouth interrupted his reverie and broke the sad pause. 'Good boy.' He stroked the dog, taking the ball from him.

'This squadron you've told me you served in as a chief lieutenant,' Milne started again. 'Was it 304? A bomber's squadron?'

'Yes. We fought throughout the entire war, from forty until forty-five.'

'How strange. You know me. As a historian, I like to explore such subjects. I asked one of my friends, an RAF archivist, about you and the squadron. She claimed she couldn't find your name anywhere. Crew lists, payroll, memos – nothing at all. How it can be?'

'I have no idea.' Mr Nowak frowned. 'Maybe she didn't search properly, or wanted to get rid of your request as soon as possible.'

'It's highly unlikely. This lady is a good friend of mine. She assists me a lot in my research.' The professor rubbed his chin. 'Do you have documents from your time there? Any medals? I'd love to have a look.'

'I've told you before, I moved constantly during my time in the RAF and after that. A lot went missing during the war and soon after it,' he snapped, turning away and pushing his clubs' trolley to another opening.

'Look, I'm sorry. I trust your words and didn't mean to offend you,' Milne mumbled, his elderly friend not moving to meet him. 'It doesn't seem right that all your military records have just vanished.'

'I don't know and don't care.' Mr Nowak waved.

* * *

The next few weekends, Milne didn't see the old pilot and started to worry about him. He didn't pick up his mobile phone either, and the professor didn't know how else he could get in touch. He asked around, but Mr Nowak hadn't appeared at his office for a while.

'He told me he was fine. He's just worked from home for a couple of weeks.' Melissa, a club's manager, shared her concerns. 'I'm not surprised he's tired. To run the entire club on his own, it's a massive task even for a much younger owner.'

Milne wanted to ask her Marek's home address, but decided against it. This information was too sensitive to be disclosed to the club's members. His search for Mr Nowak's military past turned the whole situation even more bizarre. His inquiry to the Society of Polish Veterans in the U.K. led him to a short meeting with an ex-pilot of 304 squadron.

'Marek Nowak? Nowak, Nowak… No. I don't remember this man, although the surname is quite common in Poland.' The man shook his head. 'He must've served in the squadron before my transfer there. Do you have a photo of this Chief Lieutenant?'

Milne didn't have. He wished all the best to the ex-pilot and departed empty-handed. He didn't need to wait for too long, though. A couple of days later, his friend called him.

'If you're still searching for the truth, you can come tomorrow in the evening,' Mr Nowak said after a brief greeting, his voice quiet but strict. 'I'll message you my home address.' He hung up the phone.

Chapter Fifteen

Professor Milne

Milne hesitated in front of the wooden door, finger hovering on the door bell despite the never-ending rain and icy wind. Alberich's low barking sounded behind the door before his host appeared on the doorstep.

'Ah, good evening, Karl.' Mr Nowak made an inviting gesture, allowing his guest room to enter the spacious, dark hallway. 'Please, come in.'

The dog rose from the sofa in the corner, coming closer.

'Hey, buddy.' Milne patted Alberich's neck, but the dog was unexcited to see him. After a cursory sniff, he returned to his corner.

'Please, come into the living room.' Mr Nowak gestured to another room, taking care of Milne's coat and scarf. 'Tea, coffee, or maybe something stronger for such a wet and dull evening?' His voice sounded from the kitchen while Milne seated himself on a wide leather sofa.

'Tea, please,' he replied, examining the space.

Pleasant pastel walls blended nicely with a carpet and curtains of the same shade of beige. The heavy wooden furniture and books, lots of books, two antique-looking displays full of them. New and old, classics and contemporary fiction, in English and a few titles in German, the language Mr Nowak knew well.

Nothing in Polish. Milne had never heard him speaking his native language. He never talked about his motherland. The professor kept on wondering whether Marek had visited Poland since the end of the war. A half-faded photo in a thin frame attracted his attention. Must be his ex-wife. She left him so long ago, but it seemed like he still remembered her. No kids. At least, he never told Milne about them. But then again, Milne never asked. He released a bitter sigh. He had enough trouble with Ethan.

'Your tea. Help yourself with sweets.' Mr Nowak entered the room, carrying a small tray with mugs and a bowl full of biscuits.

Dressed in a white woollen jumper and soft navy-blue trousers, Mr Nowak seemed relaxed but tired at the same time. In the dim lights of the lounge, sallow-faced, his eyes expressed fatigue, in contrast to his snow-white jumper.

'Do you feel okay?' Milne started. 'People in the club and I worried about you.'

'I'm fine, fine.' He waved, taking a seat in front of the professor. 'How's your research about the squadron going?' he asked without a preamble. 'You're here because of that, aren't you?'

'I'm here because you've invited me to come. As for my research, I can't find any records of your service anywhere.'

'It's because you're looking for them in the wrong place.' With that said, Mr Nowak rose from his seat and went to the shelf. Moving aside a few thick books, he reached into a hidden safe. Milne watched him, speechless.

He pulled out a tiny envelope, closed the safe, and settled back in his chair.

'You're looking for me in the wrong place,' he repeated, 'and for the wrong man.'

Milne swallowed his confusion back, but replied nothing. It was cool in the living room, but a sudden wave of heat overwhelmed him.

'My real name is Ulrich Schultz,' Mr Nowak started. 'And I'm not a Polish pilot.' He told him the whole story about the U-boat and his miraculous escape to Britain. 'This experimental U-boat had become not only an opportunity for me to get a promotion from first watch officer to a captain but the chance to survive.'

Milne sat without movement for a few seconds, then

asked, 'Why did Admiral Dönitz take such a colossal risk and appointed an inexperienced officer to a top-secret project?'

'Perhaps there were few experienced captains remaining in 1945.' Schultz shrugged. 'The ones who commanded conventional U-boats wouldn't have volunteered for various reasons. I was a young daredevil, hungry for promotion, and tired of following orders. I saw an opportunity to finish the war as a captain, not just a lowly officer, whatever the outcome. The High Command gambled again. If the project failed, the crew's losses would've been minimal. The death of an inexperienced captain wouldn't have been an enormous tragedy for the Kriegsmarine.'

'So there're only three of you who survived?'

'Hermann Thiel didn't make it.' Schultz bowed his grey head low. 'The device must've malfunctioned. We went through together, but he never reappeared. I could only assume he got stuck somewhere between time and space forever.'

'What about the boy? The radio officer?'

'As I've told you already, when Hermann and I entered the engine room, it was empty. There was nowhere to escape. We decided the boy had no choice but to take a risk and use Die Fledermaus. We didn't have time to think about him much. I helped Hermann dispose of the bodies before making our escape.' He paused, staring into space. No guilt, fear, or excuse in his firm gaze. 'I've not heard about Walter Dix since. Most likely, his attempt failed.'

Milne didn't know what else to ask, how to react. 'What about the Polish pilots' clothes, their documents? Where did you get them?' he asked after a prolonged pause.

'During one of our test journeys, we found the debris of a Polish plane. There were no survivors, only the half-frozen bodies of two pilots with no intact documents, but perfectly preserved flight suits. Which is how our plan took shape. I know it's hard for you to digest the story in one sitting.' He smirked, noticing Milne's confusion. 'This is the key to my deposit box in Switzerland. You'll find all the evidence there. And don't worry, I instructed my lawyer to provide access to the deposit box to the key holder. I've already notified him of your arrival.'

'Why have you told me all that?' What do you want in return?'

'First, I want you to shut up your mouth and stop sniffing around,' Schultz snapped, but rushed to compose himself. 'Second, I want you to find the U-boat. I want you to bring Die Fledermaus back. It's dangerous, it's venom. Nobody should use it for their benefit. Nobody should repeat our mistakes.'

'Do you regret your actions?' Milne choked. 'A way to repent? Are you trying to buy your redemption?'

'Whoever but you, Professor, can judge me.' The old captain banged his fist on the coffee table. 'You've never been at war. Most likely, you never will. Do you think your cushy job at your university gives you the slightest clue of what we all went through in those days? Do you believe that sitting behind a desk, scrolling through old war photos and documents all day, gives you the right to judge me? Judge me for my desire to survive, to stay alive, just live?' He stopped, closed his faded eyes, and leaned back against the chair's back.

Alberich, woken up by his owner's loud exclamations, came to the room. Without even looking at Milne, he put his big brownish head on the old man's lap, as if he tried to comfort him.

'I was young and desperate to live and live well,' Schultz continued, calming down. 'Hermann and I, we couldn't accommodate all the crew in our daring plan, anyway. Not all of them deserved to be rescued, either. Our navigator, Otto Lange, for example, was a brainwashed, fanatical Nazi. He would've reported us the next minute we'd told him about the escape. The motorman? Oh, God! This guy couldn't keep his mouth shut for a minute. The entire base would've known about our plan if we'd teamed up with that blabbermouth. Who appointed him to a top-secret mission? Well, it's still a mystery to me.'

Milne raised his eyes to him. 'So, you and Thiel brought your justice upon all these men?'

'You haven't been in a similar situation, Professor, have you?' Schultz shook his head. 'You've never had to choose between another's life and your own. You have no right to accuse me of anything.'

'Then, I leave you to the mercy of God. He, not I, will judge you.'

He left the house without a final goodbye.

* * *

Milne left the club after visiting Captain Schultz. He'd heard nothing from his old companion for almost six months. His tale sounded more like science fiction than reality, but it never left Milne. It turned the screws of his mind, torturing him with insomnia and distraction from work. Replaying his conversation with the Captain, Milne carried on feeding his curiosity and ultimately feeding his hope. Hope that if the device was as powerful as the old man claimed, if it could split space-time, or create alternate universes where the laws of physics didn't apply, where all events of the past and the future co-existed, it could help him. Help him see his little Stella again.

How she was at the end. The sallow skin of her face, her feeble body, those exhausted, sad eyes revisited his dreams and cruel memories. That damned disease had torn her away from him so quickly. Those never-ending, sleepless nights at her hospital bed and ultimately the doll-sized coffin, the lifeless mask of her pale face…

The only way to know whether the old man had told him the truth or not was to visit Switzerland. He needed to go. Needed to do it for Stella and his sanity. It was the only way.

One sunny Saturday morning, he walked through the park, where he noticed a familiar slim figure jogging along a path. The dog, an old German shepherd, looked familiar as well.

'Melissa?!' he called out to the woman.

'Ah, Professor Milne. Good morning!' The club manager smiled a broad smile. 'How're you doing? It's such a shame you've left us.'

'I'm fine, thank you,' he greeted. 'I didn't know you had a dog.' He nodded to the German shepherd. 'It looks exactly like-'

'Yes. It's Alberich. Mr Nowak's dog.' She beamed again, patting the dog behind the ears.

Milne crouched in front of Alberich. 'Hello, old friend. What's happened to Mr Novak?' He stared at the dog, although he could already guess the answer.

'Soon after you had left the club, he sold his business to another company. He'd been feeling unwell over the last few months and eventually moved to a care home. I visited him a few days before his move, and he asked me to look after Alberich. This boy wouldn't survive in a kennel. He's far too affectionate and loyal.'

'I know.' Milne continued to stroke the dog. 'He needs a loyal companion.'

Alberich extended his front paw for a pawshake, and Milne couldn't hide a smile.

'Sadly, Mr Nowak passed away in the care home,' Melissa concluded, bowing her head. 'He was a good man.'

Milne wanted to say something sympathetic. Some polite nonsense everybody should say in such a situation, but Alberich's huge round eyes stopped him. These eyes challenged him as if the dog kept his old owner's secret. They both knew the whole truth and couldn't tell a soul.

Chapter Sixteen

Stefan

Boston, U.K.
The present day

Stefan rehearsed his conversation with Zara on the way to the lift. What was he supposed to do? She still wasn't talking to him and would doubtless berate, call him a liar, and maybe slap for good measure. Perhaps he deserved it, but he hoped she wouldn't have it out with him in the lobby. He'd kept her in the dark for far too long, wanting to play it safe, saving his own skin.

The lift doors opened to the lobby, but Zara was nowhere to be seen. He wasn't a traitor like Professor Milne. Milne had simply used her. Stefan wasn't like Ethan or Captain Ferret, who had been screwing up their relationship for almost three years. He instinctively reached for his inhaler as a painful wave of sadness contorted his heart. An asthma attack was the last thing he needed.

He found Zara in the restaurant, having a late lunch. Lucky for him, they were the only guests.

'Can I take a seat?' he asked, approaching the table.

She didn't answer, just nodding to a chair opposite her.

'I know what you think about me,' he continued. 'A dodgy, lying, unprofessional, foreigner who can't be trusted-'

'We need to finish it,' she interrupted, staring out the window. 'Agent Cartwright's right. We can't allow Milne and the device to disappear. It seems like it's not just a scientific issue now, it's an issue of national security. And now, we have a score to settle.'

A chill ran down his spine. 'I'm won't leave you to deal with it alone. We'll go together.' He squeezed a reassuring half-smile.

Zara chuckled bitterly. 'I wonder how much Agent Cartwright offered you for this dangerous operation.'

'I'm not doing it for the NCA.' He retorted. 'I'm not with them anymore. This is for science…' he faltered, 'but most of all, to help you. I owe you so much.'

'You shouldn't take this risk.' Zara shook her head, smiling for the first time. 'I'm not angry. Honestly, Stefan, you'd better go back to Germany. We're able to manage it by ourselves here.'

'I'm not going anywhere while you're in trouble,' he said. 'It's my fault that we're in all this shit. I need to fix the mess I've created. I'm not a coward.'

'Oh, well. I can't force you to leave.' She shrugged. 'If you wish to help, I'd be grateful for the assistance.' Although her lips curled into a smile, her voice remained distant.

He needed to regain her trust. 'Thank you for giving me a second chance.' He said after a pause. 'The agent is waiting for us upstairs for a final briefing.'

* * *

'It would be better to operate separately.' Agent Cartwright had been circling the room while the two operatives finished fixing microphones and micro-cameras on Zara and Stefan's clothes. 'I need you, Zara, to meet and distract the professor while you, Doctor, together with one of my operatives, will search for the device in his room. Most likely, it's in a safe.'

'No.' Stefan shook his head. 'It's too dangerous for two people to go there. I'll deal with Die Fledermaus myself. I've done it before. So even if something goes wrong, at least, it will be only me who'll suffer.'

The agent frowned. 'I hope you understand the consequences.'

'I do, although I don't believe the device is in the safe,' he said.

'The cylinder itself can fit into a standard hotel's safe. However, the amount of energy required to keep black matter in place needs extremely powerful batteries. I'm sure Professor Milne is well-prepared for that, but with the batteries, the whole mechanism is too bulky to fit in the safe.'

'I can't imagine any other place Professor Milne can hide it, apart from his hotel room. My guys will give you a key. Don't worry, you won't need to climb up walls and squeeze through a window,' the agent continued without a hint of a joke. 'If by any chance Milne has stored the device in the safe and changed the code, you'll need our help to open it. But first, try to gain access to his room and locate the device.'

Stefan frowned but didn't object. Clearly, Agent Cartwright was indifferent to the technical details of the operation. 'What about this mysterious solicitor? Who're they?' he asked after a prolonged pause.

'We haven't found their true identity yet. But we know that the dark web server they used to communicate has a registration in China.'

'It's not much, isn't it?' Zara blurted out. 'The server can be based on Mars. It doesn't mean the solicitor is from there.'

'It doesn't,' Cartwright agreed. 'The last correspondence between the two solicitors, which my team intercepted, was in the morning. The solicitor is going to arrive in London at about eight o'clock this evening. We need to hurry. We haven't much time left.'

Chapter Seventeen

Professor Milne

Milne slowly sipped his Château Cissac, tasting every hint and subtle nuance of the expensive vintage, as if trying to drown any tormenting thoughts and break free. Night almost covered the restless city, and he spent the brief window of twilight in the darkness of his hotel suite, enjoying the view from the window. In a couple of hours, his life might change forever. In a couple of hours, his buyer's solicitor would complete the deal. He turned to a thick file on the table and released a meaningful sigh. He should've locked it in the safe for the time being.

Seventeen years had passed since his fateful meeting with Marek Nowak, an elderly Polish pilot, or under the guise of one. It seemed to Milne he saw him only yesterday. He knew he would never forget their last conversation, Mr Nowak's tired but still confident, almost commanding, voice, and the depth of his faded-grey eyes, staring at him. The events of the next couple of years turned Milne's world upside down, setting an alternative course in his life, giving him a new goal, and inspiring him to keep searching, searching for the deadliest and the most advanced weapon ever built. Shouldn't he stop? Shouldn't he report this information to the authorities and let them deal with it? As a historian, shouldn't he announce his discovery and engage the whole scientific community in his search? Wasn't it illegal to keep this knowledge to himself and… to sell his findings to some shady guys, maybe even terrorists?

Back then, he'd hardly believed in what he heard from the "ex-pilot". Even Mr Nowak's detailed story, his explanations about the device, his captain's logbook, the manual, and U-boat's whereabouts impressed him but didn't make him believe. How was he supposed to check whether his acquaintance had told him the truth, or was it another trick to distract him and avoid justice?

Time flew by. He gathered more and more information about the mysterious weapon, and finally, after seventeen long years, it reappeared from nowhere straight in front of him. Some random people from some offshore company brought Die Fledermaus to him on a plate. Who could imagine such luck?

With only a couple of years left before retirement, he'd kill as many birds with one stone as he could. For the money, of course. The country was going through turbulent times and he could no longer rely only on his savings; even less on his meagre professor's pension. His wife's passion for jewellery and exotic cruises; his dream of a small villa somewhere on the Adriatic coast, or even better, somewhere in sunny Florida – his savings could hardly stretch so far.

There was something else to it, though. His daughter was not the only one with such a horrible diagnosis. Hundreds of kids of her age all over the country suffered and died of the same disease every year. This money. It would help them all. Accelerate medical research and save countless lives. As for the device, oh… Milne had found it a noble purpose. A purpose he felt proud of.

A persistent vibration of his mobile phone interrupted his musing.

'Yes. Have you left Hull already and heading here? Does it go according to the plan?' he started without a greeting.

He had always been strict and abrupt with his son, believing such an upbringing would've made Ethan less unstable and more determined to achieve some goals in his life. After Stella's tragic death, Ethan was his only hope. The story about Die Fledermaus and its astonishing ability to move people and objects through time and space gave him a short-living hope to maybe… just maybe, be able to see his daughter again. If everything that the captain told him was the truth, if during the usage of the device, he had experienced moments of the past, then Milne had a chance to see his little Stella again. What wouldn't he give to see her smiling face again, even for a few seconds, where life and death were equally unimportant and time didn't exist? The deeper he probed into Die Fledermaus, the less optimistic he became. His dream of reuniting with his late daughter completely evaporated when he learned of the two divers and his colleagues' recent experience with black matter. He'd made the right decision, trying to get rid of it and take the money.

'Hey, are you still here?' Ethan's grumbling pulled him out of his reverie. 'I'm on my way to London.'

'Yes, I'm listening.'

His approach to parenting had only pushed his son away. Now, well. After thirty-eight years, it was too late to change. At first, he didn't plan to involve Ethan in this business, but his connection to the Navy and the still-bruised ego made him a perfect ally. To his surprise, his son didn't want to go into detail about the device and his buyer, only asking about his cut of the money.

'I've left the U-boat to my Chief Officer. She'll sort her out. Don't worry,' Ethan's voice sounded a bit annoyed. 'What you need to be worried about right now is Zara and her German friend.'

'What about them? They should've followed the sub all the way through to Hull.'

'Should've,' his son snapped. 'Instead of driving to the north, the pair is following the M1 down to the south. I'm on their tail.'

'Are you sure they're heading to London? But how do they know?' Milne mumbled. Cold sweat covered his forehead, and he took a seat on the bed.

'How should I know? I'm just doing what you've told me to,' Ethan barked. 'I'll keep you posted about their whereabouts. Listen out for my call.'

Shut your mouth! Milne raged, but bit his tongue. Ethan wasn't a rebellious teenager anymore. Besides, Milne desperately needed his help right now. A captain of a tiny ship, a mine countermeasure vessel, or whatever the silly little thing was called. Big deal! He chuckled to himself. What a loser! He behaved as if he was the commander of an aircraft carrier or a destroyer.

'Be careful. Don't come too close. The girl and that crafty doctor aren't idiots. They might notice you-' he started, but Ethan had hung up.

Milne exhaled, throwing the phone on the table. Where was this damn solicitor? They were running out of time. He swallowed his wine in one huge gulp, rose from the bed, and locked the file in the safe.

Now, the girl. A tiny needle of guilt prickled his soul when he thought about Zara. How she'd become just another obedient and naïve puppet in his dirty game. She'd made Ethan suffer enough, although the moron deserved that bitter lesson. And yet… blood was thicker, after all.

Chapter Eighteen

Zara

Zara kept a stubborn silence, only responding at random during the trip to London. She'd thought of Milne as one of her most trusted friends. If she were honest, she'd considered him more than that; an elder, a mentor, not only in science but in life as well.

Ethan had appeared out of nowhere. He was his father's son, so it came as no surprise. As for Stefan… She released a bitter sigh, attracting a worried look. Another man she should've never trusted. Another disappointment.

The Sat Nav chimed as they reached their destination. The twenty-storey modernist building of the Mouritz Hotel rose across the road.

Stefan sat unmoving for a minute, eyes focused on the hotel's entrance.

'Are you afraid?' he broke an uneasy silence.

'Afraid of what? Or whom? Of Die Fledermaus or Milne?' Zara smirked. 'They're both quite unpredictable. Milne's already betrayed me once. Nothing will stop him from doing it again.'

'I'm more concerned about this solicitor,' Stefan continued. 'It is possible that they're accompanied and armed. If so, I doubt the NCA can act quickly enough to protect us.'

Zara waved away his doubt. 'Our safety isn't their priority, so I wouldn't rely on their protection if I were you. The agency is only interested in the agency. Agent Cartwright needs to secure the device at any cost.'

'Careful. They hear us.' He patted the miniature microphone

secured under his collar.

Just two blocks away, a mini-van full of NCA surveillance agents, led by Agent Cartwright, monitored their every word and movement. The Hazmat Response team was also on standby somewhere close. None of this calmed Zara.

'I don't fucking care.' She grimaced. 'The person I trusted the most has used me. When we exposed all his lies, not a grain of trust remained. So, what else can I lose?'

'Yourself,' Stefan whispered.

'I'm afraid I'm lost already.' She sighed, uncomfortable under his long gaze.

Stefan patted her hand reassuringly. His bright eyes shone with warmth behind his spectacles. 'I'm with you. This time, you can trust me.'

'I don't understand what motive Milne has for this,' she said, moving her hand away from his. 'I can't believe it's just for the money. It's too simple and too rudimentary for him. Scientists aren't the richest people in the world, but we're not disadvantaged either. There should be something else. Something that makes Milne take all this crazy risk, forgetting his status, his reputation, his safety after all.'

'We'll soon find out.' With that said, Stefan left the car and made his way to the brightly illuminated hotel entrance, leaving Zara alone.

Chapter Nineteen

Agent Cartwright

'Careful. They hear us.' Stefan's voice crackled through the microphone.

'I don't fucking care.' Zara bit back.

'Cheeky little bastards!' Agent Cartwright smirked, listening to a straightforward conversation between the two historians on her headset.

She and her team of six operatives and technicians followed Zara and Stefan from their mini-van, disguised as a satellite TV installation vehicle. Surrounded by computer monitors, racks of wires, keyboards, and surveillance equipment, the team had access not only to Zara and Stefan's microphones and micro-cameras, but also a direct connection to any CCTV cameras inside the hotel and its surrounding.

'Focus on Dr Krause,' Cartwright instructed one of her aides, coming closer to the woman's desk and, staring at a screen. Showing Stefan entering the busy lobby of the Mouritz Hotel. Then, she switched her attention to another monitor on the building's top floor. There, in a panoramic restaurant, Professor Milne sat enjoying his dinner, still waiting for the mysterious solicitor.

'The room's empty, please, proceed,' she directed Stefan, who entered the hotel and headed to the room.

He opened the door and stepped in as carefully as possible, using a spoofed keycard. He switched on his torch and stopped for a second, deciding where to start.

'He's doing well so far, isn't he?' Cartwright smiled. 'Maybe he'll consider working for us.'

Another technician attracted her attention. 'Ma'am, we've got a visitor.'

'Who?' Cartwright squinted. 'Zoom in a bit, please.'

A short male figure, dressed in a slim black suit with a case in his hand, on his way along the corridor, had stopped at the professor's room.

'Captain Milne?! What on earth is he doing here?' Cartwright mumbled. 'Doctor, do you copy?' She switched on her headset again. 'You need to get out of the room. Now!'

'Scheisse! I've just opened the safe and-' Stefan's whisper sounded furious.

'Out, now!' Cartwright commanded too late. She saw Ethan Milne entering the room.

Chapter Twenty

Professor Milne

Milne couldn't resist the second glass of Château Cissac. Not a good idea. He needed to stay focused. It was too little, too late for regrets, though. A waiter had already brought him his drink. The restaurant was getting busier with upcoming hotel guests and businesspeople who chose this place for informal evening meetings.

Still no solicitor. He continued scanning newcomers, patting a thick file on the table next to him. He was about to finish his wine when the restaurant's glass doors opened, and a middle-aged gentleman in a blue office suit and a light beige trench coat entered the room. His dark eyes had been scanning the restaurant for a couple of seconds. When he spotted the professor, a wide smile illuminated his slightly tanned face.

'Professor Milne?' The gentleman nodded in greeting, coming closer to the table. 'Good evening,' he continued in perfect English.

'Ah, good evening.' Milne rose from his chair for a handshake. 'Nice to meet you finally, Mr... ehm...'

'Hussein Akkaş.' The solicitor nodded. 'Please, call me Huss.'

'I hope your flight was nice and quick.' Milne gestured to a vacant chair across the table. 'How do you find it here in London?'

Mr Akkaş beamed his perfect smile again. 'Ah, it's as busy as Ankara, but not as sunny and hot.'

'Would you like a drink, or maybe something more substantial? The steak is particularly good here.'

'Oh, no, no,' the man protested. 'Unfortunately, I need to leave London as soon as we're finished here. We should get straight to business.'

'Ah, very well.' With that, Milne moved the file closer to his guest across the table.

'What's this?' Mr Akkaş inquired, smile remaining, but a shadow of confusion reflecting on his features.

'You didn't expect me to bring the device to the restaurant? You weren't expecting its demonstration in front of all these people, were you?' Milne made a wide gesture. 'This is a technical manual, dated 1944, describing how to operate Die Fledermaus. The file also includes the manual's detailed translation into English.'

The solicitor examined the file before raising an eyebrow. 'And the device?'

'It's close. Don't worry. I expect you and your clients to pay half of the money first, as a guarantee. After completion of our transaction, I'll gladly present the device to you.'

'This isn't what we discussed with your representative, Professor.' Akkaş frowned. 'We agreed to one complete payment for one device. I'm not sure my clients will agree-'

'Don't worry. You needn't wait long. Die Fledermaus is nearby.' Milne grinned, reclining in his wide chair. 'Besides,' he added, 'please, take no offence by this, but I don't know you or your client. How can I trust a person I've never met? As for the manual, it's a vital piece of information. Die Fledermaus isn't a weapon in the traditional sense. It's not a missile launcher or a gun that any idiot could use. It's the most advanced, deadliest, and complicated piece of weaponry humanity ever designed.'

'Fair enough,' Mr Akkaş snapped. 'I'll get in touch with my client and request for a transfer of half the payment upfront.'

He pulled a secure mobile phone from his pocket and typed a message. A silhouette momentarily distracted Milne's attention, as a figure in grey trousers and a cashmere short coat walked by.

Ethan had been right. Zara and the German were heading to London. Milne didn't have time to finish his thought as Zara had noticed him.

'Good evening, Professor. What an unexpected place to meet.' She approached the table with a broad smile.

'Ah, Zara, good evening.' Milne had nothing to do but to rise in greeting. 'An unexpected place, indeed.'

The solicitor sat silently, shifting his gaze from Milne to Zara and back.

'What brings you to London? How does your wife feel? Is she okay now?' Zara asked, paying no attention to the professor's quiet companion.

'Oh, the doctors needed to put her in a medical coma to stabilise her condition.' Milne waved. 'They reckon it may take a while. I wanted to stay with her.' He released a deep sigh. 'Her family has arrived: her son, her eldest daughter with her children. You know, I've never been close to either of them. Her daughter still hasn't accepted me. I felt uncomfortable and unwelcome there, so gave them some space. I needed to be away from all of them and this horrible situation. My blood pressure jumped, and the doctors advised me to take a break. I'll be back to Portsmouth tomorrow.'

'I'm sorry to hear that. I hope she recovers soon.' Zara nodded. 'Nothing else you can do now, only pray for her health and fast recovery.'

'I pray for that every minute.' Milne bowed his head lower. 'Oh, I'm sorry. I didn't introduce you to my counterpart. We used to work together.' He turned to the solicitor. 'Dr Hussein Akkaş from the Ankara State University. He's here for a short private trip, so we've agreed to meet. Dr Akkaş hopes he can cheer me up a bit during this hard time. Miss Zara Rose, my colleague, mentee, and above all, a good friend,' he continued, introducing Zara to the solicitor.

'Nice to meet you, Doctor.' Zara stretched for a handshake.

'Pleasure is all mine.'

'What is your area of expertise?'

'I'm... ehm...'

'Hussein specialises in the financial structure and banking system of the Third Reich before and during the war,' Milne superseded.

'Yes, yes, the Professor is correct.'

Zara clapped her hands. 'I'd love to know more, especially the financing of the U-boats' program.'

'What about you? What brings you to London?' Milne interrupted. 'I thought you'd be in Boston, gathering information and bringing scientists together to discuss the issue.'

'Well, it's nothing to discuss. The U-boat is under the jurisdiction of the Navy now.' Zara shrugged. 'When Dr Krause and I arrived at the dock in the morning, the Navy representative informed they would take her to dry dock in Hull. They wouldn't co-operate or allow us to look at her one more time. After a short debate, it made sense to return to the Imperial War Museum and continue my investigation there. The Navy has agreed to pay for my accommodation here. They desperately wanted me out of the way.'

'What about Dr Krause?'

'He returned to Germany. Most likely boarded his plane at Heathrow by now.'

'Strange.' Milne nodded. 'Okay. Let me deal with the Navy when I'm back in Portsmouth.' He turned to the solicitor. 'This U-boat I've mentioned to you. She's turned into a real pain.'

Mr Akkaş rolled his eyes. 'Oh, I can imagine. Bureaucracy is everywhere.'

'Maybe we can have dinner with the three of us, and if Dr Akkaş would be so kind, I'd love to pick his brain about the financing of the Kriegsmarine and the U-boat program?' Zara asked.

A vibrating phone eased the uncomfortable pause, and the solicitor's thin lips stretched into a polite smile.

'I'm afraid I need to go now.' He bowed. 'Some private matters require my attention. I'm happy to meet you tomorrow in the morning. If we're staying in the same hotel, it shouldn't be difficult to arrange our meeting.'

Zara shook her head. 'Oh, of course. It's late now. You should relax after such a long trip from Turkey. I understand.'

'I'd better retire as well.' Milne rushed to get up. 'Today was an endless day for me. I started early in the morning and it seems I travelled all over the country this few days.'

'No problem, Professor. See you tomorrow at breakfast then?'

Milne nodded goodbye. 'Yes, see you tomorrow.'

'Goodbye, Miss Rose, pleasure to meet your acquaintance.' Dr Akkaş bowed before following Milne to the door.

'My client has agreed on your terms and transferred half the money already,' he whispered, catching up with Milne near the lifts. 'Where're we going now?'

'To meet Die Fledermaus. Meanwhile, you can transfer the rest of the amount to my solicitor's account.'

Chapter Twenty-One

Zara

Now what? She couldn't keep Milne and the solicitor in the restaurant forever. Where did they go? To his room or to some safe location where the professor was hiding the device? What if Cartwright was wrong? What if he didn't have it in the room?

'Zara, report,' Agent Cartwright's voice sounded in her ear.

'Nothing to report. You heard the whole conversation. This Turkish solicitor, disguised as a historian, received a message on his phone. I assume it was from his client,' Zara whispered, turning around in the hope nobody could hear her. 'Where's Stefan? Has he finished in the room? Milne and his guest are likely heading back there right now.'

'We'll deal with Dr Krause and these two. Your part here is over. Return to the car and await instructions.'

'What do you mean? What's happened?' Zara raised her voice, but calmed down, noticing the curious looks of the surrounding guests.

'Go back to the car and wait for further instructions.' The agent cut off.

She wasn't leaving Stefan alone there. She rose from the table and hurried up to the lift.

Chapter Twenty-Two

Stefan

Stefan entered the busy hotel lobby, heading straight for the lifts. Luckily, an empty lift arrived, and he had time to compose himself. His mission seemed to be an easy one. And yet his heart hammered. Why was he doing this? The lift began its silent ascent. He should've agreed with Cartwright's initial plan and sent one of her operatives to locate the device. He was just a historian, not a secret agent, not even a physicist or an engineer who understood how to operate the damn thing. Who did? All he knew was what Walter Dix had told him, what he'd written in his journal. Some guesswork was required, of course, and the odd speculation about his experience. And, worse still, what if he was wrong? How would he disarm Die Fledermaus then?

The lift stopped, doors opening onto the dusky corridor. He released a painful sigh, wiping cold sweat from his forehead. A sudden heaviness seized his chest. No, please, not now. He touched his pocket for an inhaler, but after a couple of deep breaths, he continued his way along the corridor.

'The room is empty. Please proceed,' Agent Cartwright's voice sounded in his earpiece.

'Room 515,' he whispered, pulling out a key-card and opening the door. Professor Milne was in the restaurant. He hoped Zara could keep him occupied as long as possible. Stefan examined the room, opening a wardrobe and checking the bedside tables. If Cartwright was right and the device was there, perhaps it was in the safe?

He turned away from the bed and returned to the large wardrobe, hiding the built-in safe. Now, the moment of truth. He smirked, inputting the code.

To his surprise, the lock clicked opened. Empty?! Although he expected such a turn, he still couldn't believe all their risks had come to nothing.

'Doctor, do you copy?' the familiar strict voice sounded. 'You need to get out of the room. Now!'

'Scheisse! I've just opened the safe-'

'Out, now!'

The door's lock clicked, and a dark male figure appeared on the doorstep. Stefan darted to the bathroom, but it was too late. Ethan jumped in front of him, grabbing his coat.

'Ah, Dr Krause? What a surprise!' His smile shone in the half-light of the room.

Stefan pushed his pursuer back. 'Verpiss dich!'

Ethan dropped the case he'd been holding, but maintained his balance. The next moment, Stefan received a powerful punch to the stomach. He bent over, struggling to catch his breath. His earpiece, his only connection to the team, dropped on the fluffy carpet.

'Why are you sniffing around here?' Ethan took one step closer to Stefan. 'Where's Zara? I see she's dragged you into all of this.'

Stefan tried to rise, but Ethan's kick knocked him to the floor.

'Who are you working for?' he continued.

Did he want to kill him? Stefan backed up towards the door.

He wanted to shout, but the words stuck in his throat. He was suffocating. The cold sweat streamed down his forehead. His chest was on fire. He gathered all his remaining strength to reach his inhaler, but the pocket was empty.

'Are you searching for this, Doctor?' Ethan grinned, squeezing the inhaler in his hand. 'Come on! Try to get it.'

This was the point of no return. Gathering the last of his

energy and overcoming the wrenching pain in his lungs, Stefan snatched the case and pried it open. Just as he thought. Cartwright had followed the wrong lead. Stefan turned the two metal disks on top of the container.

The world around him plunged into a white, dazzling abyss. Soundless nothingness surrounded him. The same experience as aboard U-4713/A.

Enveloped by a blurry, watery substance, Stefan saw the living room of his house in Kiel. The room was festive, and he was busy decorating the Christmas tree, just as he saw it for the first time aboard the U-boat. The same fancy glass decoration slipped from his hand, and again Zara caught it in mid-air.

'You're so clumsy.' She laughed.

He saw both their reflections in the blown glass. Both were a few years older, but happier.

A warm sensation of comfort poured into his soul. Fear and confusion evaporating, superseded by warmth and joy.

The image changed, coming into sharper focus. Every bombarding sound growing to an excruciating crescendo.

Stefan turned around on instinct, realising they weren't alone in the room.

A dark shadow stood in the dimly lit corridor. The figure's bald head almost touched the ceiling. The building shook.

Stefan turned to Zara, but there was nobody in the room. He stared at the shadow, unable to distinguish any features. It was too dark. The figure seemed wrapped in a dense black fog. He took a few steps into the corridor, but the shadow vanished.

The corridor looked nothing like the one in his house. The tremors stopped. He stood now in an unknown place with long tiled walls and high ceilings. Nobody around, just the loud gurgling splashing of water around him.

It looked like a corrupted memory of a hospital. He struggled to breathe in the environment and kept walking along the corridor for what felt like an eternity. A door assembled itself to him in the distance, which opened as he reached it.

Dressed in white tiles from the floor to the ceiling, the room resembled an operating theatre. Instead of an operating table, a bath sat at the centre. The sounds of hissing and splashing water intensified.

Stefan motioned closer to the bath.

It was full of water, and through its ripples, Stefan saw a man's body, pale blue, eyes closed. The man somehow looked familiar, yet entirely foreign. He had seen him somewhere. Where exactly he couldn't remember. Stefan rested his hand in the bath, trying to touch the man's shoulder. On contact with his shoulder, an eviscerating cold burning sensation sprang through Stefan's body. He yelled with perplexing pain and everything disappeared.

Chapter Twenty-Three

Agent Cartwright

Cartwright stared at the computer screen and couldn't believe her eyes. 'What the hell just happened?'

A few seconds ago, two male figures were fighting in the dim light of the hotel room. In a flash of dazzling light, vanishing as if they had never been there.

'Group B, group B, do you copy?' she demanded in her headset to her two agents who had left the shelter of the mini-van to rush to Stefan's rescue. 'Abort the mission and stay where you are.'

'Ma'am, we're at the entrance already,' the male voice broke through the cracking interferences.

'Stay where you are and wait for further instructions,' Cartwright barked.

One of her assistants zoomed in on the glowing cylinder on the floor. 'The device, Ma'am. It's still there, in the room.'

'The ideal time to pick it up,' Cartwright mused aloud.

'We've got company,' the assistant commented, still keeping the camera focused on the room.

Cartwright connected to the away team again. 'Group B, proceed as planned.'

'Copy that. Proceeding to the hotel.'

On the screen, she saw Professor Milne and Mr Akkaş discussing something, pointing at the case with the cylinder on the floor, and gesticulating vigorously.

'Have you got the solicitor's real identity?' she asked a technician.

'It looks like Hussein Akkaş is his real name,' the man responded, without turning his gaze from the screen. 'He's a Turkish citizen, but he arrived in the country using a British passport issued in another name. I'm working on it right now.'

'Anything interesting about his Turkish identity?'

'No. I'm afraid we need more time to dig deeper and request information from the Turkish authorities. Or try to break into their database-'

'Please, you can't be for real. We have no time for this.'

'Ma'am, Miss Rose,' another agent interrupted. 'She's arrived.'

'Damn! What's this stupid girl doing? I told her not to intervene,' Cartwright screamed, clenching her fists.

She could hear their heated conversation. Zara pointed to the professor and shouted at him.

Cartwright swallowed her annoyance back. 'Shit! The solicitor has got a gun.'

Chapter Twenty-Four

Zara

'Why? Why are you doing this?' Zara shouted, eyes burning with tears, unable to wipe them at the gunpoint. 'You destroyed your career, your reputation, you betrayed me. Now, two people are in the greatest danger, including your son. What are you doing? The crucial question is *why*.'

'You'll never understand this, Zara.' Milne smiled his crooked smile, holding Die Fledermaus. 'You say I've betrayed you. And you? What have you done to Ethan? You abandoned him when he needed you the most.'

She scowled. 'So, was it revenge for your estranged son's heartbreak and an opportunity to earn some dirty cash?'

'No. Nothing personal, darling, just business.' Milne shook his head. 'It's not just about the money, either.'

'So, what is it about? I deserve to know the truth, at least, before I'm shot.' She nodded to the solicitor.

'Oh, shut up! Both of you!' Mr Akkaş barked. 'Give me the device,' he commanded, turning to Milne, 'and we'll finish the deal.'

'The batteries.' Milne shot a quick look at the cylinder. His face turned pale.

'What about them?'

'They won't last long. We need to find Ethan and Stefan.'

'What will happen when the batteries run out? Were there any spare?'

'When the batteries have completely degraded, the gravitational fields keeping that tiny black dot suspended at the centre of the cylinder will collapse,' Zara replied instead, nodding to the device. 'The black matter will collide with the glowing fluid, then not only this room or this hotel, but the entire city will go to hell.'

'You haven't told me anything about the batteries.' The solicitor shifted his gaze from Milne to Zara and back. 'What if they were to die on my way back to Turkey?'

A loud stomp in the corridor made him stop. The door swung open.

'Gun down! Hands up!' The two agents burst into the room, levelling their firearms at Milne and the solicitor, but it was already too late.

'One more step, and she's dead,' the solicitor hissed, squeezing Zara's neck, pressing the cold barrel of his gun to her head.

Was this how it was going to end? Some dodgy lunatic killing her? Zara's knees weakened. She was a step away from fainting, but it would make the matter even worse.

'Drop your guns! Both of you,' Milne rumbled. 'Or I'll send all of us to hell.' He gestured to the device. 'The batteries are dying, but trust me, there's enough energy to destroy the entire building.'

The agents slowly lowered their guns, shifting their gazes from the professor to the solicitor and back. Mr Akkaş took a step back from Zara but levelled his revolver at her head.

'Why are you doing this, Professor? What's next?' Zara asked in a low and trembling voice.

'I think you've got the wrong lead,' Milne addressed to the agents instead.

'Why's that?' The closer of the two agents bit back.

'Let's ask our guest where he's going with the device and who his mysterious client might be.' He sneered, nodding to the solicitor. 'I bet Turkey isn't your final destination, is it? What is it? Iran? Afghanistan? Maybe Chechnya? Oh, come on. Tell us what terrorists' nest you're going to deliver it to.' He shook the glowing cylinder in front of his opponent, and Zara saw the black dot at its centre fluctuate, constantly changing shape.

'Syria. I'm delivering the device to Syria,' Mr Akkaş snapped.

'See!' Milne rolled his eyes in a mocking grimace. 'In less than twenty-four hours, these troublemakers wouldn't pose any threat to the world anymore. Zara told you the truth. It should have just enough charge in those batteries to allow you to leave London and to travel to the meeting with your client. And then... Bang! No problem anymore.'

'What?' Zara yelled. 'You could destroy an entire country? Because of what? Some prejudice? Your assumption, based on some hatred-spreading media? You're a historian, not a mass murderer-'

'No prejudice at all. I don't care if it's Iran, North Korea, Syria or any other rogue nation posing a global threat. When I realised Die Fledermaus couldn't solve my problems, then I'd utilised the most of its capabilities to make the world a safer place. You don't think that these people would use the device for scientific purposes, do you? For good?'

'We're historians, not politicians. Leave these problems to MI5 or the NCA to deal with.'

'Oh, really? The NCA?' Milne chuckled bitterly. He nodded to the two agents. 'How many terrorist attacks have you stopped lately? How many people need to die because of your incompetence and corruption?'

The two men kept silent.

'I can't believe I'm hearing this from you.' Zara shook her head. 'You sound like a brainwashed Nazi now. You, the person who studied them all your life, turned into one of them. No. I don't believe it. Am I missing something?'

'I hoped,' he faltered. 'I hoped it might help me see something or, better, somebody lost to me long ago, lost forever.'

'Oh, please! You're a scientist, not a medium who's able to

talk to the dead.'

Milne's deep despair bordered on bizarre naivety, if not to say more, sheer madness, pure and simple.

'You try to kill too many birds with one stone,' she continued. 'To use me for discovering the U-boat and the device, to take all credit for it, to wipe out an entire country and get paid–'

'Fucking bastard!' The solicitor barked, gritting his teeth and raising his gun to the professor.

A light vibration, a mini-shock wave went through the room, and Stefan landed heavily on the solicitor. Ethan followed him, falling between the two petrified agents. Mr Akkaş dropped his gun, but the officers reacted swiftly to pick it up and apprehend him.

'Stefan!' Zara rushed to him and fell into his arms.

'The game is over, Professor. Your concern about national security is touching, but Zara is right – leave it to the NCA and other intelligence services and give us the device.' Patricia Cartwright appeared on the doorstep, leading her small army of agents. 'Mr Akkaş, Captain Milne, hands up!' She turned to the men.

'Don't come any closer,' Milne mumbled. His hand still squeezed the case.

'Professor, please, don't do it. Let's put all the guns down and talk.' Stefan made a reconciling gesture. 'You know better than we if you use Die Fledermaus again now, it will run out of the batteries completely and–'

'No. It's too late.' Milne shook his head. 'The old captain was right, telling in his notes we would never fully understand and possess Die Fledermaus. The device will possess us. We'll never be able to control time and space using Die Fledermaus, but Die Fledermaus will always control us.'

'Father, please, listen to them, listen to me, at least once in your lifetime. Put the damn thing down and let them deal with it.' Still shocked and pale, Ethan broke into the conversation. 'If you use it now, nothing guarantees that you'll see what you want to see or meet a person you want to meet. I've just returned from there. I know what I'm talking about. You aren't imagining it. It's...' he faltered. 'It's more than your mind can bear.'

'No. There're only two routes out of it: prison or eternity.'

Stefan jumped, ready to push the professor down, but a powerful force punched him back. Like in a slow-motion film, Zara watched the black dot inside the cylinder explode, turning the glowing liquid into a pulsating ink-black fluid. The white and dazzling light made the company to turn away, bending down and covering their eyes.

Zara dropped to the floor next to Stefan. She curled up, closing her eyes, expecting an explosion, the room's collapse, the end of the world.

The light extinguished as suddenly as if it switched off. Then, the absolute vacuum of sound...

'What's happened? Where's the professor? Where's the device?' Cartwright was the first to recover. She stared into the space where Professor Milne had stood a few seconds before.

Only silence answered her.

Chapter Twenty-Five

Zara

'Dr Krause, Zara, on behalf of the NCA and MI5, thank you for helping our investigation.' Cartwright favoured Stefan and Zara with a warm smile as the trio seated themselves in the spacious Hotel Mouritz' lobby. 'I think you can clarify what just happened.' She nodded to Stefan.

'There's nothing to thank us for.' He shrugged, voice still trembling. 'We lost the device, along with Professor Milne. I was wrong, Walter Dix was wrong, we all were. We theorised black matter would produce a colossal explosion if released in such a concentrated quantity. An explosion large enough to destroy an entire city.'

'So, what exactly happened?'

'I think you're better discussing it with physicists.'

'I'm sure I will in time, although we don't even have the device to show them now. Besides, I'm interested to hear your theory.'

'I can only suggest that the enormous levels of energy the black matter emitted were sufficient not only to rip time and space apart but also to make the "segment" collapse on itself.' He stopped, shifting his gaze from Cartwright to Zara and back.

Cartwright squinted. 'Whether it's true or not, we'll never know. We've lost the device. That's all that matters now, at least.' She bit at her thin lips in annoyance. 'This time, I'm afraid we lost Die Fledermaus forever.'

Zara, who had kept silent until this point, asked, 'What about Professor Milne? What about the second diver, Pete?'

'Nothing we can do for them. We can only hope he'll be as

lucky as Ivor Kazinski and one day return.'

Zara didn't answer. She saw an arriving police car through the window, here to pick up the handcuffed Hussein Akkaş and Captain Milne. Ethan turned his head slightly and their eyes met. There was no anger or hatred in his eyes, only shock, grief, and fear. She knew it would be the last time she saw him.

'And Ethan?' Zara faltered. 'What about him?'

'We will charge captain Milne with conspiracy to assist in organised crime and terrorism, concealment of evidence, and attempted murder. Most likely, he'll spend the rest of his life in prison.'

'No. Please, he's not a terrorist. He was just confused.'

'I don't think he wanted to kill me,' Stefan interrupted. 'Zara is right. He's an arsehole, but not a cold-blooded murderer. His father dragged him into this crime. When he realised he was in too deep, he thought he had no choice but to continue.'

'He's lost his father. His Navy career is over. I know Ethan. For him, it's worse than the death penalty.' Zara squeezed Cartwright's sleeve. 'Please, Officer. I've helped you with this case as much as I could. All I'm asking in return is to save Ethan by putting him on suspended conviction or something similar.'

'I promise to do my best, but it won't be easy for him to avoid court martial.' Cartwright shook her head.

'I'm sure you'll succeed.'

They kept silent for a few minutes.

'What about you? Back to Germany tomorrow?' Cartwright turned to Stefan. 'Maybe you wish to continue your interrupted holiday here in London?'

'Thanks for the offer, but I've had enough of British hospitality.' Stefan laughed bitterly, rubbing his ribs.

'Do you feel okay?' Cartwright frowned. 'Are you sure you don't need to see a paramedic?'

'Thanks, I'm fine. Just a couple of bruises from the fist fight and my heavy landing on the solicitor. I'll stay here overnight and tomorrow in the morning I'll take a train to Heathrow.'

'Don't worry, I'll give you a lift to the airport,' Zara said.

'I'll ask my assistant to book a direct flight to Kiel,' Cartwright suggested.

'Thanks. That would be helpful.'

'So, it's time to say goodbye.' Cartwright's face illuminated with a sincere smile again. 'It seems like the Hazard Response team has finished in the room. I need to have a word with them.' She gestured to a group of three people, dressed in bright yellow protective suits, helmets, and carrying some equipment.

Zara and Stefan said a warm farewell to the agent, and she left them alone in the lobby.

* * *

Zara and Stefan retired to the hotel restaurant on the top floor, where Milne had met his Turkish contact.

'It's hard to believe in the reality of what's happened.' Zara took a big sip of her wine and, unblinking, stared at Stefan. 'I didn't wish Milne such a horrible end.'

'He wanted to escape punishment, but punished himself.' Stefan sighed. 'Ulrich Schultz, Hermann Thiel – he knew about their crimes, knew what Die Fledermaus was capable of. Knowing all this hasn't stopped him from plotting another, even worse, crime.'

'Do you think he's dead? Could we have lost the device forever?'

'I told you and Agent Cartwright my theory. Black matter destroyed itself and the device.'

'I'm sure your explanation fits perfectly into Cartwright's report, but it's not enough for me.'

'When the batteries discharged completely, and all black matter interacted with "normal" matter, it could cut a certain segment of time out of the space-time continuum, leaving

Milne in a sort of "time bubble".'

'What's happened to this "time bubble"? Where is it now?'

'I do not know.' He leaned back in his chair. 'If modern physics perceives our universe as a four-dimensional plane, with time representing the fourth dimension, then we can try to separate one dimension from the other. I suppose that's what might've happened. As soon as DF can't reverse the separation process, this "bubble" would stay separated from our space-time continuum until it eventually collapses.'

Zara didn't respond. Stress and fatigue prevailed, after all.

'I think the best thing to do right now is to postpone this conversation until tomorrow morning,' Stefan said. 'We both need to rest.'

'Thank you for Ethan,' she said, changing the subject. 'You're right. He's not a murderer. He's a lost, confused man. His entire life was nothing but constant struggle and confusion. His father's attitude can't have made it easy.'

'Do you still care about him?' Stefan's eyes challenged her for a few seconds.

'Oh, that feeling withered a long time ago, but he doesn't deserve to go to prison.'

'True. He's also punished himself in a way.'

The waiter brought their meal, and they ate it in semi-silence.

Zara sipped her wine. Tomorrow he'd return home, and she'd likely never see him again. What'd she expected? He was a divorcee, but it didn't matter that he was single. She studied Stefan's face. He hadn't told her about his wife, but that didn't mean there wasn't another woman in his life. He hadn't been fully open about his past, yet he cared for her.

'So, what's next?' he asked, finishing his dish.

'Erm… nothing really.' His question took her unawares, but she tried to hide her real mood. 'I'll continue to work on my dissertation. The University of Portsmouth will need to appoint a new dean now, so I'll have a new mentor soon.'

Stefan chuckled. 'I hope they'll be more dedicated to history than Milne.'

'And what about you?'

'The same, pretty much. Research, publications, travels.'

'Till we meet again?' she blurted. God! Was she so desperate?

'Of course, I'd be happy to see you again. You're welcome to Germany any time. Besides, the Navy will hopefully lose interest in the U-boat and release her back to a university or a museum for study. Then, well…'

'Oh, I wouldn't be so optimistic.' Zara smirked. 'When the Navy releases her, MI5 will be there straight away. She'll be classified and locked in a dry dock, away from researchers and historians like many other secrets.'

'Well, we'll see.' He sighed. 'Are you on social media?'

Zara swallowed her annoyance back.

'Ah, I've found you,' Stefan said, scrolling on his phone.

A notification pinged in her pocket. 'Yeah, thanks.'

Her body weakened under the pressure and stress she'd experienced. 'I should go to my room.' She rose from the table, ready to leave. 'Cartwright's assistant promised to book rooms for us. I'm sure they'll be ready by now.'

'You haven't finished your meal.'

'I know, I'm too tired and-'

'Finish your drink, at least.'

'I'll order mulled wine to my room; always helps me to fall asleep after a long and stressful day.'

'Then I will see you tomorrow morning.' He rose as well, opening his arms for a hug.

They shared a soft embrace, and Zara could feel the warmth of his breath on her neck. Even after those fraught hours, he still smelled of aftershave.

Zara rushed to move away from him. 'Good night.'

* * *

A hot bath and an aromatic glass of mulled wine were enough to relax Zara, even just a little. She sat on the vast bed in her stylishly furbished room. The NCA had gone over its budget with this one. She chuckled, making herself comfortable under the fluffy duvet. Her eyelids grew heavier, and she yawned, shutting her eyes just for a second.

A succession of ear-splitting explosion erupted around her. An endless salvo of explosions and hiss of water around. The painful rattle of the metal floor plates under her feet.

She looked around in horror. A U-boat control room?

'Zwanzig, einundzwanzig, zweiundzwanzig,' a male voice counted the explosions in German behind her.

The compartment was full of Kriegsmarine's crewmen, dark in the dim, erubescent emergency light, they looked like the ghostly shadows of the room. Zara tried to focus her eyes on the nearest of them, but the dusk and the constant reverberations made it impossible. Two more monstrous explosions sounded, creeping closer.

'Dreiundzwanzig, vierundzwanzig, fünfundzwanzig…' The monotonous count continued.

A cold sweat covered her forehead. Depth charges?

These lightning balls, these incandescent suns, designed to explode at a certain depth and rip U-boats apart. They didn't even require a direct hit. The intense pressure wave created by the charge would've been substantial enough to tear the hull asunder.

'Bearing two hundred forty degrees. Getting louder.' Another voice made her jump. 'It sounds like another destroyer.'

Five more powerful roars. Half-stunned, Zara squeezed her head with her hands. Her hands… smeared in machine oil and dirt, looked alien.

A dull boom. The water rushing back into the vacuum created

by a depth charge.

'The bow is taking on water! Quickly.' A low yell from another compartment broke through the roaring of the water and the cannonade of explosions.

Another violent explosion ripped through the water, forcing the whole boat to scream and groan. It thrust Zara onto the dancing plates of the floor. A sharp dagger of pain pierced her head and… the darkness flooded in. The murky, icy water filled her lungs, burning and ripping them apart.

'Father! Please, help me!' The last flash of consciousness illuminated her mind. This time, the brawny arms of her father didn't protect her, pulling out of the water to the light. Now, there was no one to save her.

Zara gasped in a desperate urge for air. She awoke, staring into space, and it took her some time to realise she was back in her room.

What a bizarre nightmare, she thought, getting out of the bed and making her way to the bathroom. So vivid, so realistic. She splashed cold water on her face. Depth-charged by a destroyer. She nodded to her dishevelled reflection in the mirror.

Rushing to clear the heavy veil of her nightmare, she turned her thoughts to the events of the past few days. It seemed to her a decade had passed without the need of Die Fledermaus manipulation. A good friend turning into a criminal, a dodgy solicitor, a crazy NCA agent, a delusional ex-boyfriend, and a kind German historian accelerated her life like a ballistic missile.

Thinking of Stefan's pale face and bright-blue eyes, a warm smile stretched across her face. Some seventy years ago, they would've been enemies. Now they were working together, helping each other, becoming friends, saving each other's lives, joining against a common enemy. History was a strange thing.

Stefan was so different from Ethan, so calm and balanced, soft but brave, quiet but persistent. Ethan tried to cover his insecurity with cynical masculinity, nothing like Stefan. Or was it just coldness? This detached, methodical attitude like that of his ancestors who swamped Europe during the war? His demeanour, his manners, his speech were so smooth, so ideal, almost sterile. Of course. There were no feelings there. Embedded in his archetype, in his psyche. He didn't even realise what he was doing, didn't even know how he hurt her, dragging deeper and deeper into his ideal but deadly web. He'd helped her, but he'd not cared. The NCA, science, and himself were his motivation.

God! Where had all this come from? And then, the same heavy, bitter sadness squeezed her heart again. He'd called Milne biased, but the irony was clear to her now. She was no better thinking of Stefan like that. Maybe it was her bruised ego? And why should he run after her? A sudden wave of nausea forced her into the bathroom. Zara looked in the mirror. Her tired face and extinguished eyes reflected the stress of the day. Milne was right. Die Fledermaus was venom, it possessed everyone it touched, poisoning their soul. Black matter infused their minds, inducing suspicion and paranoia. Schultz and Thiel had worked with it for a while, and they'd killed their crew. Milne spent a day with the device and was ready to kill them all. As for her, she'd called Milne a Nazi, but she was no better than he was, accusing Stefan of sins he hadn't committed. She washed her face with the cold water. Her nausea fading. She sat on the edge of the bed and dialled room service.

Chapter Twenty-Six

Zara

'Good morning, how did you sleep?' Stefan greeted Zara with a wide smile. She'd come down to breakfast half an hour later than planned. 'I was worried you might've felt ill. I was going to check on you after finishing.' He nodded to an almost empty plate. 'Are you alright? You look so pale.'

'Ah, I'm fine.' She waved, sinking into the chair and arranging the plates. She gulped down a glass of water in a futile attempt to irrigate the desert-dry throat. 'Just had one too many yesterday, got carried away with myself.'

He chuckled. 'Celebrating the end of our mission. Where was my invite?'

'More an attempt to drown my sorrows.'

'I think you'd better stay in bed for the next couple of hours. I'll take a train to the airport or ask a receptionist to call a taxi for me.'

'No. I'll take you to Heathrow. I'm sober enough now, don't worry. A strong espresso, and I'll feel great.'

'If you insist.'

As they finished their breakfast, Zara struggled to pull her thoughts together. A severe self-induced headache certainly didn't help. Stefan seemed distant, submerged in his musings. When their meal was over, he checked out, and the two headed to Heathrow Airport.

Although rush hour had passed, the multicoloured python of heavy traffic crawled through the city centre, and Stefan shifted in the passenger seat. He tried to make a few jokes about London's transport, but Zara replied at random, and soon their conversation fell silent.

'This is it, it seems. Time to say goodbye.' Stefan smiled shyly as they finally reached the airport. Zara parked the car in the short stay car park. 'I wish we had more time, enough for a drink in a café and chat.'

'Oh, it wouldn't help.' Zara waved. 'I hate long goodbyes. They make me emotional.'

An uneasy pause hung in the air. She wanted to say so much that the whole day wouldn't be enough to express her thoughts and emotions. She didn't want to leave an awkward impression, and more importantly, she didn't want Stefan to suspect her feelings for him.

'Well, I hope we meet again soon.' He unfastened his seat belt and opened his arms for a hug. 'Thank you for everything you've done for me and for this crazy journey.'

They shared a tender hug and a shy kiss on the cheek. He left the car and pulled his suitcase out of the boot.

Zara's melancholy flooded back, prevailing over the headache. Stefan headed to the lifts, turning to wave as the doors parted. She swallowed back her tears and squeezed out a tentative smile. As the doors closed and Stefan disappeared out of sight, the minutes passed, but she couldn't start the engine.

A knock came at the glass. 'What are you doing?' she started. 'Your plane's about to take off in half an hour and-' She opened the passenger's door for him.

'Forget about it.' He waved. 'I need to stay with you. I promised not to leave you. Remember? I need to keep that promise.'

'What are you talking about?'

'Die Fledermaus showed me my future, a future without you.' He opened the driver's side door, embracing her shivering shoulders. 'There's nothing in it, just hollow solitude and regrets about things I should've done, but never accomplished. Words I never said. Zara…' he faltered, eyes looking brighter with tears he tried to hide. 'I want to be with you. In England, in Germany – wherever.'

'We've only known each other a few days,' she mumbled. 'How can you trust Die Fledermaus? How can you believe something you can't even fully explain?'

'It's not only because of the device.' He beamed, pulling her closer. 'Let's give it a chance. Let's give ourselves a chance. Listen to your feelings. What do you feel?'

She raised her tearful eyes to him, and finally, their lips met in a soft tender kiss. Just as she'd imagined, just as she craved. Delicate, warm, and loving.

'We should head back to the hotel.' She exhaled, more suggestive than she'd intended. 'My room's booked for another day.'

'Do you want to drag me through that horrible London traffic again?' He chuckled, taking her hand in his. 'I can continue my interrupted holiday in London, I suppose.'

* * *

Zara curled up against Stefan in her king-size bed in the Mouritz Hotel.

'I thought you were being cold and indifferent.' She sighed, putting her arm around his naked chest. 'You hid your feelings well.'

'I hid them well even from myself.' He chuckled. 'I was afraid of being rejected or misunderstood. I've always been reluctant to open myself to new possibilities. And we only a few days ago. I'm not the kind of person who looks for quick hook-ups, you know.'

'Neither am I.'

'I've made huge mistakes in the past, getting married at such a young age. I'm anxious about making the same mistake again. What if it's just a whim? Just physical attraction? I've asked myself all these questions. What if I misunderstood the message from Die Fledermaus?'

'You told me the device showed you your future? How is it possible?'

'It threw you into the past or a version of the past, and it cast me into the future or a version of my future,' Stefan started, climbing out of the bed to pace the room. 'I saw my living room in Kiel, surrounded by a blurry, watery substance. The room looked festive, decorated with a Christmas tree, and empty boxes all around. But I felt cold and alone in the room. I glanced at the snow-covered street outside. The neighbours were decorating their house with lights. Their joy and laughter turned my mood even colder. A piece of decoration slipped from my hand and smashed on the floor. Its debris scattered all over the room.' He narrated as he paced. 'I went to collect the larger pieces, but noticed my wrinkled, shaking hands. They aged in a second and caught my reflection in a splinter. An old man in the late eighties. Sad, lonely, and forgotten.'

'So, how do I fit in all this?'

'I didn't understand the vision at first. But when Ethan attacked me in the hotel and I used the device again, the vision repeated, but that time it had changed,' he continued after a pause. 'The same place, the same weather outside. The same neighbours decorating their house. Though, my mood had changed. Warmth and peace poured into my soul. The same fancy glass decoration slipped from my hand, but the next moment, your hand plucked it from the air. You're so clumsy. You said and laughed at me, and I saw both our reflections in the bauble. We looked a few years older than we are now, but smiling and happy. And there was something else in it.'

'What was it?'

'A long corridor. Could've been a hospital.' He waved. 'I don't remember much. The main thing is that I remember us together.'

Zara didn't reply, just took his hand in hers, making him take a seat on the bed.

'The visions almost drove me insane. I couldn't sleep the whole night, analysing what Die Fledermaus was telling me. Leaving you at the airport, it came to me. There's no future, only the endless funnel of opportunities, defined by our actions in the present. Our present creates our future. Our actions or lack of them determine our near or far future.'

'So you think the device showed you two different futures, depending on your choice to stay or leave today?'

'I believe so.' Stefan nodded. 'If physicists are right and the future is a funnel, turned upside down, with its top being the present second, then the number of possible futures increases the further we go from the present.'

'Physics again? Boring.'

'I agree. Anatomy is far more exciting.' He tickled her belly, producing a giggle. 'Yet, it was physics that brought me back to you.' He stared at her, eyes serious.

She turned away and rose from the bed. Coming closer to the window, she glanced outside at the buzzing city. Her thought turned to her nightmare.

'Die Fledermaus has changed our lives,' she started after a thoughtful pause. 'Milne was right, it's more than just a device capable of moving objects through space. DF doesn't experience time. It knows neither the past nor the future. Able to push our minds and souls beyond their limits. Prepared to go beyond life and death, dragging our psyche through alternative pasts and futures. There's something else in it, though. Nightmares that feel so real.' She closed her eyes, a sudden weakness swallowing her like the night before.

She was there, on the conning tower of a U-boat, scanning the sea with her binoculars and giving the orders to her crew. The taste of salt on her lips. Gusts of the icy storm lashing her face.

She sank beneath wind and sea spray into the bowls of the vibrating metal monster. The fierce and curious faces of her crewmembers morphed from the darkness of the compartment. She heard them joking in German, grinning at her. The stink of metal, diesel, machine oil, sweat, and damp leather wrapped her senses.

Stefan's figure emerged from the dusk, face a lifeless mask. Eyes, dark and alien, hypnotised her, making her weak. He snatched her back from her surreal reverie, coming closer and squeezing his hips to hers.

'Bizarre.' She took a step back into the shadows of the room. 'My nightmare, the one I've told you about. What if... what if DF created all these weird dreams?'

'I wouldn't be so sure about the device's influence on dreams. Dreams are just dreams, a product of our exhausted subconscious minds. I know the past couple of days have been crazy for all of us. I can imagine how upset you are now the device is lost and how pissed off you must be about the U-boat. But please, try to relax and don't dwell on it too much.'

'I'm sorry.' She sat on the edge of the bed. 'You and Cartwright are right. Nothing much we can do now. As for my strange dreams, let's hope it's just a side effect of using DF.'

A knock at the door made them jump, and they exchanged curious looks.

'I'll open it.' Zara volunteered, waiting for Stefan to disappear into the bathroom before opening the door. 'Officer? What are you doing here?'

The tall figure of Agent Cartwright appeared from the silent dusk of the corridor.

'Good afternoon. Can I come in?' She shifted on the doorstep.

'Ah, yes, of course.' Zara stepped back to let her in.

'I have a small gift for you and some great news.' Cartwright made a circle around the room and took a seat in the corner.

'I assume it's something important if you came without calling or sending one of your operatives,' Zara mumbled.

'Ah, Dr Krause?' Cartwright shouted for Stefan, without paying attention to Zara's confusion. 'Please, join us. Don't be shy. I'm sure you'll be interested in hearing my news as well.'

'Christ! Have you never heard of privacy?' Stefan muttered, exiting the bathroom, wrapped in a dressing gown.

'I see you're enjoying your holiday in London, Doctor.' Cartwright smirked. 'To make it even more memorable, I've brought you something you might like.' With that said, she pulled a file from her briefcase.

Zara frowned. 'What's that?'

'It's a copy of the device's manual. The original, written in 1944 for the U-boat's crew, we found it in Mr Akkas's belongings. He claimed he received it from Professor Milne. I'm sure this document will help with your research.' She handed the file to Stefan.

'Thank you.' Stefan nodded, looking through the document. 'What about the U-boat?'

'She's still with the Navy. As soon as their specialists are satisfied, she'll retire in a dry dock in Gosport.'

'I need unlimited access to her as soon as she's released,' Stefan demanded.

'Well, she's not under my jurisdiction anymore, but we should be able to organise that.'

'What was the news you were going to tell us?' Zara asked.

'Ivor Kazinski has awoken from his coma. Doctors believe his speech will return in a few days.'

Zara clapped her hands. 'Great. I wonder what he'll be able to tell us about his experience.'

'That's not all,' Cartwright continued. 'The authorities found a gentleman in his mid-sixties, unconscious on a bench in the park of St. Helier this morning. Luckily, his ID was with him. This man's name is Professor Karl Milne.'

'What?' the two asked in a chorus.

Stefan rubbed his forehead. 'St. Helier?'

'The Isle of Jersey.' Cartwright nodded. 'His condition's similar to Mr Kazinski; a deep coma, but no damage to the internal organs.'

'He's alive,' Zara repeated in shock. 'The device threw him as far as the Channel Islands.'

'I'm grateful Die Fledermaus operated at a relatively short range within one country,' Cartwright said. 'It would've been much worse if our professor had re-materialised somewhere in Alaska, Siberia or New Zealand.'

'True.' Stefan nodded. 'What about the device? Any debris? The empty container? Anything at all?'

'Unfortunately, it's nowhere to be seen.'

'I want to talk to the diver first and pray for Milne to gain consciousness as soon as possible,' Zara said.

'I'm sure he'll be more open with you two than with my officers.' Cartwright nodded.

'Ah, that's why you're here.' Stefan grinned. 'You need us to get closer to the professor and let him tell you everything he'd likely hide from the NCA. Without the device, it would be problematic to support any accusations against him in court. If only he could make it to the court at all.'

'Trust me, the Channel Islands are gorgeous at this time of the year, much better than overcrowded London. Romantic as well. Besides, you claim you need access to the U-boat, so-'

'I'm familiar with the islands. I've been there a few times,' Stefan said.

Zara touched Stefan's shoulder, pulling him to the bedroom. 'Excuse us for a moment.' She nodded to the agent. 'Ivor and Milne are the only living witnesses to have experienced Die Fledermaus for a long time. Their evidence is our only chance to understand the effects of black matter, and how it influences people. Cartwright is right. If Ivor has nothing to hide, then Professor Milne wouldn't be as open with the NCA as he might with us.' She lowered her voice so Cartwright couldn't hear her. 'Please, Stefan, help me get to the bottom of this.'

'What makes you think he'll talk to us at all?'

'Milne isn't a criminal. If there's still something good that remains in him, making him feel his guilt and burden of responsibility is the only way to get to the truth.'

Chapter Twenty-Seven

Professor Milne

A loud metal clanking reverberated through his skull. The teeth-aching cry of a crooked violin with frayed strings. Then, the howling of a storm and the rumble of thunder, raging in the background.

Dazzled by the white light of the device, Milne finally opened his eyes. What was this place? He glanced around, standing in the middle of a wide street, squeezing the case with the device in his hand.

Buildings, ghostly derelicts with empty eyes sockets of windows, dark trees with blackened branches instead of green canopies, and shadows of people, featureless and hollow. He was the only living being in this phantom city.

The crimson sunless sky hung low above the city's skyline. The pitch-black darkness covered the horizon, advancing from all directions. A few shadows came closer, surrounding Milne, before exploding into thousands of glittering black orbs.

Milne realised that all the noise had subsided. The broken violin ceased its cry. The street was completely still, as if suspended in a vacuum. Wrapped in absolute silence, but so deafening that he could hear his staggered breath.

'Daddy...' a familiar high-pitch voice called.

'Stella?' He turned around.

'Daddy, daddy...' the girl's voice called, coming from the first-floor window of the building ahead of him.

'Stella!' Milne burst into the half-smashed double door of the building and stopped, submerged by absolute darkness. The floor vibrated under his feet.

'Stella?' he called again, but heard nothing.

With a loud clang, the light returned, and Milne found himself in the middle of an enormous circular chamber, a rotunda without windows. He raised his head to the ceiling, but the dome was so high and wide that he felt dizzy. The light came from the narrow windows in the dome's turret. The thunder still rumbled somewhere in the distance. Semi-circular rows with thousands of seats took almost the entire width of the hall. A speaker's platform rose high above them. A massive metal eagle, clenching a swastika in its talons, adorned the wall behind the platform.

Milne glanced around. The domed building looked like a grand film set, but he'd seen it somewhere before; maybe in an old photograph.

'Why are you here?' A male voice with a pronounced German accent made Milne jump.

Milne turned around to see a young blond man, dressed in a white jumper, a black leather jacket, and a white captain's cap with an eagle on its front. The man's cold, blue eyes challenged Milne for a few seconds. He could swear there was nobody in the chamber a second ago.

'Why are you here, Professor?' the man asked again.

'You... you know who I am?' Milne stepped closer.

The man's pale skin almost glowed in the chamber's dusk. No older than twenty-five or twenty-six, his eyes... Milne couldn't bear their gaze. It felt as if these eyes, these massive icy lakes, were staring into his very soul as if they had already experienced the sorrow and fear of the entire world.

'I know you well.' The man nodded. 'What I don't understand is why the hell you appeared here, crashing through everything on your way,' he snapped, annoyance in his voice.

'I'm looking for someone,' Milne mumbled.

The man smirked. 'You're in the wrong place.'

'I'm looking for my daughter.'

'You're looking in the wrong place.'

'But I heard her,' Milne yelled. 'Heard her voice there, on the street, then in this building. She was playing the violin. I followed her voice and ended up here.' He made a wide gesture. 'What is this place? Some kind of ritual chamber?'

'You could call it so, I guess.' The man shrugged.

'And who are you? Judging by your uniform, you're a naval officer?'

'Captain Engel, the ruler of this city. At your service.' The man smiled his ideal smile and bowed slightly.

'What the hell do you mean?' Milne laughed but fell abruptly silent as a powerful tremor ran through the floor, making him almost lose his balance.

'Why did you use Die Fledermaus, if you don't have the slightest clue how to deal with the effects?'

Milne squeezed the case tighter. Had the device caused the earthquake and the thunder he'd experienced? 'I had the technical manual. I used it to navigate-'

'Your ignorance is going to destroy the city.' The captain clenched his fists. 'And both of us together with it.'

The chamber grew darker as the howling storm neared and the floor shook vigorously. Milne struggled to keep his balance.

The far wall behind the captain dissolved into crashing waves, which rushed to fill the bowl of the auditorium. Milne watched as a U-boat's conning tower rose out of the sea. Three figures stood on the bridge.

'Zara?' Milne squinted. Perhaps it was his imagination. Or a vision created by this place. 'Is it the past or the future?' He turned to the captain.

'Countless pasts and futures fluctuate around us.' The man shrugged. 'All that matters is that she will return. I've seen it, but I'm unable to stop it.'

'Nothing makes sense here.'

'For you? Maybe not.' The captain raised his voice, trying to shout down the raging storm outside. 'Why are you so ignorant of what can be? To think your primitive logic would work here?'

Another powerful tremor shook the building, and the sea spray slashed Milne. Captain Engel squeezed his stomach as if in pain, but pulled himself together.

'Give me the device and leave.' The Captain stretched his hand to snatch Milne's case.

'I want to see my daughter. Bring her to me and you'll have it.' Milne clutched the case to his chest.

Another tremor opened a wide crevice in the mosaic floor before them. Above them, the windows shattered inwards, raining glass and debris of glass onto Milne. He covered his face, only to see the captain's body collapse into a shower of tiny pulsating and glowing orbs. They surrounded Milne, causing him to scream and cover his face.

'I've told you already. You're looking for her in the wrong place.' The captain's disembodied voice sounded behind Milne's back.

A heavy hand grasped his shoulder. The black orbs coalesced, morphing back into the captain. 'Have you ever looked into your heart?' the captain whispered in Milne's ear. 'What would we see?'

Milne jerked, trying to break free from the captain's grip, but the sharp pain in the chest made him hold his breath. He dropped the case and felt something hot and viscous pulsating in his hands. A real human heart beat in his hands. Milne roared in horror.

The Captain knelt before the terrified professor and collected the case, a chilling smile ran across his big lips.

Another wave of pain wracked Milne before his world dissolved into nothingness.

Chapter Twenty-Eight

Zara

St. Helier, the Isle of Jersey
Two weeks later

'I'm not sure he's ready to see you now.' The nurse shook her head and glanced at Zara and Stefan. 'He fell asleep about twenty minutes ago, and I don't want to wake him. Professor Milne is too fragile to accept so many visitors.'

Zara shot a look through the thin glass door where the ghostly pale Karl Milne rested in a bed.

'First, the NCA officer insisted on seeing him, now you,' the nurse continued.

'Cartwright's got ahead of us,' Stefan mused aloud. 'Couldn't she wait a couple of days? God, she's so desperate to close this case.'

'I don't remember her name, but she was pushy and insisted on taking his notepad.' The nurse nodded. 'It upset Professor Milne, and I had to ask her to leave. The officer argued, but I requested the matron, and she removed her from the room.'

Stefan chuckled and nudged Zara's elbow. 'I'd have loved to see that.'

Zara wasn't listening. 'She took his notepad?' she asked the nurse.

'Well, yes. As I've already told you, his speech hasn't returned, but he can write. He asked for a pen and paper. When he's not sleeping, he draws. It tires him, though. He hardly eats, and I'm afraid he may exhaust himself even more.'

'May we…?' Zara stumbled and glanced at Stefan, but he only nodded. 'May we have a look at these drawings?'

The nurse protested, but the quiet groan from the ward made the whole group turn to the glass door. Milne had woken and sat straight on his bed. His outstretched pale hand waved the two to come in.

The nurse mumbled, but had little choice but to open the door and let the pair in. 'You have five minutes,' she snapped and left them alone.

'Professor.' Zara rushed to her ex-mentor and took a seat on the edge of his bed.

Stefan followed her and occupied a chair in the corner.

A weak shadow of a smile ran across his colourless lips. Milne squeezed Zara's palm and produced a low groan in a fruitless attempt at speech.

'Karl, please, you need a rest.' Zara patted his shoulder. 'I'll talk to Agent Cartwright and ask her to postpone the investigation until you're better. Don't worry. She won't disturb you again.'

The professor replied with a sad moan and reclined back on his pillows. His eyes reflected nothing but exhaustion and sorrow.

'You'll recover. Stefan and I will be here for you,' Zara continued, but Milne shook his head.

Stefan rose from his chair and came to the bed.

'Can we have a look?' He nodded to a small notepad on the bedside table. Zara hadn't noticed it when they came.

Milne handed it to Zara.

Two dozen drawings in multicoloured pens and pencils. Zara could remember from their long chats that Milne's parents had insisted on his attendance at a fine arts school when he was younger. However, he had neither the talent nor the desire to draw, and finally gave up. Zara had never seen Milne draw, but the sketches were superb for a person who'd not expressed a creative flair in fifty years or so.

'What is this place?' Zara asked, looking through the images.

There were skylines of a bizarre city, with enormous domes

and wide alleys, orbs suspended in the air, dark silhouettes of people, seascapes, and the slender shapes of U-boats.

'Where is this place, Professor?' Stefan demanded, joining Zara on the edge of the bed. 'Is it… where Die Fledermaus sent you?'

A tear ran down Milne's pale cheek.

'You must've panicked. You were afraid, but I know you didn't mean us any harm when you used the device.' Zara squeezed Milne's hand. 'We're not here to accuse you or take revenge. We're here to learn what Die Fledermaus showed you, what black matter did to you. I need to understand where it is now and how to deal with it.'

Milne shook his head again, bowing lower.

'Who's that?' Stefan frowned, pointing at the drawing of a man's head in a white Kriegsmarine's cap with an eagle badge.

Huge ocean-blue eyes, narrow chin, and sharp cheekbones – the same young man appeared again and again on the pages of Milne's notepad. On the last page of his sketches, Zara distinguished his writing.

Entering the Chamber, I've met the Captain.

She shifted her look from Milne to Stefan and back. 'What does it mean?'

Her ex-mentor arched his eyebrows, but only a couple of sad moans broke the silence of the ward. Zara wanted to ask him something else, but rushed steps and loud voices from the corridor interrupted her. She turned to the ward's door.

'You've allowed random people to visit him, but you're trying to stop his son,' yelled a familiar male voice, his screams reflected all around the long corridor. 'Where's the logic in that? What? I don't give a damn about your rules. I came here for the second time and I'm not going anywhere until I see my father.'

'God. Ethan.' Stefan released a deep sigh. 'We should go now. The last thing we need is a scandal.'

'We'll be back tomorrow.' Zara turned back to Milne. 'Please, take care.'

He released her hand and reclined back on his pillows.

Saying goodbye to Milne, the two rushed to the door, but it was too late. Ethan met them on the doorstep.

'Zara?' He frowned, skipping greetings. 'Why don't you leave us alone?'

'Ethan, please, this isn't the place to quarrel,' she started. 'We came here to see your father because we believe that-'

'That you can cause me and my family even more pain?' Ethan snapped. 'My father was in a coma. He's still not fully recovered, and nobody knows when it's going to happen. I need special permission every time I leave my house along with this piece of "jewellery" the NCA provided me.' He nodded to a black bracelet on his wrist with a tracker in it. 'My father has created lots of problems. We've made lots of mistakes and paid for them already. We'll be paying until the end of our lives. Is that not enough for you? What else do you want? To torture my father again and again? To take your revenge?'

'Typical Ethan.' Zara chuckled bitterly. 'Look at you, playing victim now. It's everybody else's fault you almost killed Stefan and tried to stop the agency. I regret ever helping you and saving your sorry arse from rotting in prison.'

'Please.' Stefan touched her shoulder, standing between her and Ethan. 'Let's go.'

Zara swallowed her rage and followed Stefan to a lift, never looking back. She knew Ethan's blind anger would've burned her to the core.

* * *

'Now what?' Zara asked as they left the hospital, walking down across an overgrown lane beside the carpark.

Visiting Milne had clarified nothing. Zara's health – her constant insomnia, mixed with heavy nightmares, loss of appetite, and fatigue as a result – didn't help the matter.

Stefan yawned, walking to the car park where their rented Renault waited. 'We need to rest. Let's go back to the hotel. Nothing much we can do right now.'

Zara nodded. The burden of fatigue pressed on her shoulders.

'What do you think about Milne's drawings? What are they? Just the result of his condition? Or does this place exist?' Stefan asked after their car left the car park and took the main road leading to the town's marina. 'If so, what is the significance of it? Do you think we need to discuss it with Cartwright?'

Zara shook her head. 'We have little choice, but I doubt she found anything more than we did.'

'Perhaps not. Now, Cartwright is playing "bad cop" to our "good cop". Her agents will have questioned Ivor Kazinski. She might have more luck with him.'

'Even if Ivor can speak, it doesn't mean Cartwright will share that evidence with us.'

Stefan shrugged; eyes fixed on the busy road. 'At least we'll show our willingness to help with the investigation again. Remember, she has more abilities, resources, and authority than we do, but it was Cartwright who asked us to help. And you agreed first.'

Zara remained quiet.

'Besides, she promised us access to the U-boat when they're finished with their investigation,' he continued.

She sighed. 'We can only try.'

They finally arrived at the hotel, just a stone's throw from the shore. Spring came much earlier to the Channel Islands. And at this time of the year, the town's promenade was full of tourists and the marina packed with yachts of all shapes and sizes.

The two had neither the time nor the desire to spend their day outdoors and headed straight to the hotel room. After a quick shower and sorting out luggage, they could finally relax.

'Don't you want to have a few hours' sleep?' Stefan asked,

stretching in the bed, patting a space next to him. 'We woke early this morning.'

'No, I won't sleep at night, if I do.' She took a seat on the edge of the bed.

'Oh, come on! You look tired. I noticed it in the airport, but didn't want to upset you.'

'I know. I haven't slept well for the last week or so.' Zara nodded. 'Insomnia makes me lethargic. I struggle to focus.'

Stefan frowned. 'Did you see a doctor?'

'No, but they checked all of us straight after the black matter's explosion. There were no traces of radiation, chemical toxins or anything like that.'

'Zara.' He moved closer, scrutinising her. 'I'm regretting now going back to Germany and leaving you alone. I should've stayed with you in England. We don't know what the hell we're dealing with. You need to report your symptoms. You were the one who believed black matter could affect us in some unpredictable ways.'

She chuckled. 'And how do you expect me to explain my condition to doctors?'

'Ask Cartwright for a referral. I'm sure the NCA has special facilities, specialists, and equipment for such an occasion.'

'She's the last person I want to discuss it with.' Zara shook her head.

'Why didn't you tell me you felt unwell? Have you continued to see those strange visions like you experienced the day after the explosion? Nightmares? Anything else unusual?' He leaned back on his pillows. 'Why don't you tell me anything?'

'You were busy at work,' she squeezed a tired half-smile. 'Worrying about the NCA testimony we'll need to give, as if our close collaboration with Agent Cartwright wasn't enough. I hoped Milne would feel better by now, able to help us. But it seems all our hopes are in vain.'

'Please, don't think about it too much and promise me to see a doctor when we finish here.' He moved closer to her, opening his arms for a hug, kissing her pale forehead. 'I couldn't wait to see you again.'

'You need to rest after such a long trip.' She pushed him back slightly. He didn't insist and reclined on his high pile of pillows.

Ten minutes later, the room filled with silence, and only Stefan's quiet breathing disturbed Zara's musings. She moved to the wide chair at the window and switched on her laptop. Smiling to herself, she shot a glance at her dozing partner. If that's what they were now. Tied by circumstance. Without his heavy-rimmed glasses, face relaxed and peaceful, he looked much younger than his age.

What if they were both wrong? Dark waters of hesitation rose again. Everything had happened so quickly. The shock and excitement of their crazy adventures would eventually subside, but what would that leave? She turned back to the bright screen of her laptop, hoping the latest news might distract her from her pointless fears, but she struggled to focus. Milne's eyes, full of hope and pain, emerged in front of her. His strange, surreal drawings floating in her mind.

Entering the Chamber, I've met the Captain.

What was that supposed to mean? Who was their mysterious Captain, and where was the Chamber? Those cold, blue eyes. His features seemed familiar, somehow. Had Milne meet a young Ulrich Schultz? Was that even possible? If so, why wouldn't he call him by his name?

Recalling the professor's scared expression and his body language, she refused that idea. Her phone vibrated, slipping off the wide wooden window sill. She jerked in her chair, and Stefan turned around in the bed.

'Ah, good afternoon, Patricia. How are you?' Zara put it on a loudspeaker so Stefan could hear their conversation.

'Hello, Zara.' Cartwright's voice echoed around the room. 'Doctor, are you somewhere nearby?'

'Hello, hello. Nice to talk to you again.' Stefan didn't hide a chuckle.

'I hope you're enjoying spring on Jersey,' she continued. 'Have you visited our patient?'

'We visited Professor this morning,' Zara said. 'He still can't talk, but he's writing and drawing.'

'I must admit, Professor Milne's artistic talent impressed me. However, I had little time to enjoy them. The hospital staff were less than helpful to our investigation. Luckily, I've taken a few photos of his drawings.'

'So, what do you think?' said Zara, as Stefan got off the bed to move closer to the phone.

'That's was my next question.' Cartwright sounded surprised. 'I thought you might've recognised the place, might've seen it while dealing with the device. What about the mysterious male figure? The Captain, as Milne names him. Have you seen this person before? A famous U-boat's ace you can recall?'

'It's hard to compare a crude pencil drawing to a real person. Milne's sketches are good, but he's far from Leonardo or Rafael.' Zara shrugged. 'My first thought was a young Ulrich Schultz, as Karl knew him personally.'

'A good guess,' Cartwright agreed. 'I'll ask my team to search for the old photos of the captain.'

'No, I don't think it's Schultz.' Stefan cut in, shaking his head. 'Why wouldn't Milne call him by his name? He looked so sad and scared when we tried to talk to him, as if-'

'As if he was afraid,' Zara continued, 'as if something or someone threatened him.'

'We need to identify our captain,' Cartwright said. 'He may lead us to the device or even to the missing diver.'

'What about Ivor Kazinski?' Stefan asked. 'Can he talk? Has he given testimony already?'

'No. He didn't speak. Neither did he leave any visual representation of his travels through time and space.'

Zara frowned. 'What do you mean, *didn't*?'

'Mr Kazinski is dead,' Cartwright's voice faltered.

'What?!' Zara jumped from her chair, and Stefan shifted his gaze from Zara to her phone and back.

'He died two days ago in the hospital,' Cartwright continued. 'A nurse found him dead in his bed.'

'There's nothing about it in the local news,' Zara mumbled.

'It's a classified case, so we don't want any noise around it.'

'What was his cause of death?' Stefan asked.

'He drowned.'

'What?!' the two asked in a chorus.

Stefan grinned a bitter smile. 'It looks like Cornish hospitals don't look after their patients well, allowing them to wander around the seashore in the middle of the night.'

'Ivor didn't leave the hospital premises. He was too weak even to get out of bed. Nor did anyone visit him during the night. The hospital's CCTV cameras confirmed that.'

'Then how did he drown without leaving his bed?' Zara almost yelled.

'His bed and hospital gowns were soaking wet when the nurse found him in the morning. His lungs were full of sea water.'

Stefan said nothing, only shook his head,

'Do you have the samples of the water from his clothes and lungs?' Zara asked.

'We've found nothing unusual in them. Just salt water from the sea. No fingerprints on his body or in the ward, either.'

'What about Milne?'

'Meaning?'

Zara released a deep sigh. 'If there's a connection between Ivor's death and Die Fledermaus, we're all in danger, and Milne is the logical target. We all need protection, but he needs it the most now.'

'I envy Ethan. The police are looking after him twenty-four-seven already.' Stefan chuckled.

'Doctor, please.' Cartwright made a meaningful pause. 'The last thing we need is to panic and blame the device for all our misfortunes. I can't stretch my limited resources further, unless I believe you and other witnesses are in real danger, but I don't believe you are.'

'And Ethan? What was his experience with Die Fledermaus?' Zara asked. 'We don't know anything about his encounter at all.'

'We didn't get much information out of him. It seems like his experience with black matter was too short. He claims he saw his deceased sister, Stella, in her adulthood as if she'd never died. Along with other people from his past. Nothing which helps our investigation.'

Stefan sighed. 'In the Mouritz Hotel, Ethan didn't remain silent about Stella to Milne. Why? Did he lie to him, trying to save him? Lying to conceal the truth about his genuine experience with black matter? There's no way to check any of his testimonies, so we have no choice but to believe him.'

'Wait a minute,' Zara interrupted. 'How could he see Stella, if Die Fledermaus can't travel to the past and can show us only the alternative futures, based on our current events at the present? What was it? Another alternative reality? Another dimension where Stella didn't die?'

'The device had shown you U-4713/A crew when you experienced it for the first time aboard the vessel. Remember?' Stefan shrugged. 'What was it? An alternative past of U-4713/A?'

'I thought I saw her genuine past. But I'm not so sure now.'

Stefan shook his head. 'I wouldn't use the terms "past" and "future" regarding black matter.'

'All your theories sound very exciting,' Cartwright cut in. 'However, we're running out of time.'

'What do you want us to do now?' Stefan asked.

'It would be helpful if you could get Milne's notepad and get more details out of him. Apart from that,' she paused. 'There's nothing you can help us with currently. Enjoy your stay on Jersey.'

They said goodbye, and Zara hung up the phone.

'God, Ivor.' She rose from her chair and stared outside. 'I hoped he'd make it. I was one hundred per cent sure he would be fine.'

Everyday life went by. The sea, overcrowded with yachts and pleasure boats, blinked with its dark waves, reflecting the dazzling sun. Tourists filled up the marina, and all bars and fancy French patisseries were heaving. The light breeze swung multicoloured baskets full of petunias and daisies.

'There's something I need to tell you.' Stefan broke the oppressive pause first. 'I saw Ivor drowned.'

'What?' Zara turned from the window. 'Where? When did you see it?'

'When Ethan attacked me in the Moritz Hotel, Die Fledermaus showed us together in my house in Kiel, but it was only a fraction of what I saw there.'

'So, what else did you see?'

Stefan told her the rest of his vision. 'The dead man in the bath looked familiar to me, but I didn't recognise him back then. Now, I know why. I saw Ivor's photo in a newspaper or on TV, but the pieces have only just fit together.'

'Why didn't you tell me about it?'

He shrugged. 'You were confused. Your nightmares and visions. I didn't want to upset and scare you even more. I thought the most important part of it was that we were together.'

Zara sat on the bed and closed her eyes. 'What are we going to do now? Will you tell Cartwright?'

He sat next to her, taking her hand in his, and kissed it. 'The weather's great; we should go have lunch. I'm starving. We need some fresh air to clear our heads and think everything through.'

'There's nothing to think about.' Zara shrugged. 'One of our witnesses is dead. Milne is silent. Our experience with the device is driving us mad, and Ethan... well, he won't tell the truth. At least, not to Cartwright and her operatives.'

He embraced her waist, kissing her neck slowly as he turned her around and looked into her eyes.

'I know what's on your mind.' He lowered his voice. 'You know we can't prove what we've seen. We can't measure the traces of black matter. As for Ethan, he made it crystal clear – he doesn't want to see us.'

'There has to be a connection with Ivor's death.' Zara shrugged, trying to avoid his gaze. 'You saw it long before he died. I don't believe in coincidence. It has to be related to black matter.'

'Zara, please, there's no time to despair.' He cupped her cheek, his lips touched hers. 'Please, forget about the case for a moment,' he whispered in her ear, pushing her gently onto the bed.

She chuckled. 'I thought you were starving.'

'I can wait an hour.'

Chapter Twenty-Nine

Zara

'Oh, please, at least finish your ice cream. It's delicious.' Stefan nodded to Zara's plate with the already half-melted dessert. 'You've left most of your main dish untouched.'

They found lunch at one a café on the marina, but Zara's dark mood had followed them.

'I don't have the appetite today.' She waved. 'Besides, I don't have as much of a sweet tooth as you.'

Stefan couldn't resist the treat, taking Zara's ice cream and devouring it within a couple of minutes.

She couldn't hide a chuckle. 'See? I told you.'

'Okay, let's take a stroll,' he said once they'd paid their bill. 'You need some fresh air. You'll sleep better after a walk.'

They wandered down the wide promenade, edged by stumpy palms and multicoloured clouds of blooming rhododendrons. The calmed sea breeze crawled to the shore and waves rustled quietly in the background.

The couple kept silent for a while. Cartwright's revelation of Ivor's death and Ethan's silent testimony preoccupied them both.

'Milne hoped Die Fledermaus would let him see Stella again. When he realised it was impossible, it broke him.' Zara broke through a lengthy pause. 'Black matter corrupted him.'

Stefan nodded. 'But it was Ethan who met Stella after all.'

'Showing the past, the future, or any other slice of reality, is black matter conscious somehow?' She shot him a worried look. 'Does it choose where, in what corner of reality to take us?'

Stefan shrugged. 'If so, what's the purpose of our visions?'

'I don't know. We thought we understood the fundamental principle of Die Fledermaus, but I question it now. Especially after Milne's drawings and Ivor's death.'

'Please, Zara. Give your poor, exhausted mind a rest.' Stefan stopped and took her chilly hands in his. 'We don't know whether Ethan is telling the truth. As for Ivor... remember Walter Dix and Ulrich Schultz? They dealt with the device much longer than anyone of us, yet they both lived long lives and died in their eighties. In his memoirs, Walter Dix mentioned no side effects of black matter.'

'Maybe he didn't pay any attention or didn't relate them to the device?'

Stefan's face illuminated with a smile. 'Maybe that's why he lived such a long and happy life? Because they didn't dwell on questions without the answers?' He winked and turned to a kiosk selling flowers and postcards. 'What are your favourite flowers?' He nodded to the enormous bouquets and baskets.

'These.' Zara couldn't hide a smile and pointed to a huge pink-and-white cloud of fluffy peonies.

'Great choice!' Stefan nodded and bought the bouquet.

They continued their way, joking and smiling, and finally took a seat on a wide bench at the seafront.

'Thank you.' Zara put her head on Stefan's shoulder. 'You know how to cheer me up.'

He didn't answer, just stroked her hair. His eyes scanned the low horizon.

Bleep, bleep, bleep…

'What's that?' Zara raised her head, looking confused.

Bleep, bleep, bleep…

'What? What do you mean?' Stefan frowned. 'I can't hear anything, just the sea and seagulls.'

Bleep, bleep, bleep, bleep… The irritating drone grew louder, drowning all others.

'The sound,' she mumbled, trying to rise from the bench, but her knees weakened as a sudden heaviness pressed her chest. She struggled to inhale. The world blurred around her. 'It sounds like…'

'God, Zara! You've gone pale.' Stefan's distorted face came into focus. 'Are you okay?'

'I… I don't know.' She filled her lungs with air in a great gulping breath. The pulsing sound was gone as suddenly as it had appeared.

'I heard it,' she faltered, still unable to move.

Stefan squeezed her palm. 'Heard what?'

'A U-boat. Then I saw him in the mirror. I know who he is.'

'What are you talking about?'

'The Captain,' Zara whispered. 'The man in Milne's sketches. I've seen him before a few times: aboard the U-boat when I saw the crewmen, then in the hall with the pods, and in the mirror in my hotel room. It was-' She drew a deep breath and exhaled loudly. 'He appeared from the sack. I don't remember details. I hoped my visions would subside, but it seems like Milne's drawings have brought them back.'

* * *

'After we visit Milne, you'll see a doctor immediately.' Stefan shot her a worried look as he drove the car out of the hotel car park, heading to the hospital.

Stefan fussed over her the whole evening, although she neither felt nor heard anything unusual.

'I don't know how it works in Germany, but there's no chance to get to a specialist in the hospital without a referral from my local GP. Besides, I don't even know which specialist I need to see,' she mumbled in annoyance.

'I'm sure Cartwright will help.' He waved. 'I'll ask her to press them if needed.'

'Let's just focus on the task at hand.'

A few minutes later, they reached the hospital, parked the car, and made their way straight to Milne's ward.

'Karl Milne?' A receptionist's friendly smile faded away. 'I'm sorry, but-'

'Zara, Dr Krause?' Cartwright's familiar voice sounded behind them. 'Please, follow me.' She waved to one of the vacant waiting rooms.

'What's going on?' Zara squeezed Stefan's hand.

He followed the agent to the office. 'We'll soon find out.'

'Professor Milne is dead,' Cartwright announced, closing the door behind them, and taking a seat on a low settee. 'I'm sorry, Zara.'

Stefan sank into a wide leather chair, swearing in German under his breath. Zara covered her mouth with a quivering hand, afraid to scream in despair. Tears stung her eyes, but she couldn't move to wipe them.

'How?' she squeezed finally.

'A heart attack early in the morning.' Cartwright exhaled. 'He complained about chest pains in the evening. He was unresponsive to normal treatments and struggled to sleep, lost consciousness, and his condition deteriorated overnight. Doctors tried everything, but he was gone.'

Silence hung in the room, only disturbed by Zara's choked sobs.

'I know how hard it must be for you.' Cartwright touched her sleeve. 'He was more than a colleague or mentor. The events of the last few weeks have turned your entire world upside-down, but you need to stay strong. We all need to-'

'Can I see him now?' Zara asked through tears.

Cartwright sighed. 'I don't think that's a good idea. Milne's wife and other relatives are about to arrive. Ethan is here already.'

Zara just shook her head. The white walls of the room with its low ceiling closed up around her. The air became hotter and stuffier. She needed to get out of there; she needed some space.

'I'll wait for you outside.' She nodded to Stefan and left the room without saying goodbye to Cartwright.

Chapter Thirty

Stefan

'Give her some time.' Cartwright made a warning gesture to a shocked Stefan.

'What caused the heart attack?'

'The doctors don't know yet.' She shrugged. 'At least, he didn't drown.'

'What about his sketches?'

Cartwright took the notepad out of her case. 'I'll send you the copies later.'

'The Captain again?' Stefan raised his eyes from the pages.

She nodded. 'And the U-boat.'

Stefan looked through the pages. 'Judging by these drawings, this isn't U-4713/A.' He rubbed his chin. 'There's no number on the conning tower, but I can tell straight away it's not XXIII-class. It looks more like type VIIC, an Atlantic version.'

'What? Another submarine? Another captain?'

'I wouldn't jump to conclusions.' Stefan grimaced. 'What's that?' Milne's sloppy writing on the last page of the notepad attracted his attention.

She will return.

'What does he mean?'

Cartwright shrugged. 'His daughter, Stella, perhaps? Ethan claimed he saw her.' She took the notepad back from Stefan and returned it to her case. 'Whatever it means, I have no time to guess right now. The dead bodies are piling up around me, and I don't know how to stop it.'

'So, you think there's a connection between Ivor and Milne's deaths?'

Cartwright rose from the settee and made a circle around the room. 'The cause of their deaths are completely unrelated. Ivor was murdered, I have no doubts about it. The question is how, by whom, and how we're going to prove it. Professor Milne died of a natural cause with no traces of poisoning or anything that could cause his heart attack.'

Stefan bowed his head lower. 'The only thing connecting these two men is black matter.'

'You know I can't attach our speculations to the report.' Cartwright approached, resting her hand on his shoulder. 'Go to Zara. She needs you the most now. I'll keep you posted if something new comes along.'

'Zara.' Stefan exhaled. 'I worry about her.'

'Why?'

He told Cartwright the full story about Zara's condition. 'She's convinced she saw the man whom Milne called the Captain,' he added finally. 'She saw him during one of her episodes.'

'So, who is he? Why is he so important?'

'If only we knew.' Stefan bowed his head low.

'Doctor, you understand I can't write my report based on Zara or anybody else's nightmares or visions.' Cartwright sighed.

'I understand.' He nodded. Should he have told her about Ivor? What was the sense in doing so if she didn't believe Zara?

A prolonged pause filled the room.

'I feel terribly sorry for Zara. Let me have a word with the doctors about her hallucinations,' Cartwright said. 'I'm sure they won't refuse to assist us.'

Chapter Thirty-One

Zara

Zara stood at the window in the long hospital corridor. Despite the bright sunny day, the gusty wind from the sea bent trees to the ground. Milne was gone, leaving her confused and angry, feeling betrayed, but she'd never wished him such a horrible end. Alone and scared in a cold and unfamiliar hospital ward, surrounded by unknown, indifferent people. She wondered what his last thoughts were. A tear ran down her cheek. She was glad she'd had enough time to forgive him.

'Zara?' Stefan's calm voice interrupted her thoughts.

She felt his warm breath on the back of her neck as he gently embraced her shoulders.

'If we wait here for another half an hour, a doctor will see you,' he continued. 'Cartwright had a word. They'll also take a blood test and whatever else they need.'

'Okay.' She exhaled.

It was pointless to object. She didn't have the energy to fight.

* * *

They strolled down a public trail, along sheer cliffs, to a deserted beach. Zara walked slightly faster, intrusive thoughts occupying her. Stefan walked behind at a respectful distance. The perfectly preserved remains of a German bunker rose in front of them. This concrete guard from the island's dramatic past attracted groups of tourists during the high season but stood grim and lonely in the brisk morning air. Zara ran down the path, closer to the dark witness of the occupation.

'I think we need to book our tickets home,' she started, circling the building without looking at Stefan. 'The hospital tests have found nothing unusual. As expected.' She chuckled. 'We haven't heard from Cartwright, either. So, there's no point sitting around?'

Stefan came closer, his voice calm. 'You don't want to spend a bit more time with me?'

'Oh, please, we've discussed it already.' Zara grimaced. 'And I've already told you we don't need to rush things. We both need some time. Let the dust settle.'

'I understand.'

'I don't want you to think I'm trying to get rid of you.' She shook her head. Lost in translation. She needed more time. They both did. 'The best thing to do right now is to go back home and think what's best for each other-'

'All I want you to know is that I'm here as long as you need me.' He took her hands in his. 'A bit of normality will help your recovery, I'm sure.'

She nodded with a tired smile, but remained silent.

They made a full circle around the bunker. The doors locked. The blasts of wind hit its thick grey walls and howled in the narrow windows and between the rusting rebar.

'They've already returned Milne's body to Portsmouth,' Zara started again after a few minutes of silence. 'I'll attend the funeral. His colleagues from the University know the exact date. I feel I need to say a last goodbye. I need to confront Ethan.'

'I don't think that's a good idea. He's not in the right mood to talk, especially now.'

She winked. 'Are you jealous?'

'I'm too old for such infantile jealousy.'

'Ethan talked to his father before he died. He might've learnt something.' Zara continued seriously. 'Something about the Captain and the Chamber or the other U-boat, Milne drew before his death.'

'Yeah, and his daughter who will return.'

'It'll be hard, but I need to do it.' She put her hands on his shoulders and stared into his deep eyes behind the thick-rimmed spectacles.

He cupped her face in his hands. 'I know. Please, be careful.'

Chapter Thirty-Two

Zara

Portsmouth, U. K.
One week later

A black stream of smartly dressed mourners flowed out of
the entrance of the tiny chapel, attached to a crematorium.
The service was over. Zara waited in her car. Her anxiety
had kept her out of the chapel. She couldn't face Milne's
tearful relatives and grieving friends. In the crowd, she
recognised a tall, elegant lady in her earlier sixties, dressed
all in black. Milne's widow. Another, much younger woman
clung onto her elbow, talking to her. She must've been Karl's
stepdaughter. Zara wrapped her jacket tighter, scanning the
crowd. The ever-changing spring weather brought rain and
storms, and Zara caught herself thinking about her trip to
the warm, blooming Jersey. Ethan. She noticed his slim
figure in a black trench coat. No sight of his mother, though.
Zara chuckled ruefully. What a dysfunctional family!

The guests slowly disperse. Nobody wanted to stay outside
on such a gloomy day, but Ethan didn't rush. He stood still,
staring at the richly decorated neo-Gothic facade of the chapel
as if trying to find an answer to a tormenting question.

Zara left the car and approached him. 'Ethan?'

'Oh, you again?' He bowed his head, body language reflecting
his exhaustion and faux-humility. 'Still don't want to leave me
and my family alone?'

'I came to say a last goodbye to your father. He loved me

once. I'm not angry with him.' She swallowed her approaching tears. 'I forgave him. All I want now is to make peace with you as well.'

Ethan grinned, hints of madness in his black eyes. 'My father loved you because you reminded him of Stella. But you're not my sister. Which is why he didn't think twice before betraying you.'

'Did you see her? Is it true?' Zara blurted.

He shot her an anxious expression, but gave no reply, just turned to walk to his car.

No. It couldn't end like this. She'd not made it all the way from Jersey back to Portsmouth to meet a concrete wall of cynicism. She clenched her fists. 'Damn you! Face it! Your father is dead, and so is Ivor Kazinski. Can't you see a pattern here?'

'The diver? I didn't know…' He turned to meet her, a shadow of confusion on his face. 'What do you want from me?'

'What did Die Fledermaus really show you? Do you know about the Captain? Did you see your father's last record in his notepad? "She will return." Did he mean Stella? Did you see her?'

A cruel pause hung in the air.

'Yes. I met my sister there,' Ethan pressed finally. 'Though she wasn't Stella anymore. It's hard to explain.'

'What do you mean? Did you talk to her? Did you see her as a child or as an adult?'

Ethan waved. 'I told everything I know to Agent Cartwright. I didn't lie to my father in the hotel either. Despite the fact he didn't care to share all the details about the device, I knew what he was after. I knew why he was so obsessed with getting it and why he was so incensed when the damn thing didn't meet his expectations. I knew my father well enough.'

Zara frowned. 'Why didn't you tell him the truth? Did Stella tell you something that Milne wouldn't like?'

'It doesn't matter now.' He continued his way to the car.

She kept silent. Ethan was uncompromising. Holding so much anger, hatred, and pain in his heart, and never wanting to let it go.

Even at his father's grave, he couldn't find peace, forgiveness, or move forward. If only "forward" existed for him now.

Chapter Thirty-Three

Zara

'How long since we last met?' Yvette Moreau shook her curly black hair and smiled. 'I must admit, I'd prefer a more cheerful time for our meeting.'

She took a big sip of coffee while glancing outside. The grim, windy weather wasn't right for a long stroll along the sea or a spot of shopping in town. The leaden clouds hadn't parted, so the two friends had agreed to meet in a small café close to the harbour.

'It's been a long time.' Zara nodded. 'I should've called you as soon as I arrived from Jersey, but Milne's funeral and the investigation… it's been a lot. I'd not planned to stay long in Portsmouth, but I don't want to go back home either.'

'You know you can always stay at my place,' Yvette welcomed. 'Remember the good old days when your university sent you to work in our faculty?'

'Of course, we had a great time back then.'

'Nothing stopping us from doing it now.' She clapped her hands. 'Check out from your hotel and move in. Since my little sister returned to Strasbourg, I've had the entire house for myself.'

Zara chuckled. 'And what will we do? Just two of us?'

'I'll bake you proper croissants.' Yvette shrugged. 'The English can't make them. You know it better than I.'

Zara squeezed a tired smile. 'Oh, please! Bribe me with baking. Your pastries and cakes were always amazing.'

Her friend's expression turned serious. 'I'm won't ask about the investigation. I know it's all top-secret, blah, blah, blah, but

I'm worried about you, seeing you like this. Hopefully, your new boyfriend cheers you up.'

'Stefan.' Zara nodded. 'There's no jealousy or selfishness in his heart, and yet, he's another link in this long and painful chain of misfortunes. I can't think about him without recalling everything we've been through.'

Yvette squeezed her icy hands but said nothing. They kept silent for a few moments, enjoying their coffee. The weather had turned from bad to worse, and the first fat drops of the rain bounced off the café's wide windowsills.

'With him staying in Germany for a while, it'll give you some time to heal,' Yvette encouraged. 'Take a few days off work, and spend some time here, hanging out with me.'

'It would be good.' Zara smiled, finishing her drink.

Bleep, bleep, bleep.

A sharp pain pierced her temples, causing her to grimace. A wave of nausea swirling in her stomach.

Yvette frowned. 'What's wrong?'

'Ah, just sudden nausea,' Zara mumbled. 'I hardly had any breakfast today.'

Bleep, bleep…

The noise in her head faded away.

'Can you bring us a glass of tap water, please?' Yvette asked a passing waiter, before turning back to Zara. 'How long have you been suffering from it?'

'A few weeks, I think. Why?'

'Well, don't you think you…' She rolled her eyes, 'attends un bébé?'

'Oh, piss off! Don't be daft! That's not funny.' Zara waved, annoyed. 'Besides, I've been to the doctor recently.'

'What did they say?'

'What can they say? Especially if all tests showed nothing wrong? My GP's given me three weeks of sick leave for severe anxiety and stress.'

Yvette shrugged. 'Maybe it's close to the truth. You need to rest. That's for sure. If you insist on staying in the hotel, at least promise to go shopping with me on Saturday.'

'I promise.' She exhaled with a smile.

Bleep, bleep, bleep…

Sonar thrummed like an orchestra. Zara turned to the window, and in the smears of the rain on the glass, she saw a man sitting a couple of tables away from them. She recognised his chiselled profile and stubborn chin, his sharp cheekbones, and narrow eyebrows. He wore a white, high collared jumper, which made his pale skin look almost glowing. Zara could distinguish the minute blue veins of his temple and long, dark eyelashes. The reflection turned to her and nodded with a half-smile. The vision lasted only a few seconds, but as Zara turned away from the window to look, all the surrounding tables appeared empty.

'Where is he?' she panicked.

'Who?'

'The young man in a white jumper.' She rose from her chair, scanning the café. 'He was sitting at that table, right there. But he's gone?'

'Zara, nobody's left the café for the last twenty minutes. That table's empty.' Yvette touched her sleeve, lowering Zara back into her seat. 'I'm sitting in front of the entrance. I can see everybody coming and going, but look…' She made a wide gesture around. 'There're hardly anyone here.'

'He was there.' Zara shook her head. 'The young blond man. He nodded and smiled at me.'

'I thought you'd have stopped pursuing young men since you met Stefan.' Yvette chuckled.

'No. You don't understand. I recognised him.' Zara raised her voice. 'I'm sure it was he.'

'Who? What are you talking about?'

'It was the Captain,' she mumbled to herself.

'Pardon? What did you say?'

Zara sunk into her chair. 'Nothing. Never mind.'

* * *

Yvette stopped her car in front of the hotel, giving Zara a worried look.

'Please, try to get some rest and call a doctor if you feel unwell again,' she said, pulling her friend in for a hug.

'I will do.' Zara nodded. 'I'm sorry I scared you to death.' She added with a shy smile.

'I'll pick you up on Saturday afternoon. We can go to the new mall if you fancy shopping.'

After a warm goodbye, Zara retired to her room. What was happening? The image of the young captain flickered into her mind. She didn't know what was worse – Yvette thinking she was pregnant or thinking she'd gone mad. She took off her coat and shoes and sank into the double bed. First, Milne. Now, her. What if they had all seen him? An icy chill ran down her spine. Ethan wasn't telling the whole truth. What if Stefan could see him as well?

The sound of Stefan's voice would calm her, but she couldn't tell him about her encounter with the Captain. The last thing she wanted was for Stefan to drop everything in Kiel to babysit her.

A bubble bath always relaxed and calmed her. She smiled, stepping into the hot water. Closing her eyes, she inhaled the sweet and musky scents of ylang-ylang, lavender, rose, and other scents she couldn't quite name.

Zara thought of Yvette's tanned, smiling face, the busy harbour, frothy milk in her coffee cup, heavy drops of rain, hitting the café's window.

Bleep, bleep, bleep…

She opened her eyes, struggling to catch her breath. The bath water rippled and the entire room shook. The temperature sank as she slipped beneath the water. Resurfacing, she felt salt water on her lips. Zara clambered from the tub, shivering, water sloshing over the floor. Her vision blurred, but she grabbed a towel and wrap it around her chest.

Bleep, bleep, bleep...

Zara crawled to the toilet just in time to vomit. She sat back against the bath, gathering her hair in a ponytail, eyes, and nose watering. A cold draft filled the bathroom, and as she turned, her eyes met his.

The young blond man from the café stared at her, unmoving. His deep blue eyes hypnotising her, body and thoughts paralyzed. His features were close to distinguish every long black eyelash, every thin vein pulsating on his temples. The same half-smile crossed his big lips.

She screamed, backing down and grabbing the wet edge of the tub, but slipped and banged her head on the toilet.

The world sank.

Chapter Thirty-Four

Zara

Zara awoke in her hotel bed, wrapped in her towel. An aching, dull pain at the front of her head growled to life, and she slid back into a prone position. Daylight had diminished, colouring the room in dull grey, casting long shadows on the floor.

One of the long shadows moved in the far corner. The Captain. Still haunting her. Dressed in a long black coat with the Kriegsmarine's insignia, he looked changed now. Or maybe she could finally define his features? He was handsome, even delicate in a way. "Delicate" and "U-boat commander" sounded dissonant, but Zara could think of nothing else as she stared at him. The evil storms of the Atlantic and the North Sea hadn't left their marks on his smooth skin. The man came closer to the bed, a gentle smile painted across his lips.

'Ah Zara, I'm glad you're finally awake. I've waited a long time to meet you.' His accented voice sounded friendly. His accent similar to Stefan's, but more pronounced. 'I'm terribly sorry for the bruise. I'd not meant to alarm you.'

'You know my name?'

'We've not been formally introduced, but I know you well.' His eyes mesmerised her.

'Are you..?' she faltered. 'The Captain?'

'Commander Julius Engel of the 11th U-boat Flotilla.' The man nodded. 'At your service, Miss Rose.'

Zara's hands trembled. 'Why are you here? Why are you following me? What do you want?'

'You're the only one who can help me. So, I'm here to ask you for a favour.'

'Oh, I see.' She smirked. 'Did you ask Ivor Kazinski and Karl Milne for a favour before killing them? I assume they refused.'

'I had nothing to do with the old man's death. His poor heart couldn't cope with stress, and he died of a heart attack. You know that better than I.' The man shrugged. 'I didn't kill him. You can have my word for it.'

'Milne saw you. He left drawings of your encounter.'

'Yes. Die Fledermaus threw him into my lifeline and almost destroyed everything there. He didn't know how to operate the machine correctly, but still took the risk. What he saw scared him. But I had nothing to do with his death.'

'And the diver?'

'What about him? He wouldn't have been able to return to normality. Black matter corrupted too much of his psyche.'

'The hall with deformed bodies in the pods. I saw you there. Then, in the mirror of my hotel's bathroom.' She paused. The pain in her forehead stopped her from focusing.

Julius frowned. 'I have no idea what you're talking about.'

'The tunnel, the man in an SS tunic, who called himself Der Meister and showed me the bodies in the pods-'

A grimace of horror distorted his face. 'You saw Der Meister? Did you talk to him?'

'We spoke.' Zara clenched her fists. 'I saw you there too, straight on the floor, appearing from a slimy sack attached to the ceiling. Now, can you tell me what this all means? Why do I keep experiencing these bizarre visions? Why are you stalking me?'

'I need you. You're the only candidate left for this mission, and I'm sure the correct one.'

A chill ran down Zara's spine. 'What mission?'

The hotel phone rang, making her jump as shed turned to the bedside table.

Zara picked up the receiver. 'Hello!' She turned back to Engel. But he'd vanished.

'Zara. How're you doing?' Yvette's voice sounded on the line. 'I've tried to reach your mobile, but you must've switched it off. Are you okay?'

'Ugm… Eh… Hi,' Zara mumbled, staring at the dead screen of her mobile. 'I'm okay.'

'You don't sound like it.'

'I've… I've just had a nap.'

'Oh, sorry if I woke you.' She paused. 'Nothing urgent. I'm just calling to tell you I won't be able to do it on Saturday. Our shopping, I mean. I have builders coming in the afternoon. They can only do it this Saturday.'

'That's fine.'

'I want to meet again, but this damn bathroom is my never-ending pain.'

Zara nodded. 'It's fine. Sort out your bathroom. We'll check out the new shopping mall when I'm back to Portsmouth.'

'Thank you. Promise me to take care of yourself until then.' The warmth in Yvette's voice meant everything.

They said a warm goodbye and hung up.

Zara reclined on her pillows. She touched her forehead. Unfortunately, the growing lump left her with no doubts. She tried to recall what had happened, a makeshift icepack pressed to her throbbing forehead. The captain's words swirled in her head. Where had he come from? A multi-dimensional being who could travel between her world and others, if other worlds existed? If so, he didn't need Die Fledermaus. She released a deep sigh. Milne had been there. The crucial question was, what did Engel want from her?

The mobile phone came back to life, interrupting her thoughts.

Zara rolled her eyes, reading the name on the screen. Cartwright always knew the right time to call. Zara picked up. 'Hello. How are you doing?'

'Good evening, Zara. Have you watched the news today?' Cartwright started.

Zara smirked. 'No. I'm not a fan of horror movies. Why?'

'A badly damaged container ship has been rescued in the North Sea and taken to the port of Ipswich,' Cartwright continued, voice strict. 'Ring any bells?'

'Well, yes. I recall reading an article about the accident yesterday. It said the ship's engine had blown up or something. As far as I remember, there were no fatalities or injuries when the explosion happened.'

'They analysed the damage as soon as the vessel arrived at drydock.' Cartwright paused. 'They've found torpedo debris in the ship's hull. Specialists believe the torpedo was German made. 1943, to be precise.'

Zara jumped from her bed. 'What?'

'The officers claimed the ship's radar had picked up a signal from another vessel in the proximity of the container. They swore to God there were no ships around, not even on the horizon. The charts have confirmed that.'

'A submarine?' Zara frowned. 'Why would somebody attack a merchant vessel straight under our noses? What the-'

Cartwright continued, 'This morning, an unidentified submarine emerged off the coast of Crete, and tried to shot down a Greek coastguard helicopter. The pilots, who luckily avoided the fire, said they could distinguish the unusually shaped conning tower and two gunmen in black leather jackets and white caps.'

'A kind of historical re-enactment or something?' Zara couldn't hold a mocking smile.

'Zara, I'm serious!' Cartwright snapped. 'My boss received a call from MI5 today. I'm sure the Ministry of Defence will be on us soon. We can't just turn to Germany and ask whether they've started Word War Three already, and we're still unaware.'

'*She will return.*' Zara exhaled.

'Pardon?'

'Remember Milne's last record in his notepad?'

'Yes, but-'

'He didn't mean his daughter, Stella.' Zara choked; throat dry. '"She will return". She. The U-boat.'

'Close,' Cartwright replied. 'We're dealing with another submarine and, potentially, with Die Fledermaus mark two.'

'It explains the sudden appearance and disappearance of the vessel.'

'Any ideas on what kind of U-boat it can be?'

'Stefan's researching it, based on Milne's sketches, but without success so far. He swears it's a VIIC-type, but we need more information.'

Cartwright sighed. 'I tried to call Dr Krause a few times today. No answer.'

Zara's heart dropped. God, no! Had Engel found him? He said he was uninterested in anybody beside her. Could she trust him? 'I'll try to reach Stefan later in the evening,' she said finally.

'This situation is extremely delicate. We need to get in contact with this U-boat first, whoever's navigating her,' Cartwright said. 'You're needed in London as soon as possible. I know you're on sick leave now, but I may need your advice. With any luck, we'll avoid the involvement of German Navy officials or any other country in this investigation.'

She continued her musing aloud, but Zara's thoughts were miles away, on the grim and windy coast of Kiel.

* * *

'Stefan?' She breathed a sigh of relief when he appeared on the screen. 'How are you doing?'

'I'm okay. Needed to go to the office for a few hours and forgot my phone at home. Nothing exciting, just boring statistics and reports,' he greeted her. 'How was your day?'

'It was good.' She nodded, continuing casually, 'by the way, Cartwright tried to contact you.'

'Ah, I've missed her calls. Is it about the gunfire and helicopter near Crete?'

Zara frowned. 'So, you've watched the news?'

'The media here tried to make a big sensation out of it. An alien invasion, Russia or North Korea are testing a new weapon, and so on.' He waved. 'The helicopter's camera "suddenly" corrupted and erased the film.'

'What about the torpedo debris in the hull of the container ship?'

Stefan's expression turned serious. 'My office hasn't received official requests yet. It looks like the British are trying to keep this news under wraps. Cartwright has requested my help, but I can't go behind the backs of my boss or my government again.'

'I'm sure she would prefer you to deal with this case from the German side. You know how persistent she can be.'

He snorted. 'She can try.'

'What about Milne's drawing of the U-boat? I believe Milne meant the U-boat, not Stella when he wrote, "She will return". If so, we need to find out what happened to the sub.'

'That's a good point.' Stefan nodded. 'I didn't think it would be a boat.'

Zara hesitated, but finally said, 'We need to narrow our search to the 11th Flotilla.'

Stefan arched his eyebrows. 'Why's that? Where did you get that information?'

'The 11th Flotilla was based in Bergen. So, we may need to have a look at all the U-boats which went missing between the creation of Die Fledermaus and the end of the war.'

Stefan interrupted. 'I'm well aware of the 11th Flotilla in Norway.'

'Do you have any useful connections there? We may need to ask our Norwegian counterparts for a huge favour.'

'I can pull a couple of strings, but… how did you know all this?'

She hesitated. What if the Captain lied? 'The Captain told me that,' she exhaled.

'What?' Stefan leaned forward in his chair.

'I met him today,' she whispered. 'I talked to him.'

'I'm coming to England.' He sighed. 'I shouldn't have left you alone in your condition. If British doctors can't help you, maybe you need to try a German one.'

'Stefan, I'm not ill.' With that, she told him about her meeting with Engel. 'We need to find who he is, what he wants from me, and how this new U-boat fits into it all. We can be certain that the Captain can travel in and out of our continuum without the use of black matter.'

He frowned. 'Are you sure you don't need my help after your latest "encounter" and that massive lump on your head? Please, promise you'll see a doctor tomorrow. You might have a concussion.'

'I promise.' She shook her head.

A long pause filled the call, but she didn't want to leave Stefan in worry. 'What happened to Dr Gerhard Stromm?' she asked.

'What do you mean?'

'Was he trialled like most high-ranking SS officers? Did he run abroad to South America or the US like other Nazi scientists?'

'It's another unsolved mystery.' Stefan shrugged. 'Dr Stromm vanished a day before the Allies' bombed his lab and they never found his body. Differing testimonies recounted by his driver and housekeeper when questioned. The driver claimed he drove Dr Stromm to the airdrome. However, no flights departed at that time of the night. The housekeeper swore to God that he took a cyanide pill on the same night. Both witnesses subsequently changed their testimonies, agreeing that, most likely, Dr Stromm had escaped.' He paused. 'Why are you asking?'

Zara closed her eyes and cupped her head in her hands, groaning quietly.

'What's wrong?'

'Something tells me Dr Gerhard Stromm may be very much

alive.'

Chapter Thirty-Five

Stefan

Kiel, Germany
Three days later

Stefan opened an email from Ida Moen, a good friend and lead historian at the Royal Norwegian Navy Museum archives. He'd made a few research visits to Norway, and Ida had become his first point of contact. She'd discovered a few documents to help his investigation after his request to the German archives yielded no result.

Stefan stared at the screen. An order of appointment: a black-and-white photo portrait of the man. Just as Milne had depicted the Captain in his sketches. If he were to upload this picture into a facial recognition program, he might find the Captain's face in a German archive.

The microwave pinged, distracting his musings. He pulled out the steaming plate of stew, poured coffee from the percolator, and returned to the settee. He opened the file and continued reading.

His thoughts turned to Zara. Their time on Jersey had felt like a hundred years ago. His fingers running through her thick auburn hair and over her bare shoulders. Her smooth skin scented in her favourite perfume with warm notes of peony, lilac, and lavender.

The loud chime of the wall clock pulled him out of his sweet reverie.

He shot a glance at it. Nine o'clock in the evening. It would be an hour earlier there. Hopefully, he wouldn't wake her. He finished his meal and turned back to the laptop. He didn't need to wait for too long.

Looking a bit tired, Zara's face appeared on the screen.

'Evening, angel. How are you? I hope it's not too late,' he started.

'Ah, I'm okay. The weather's worsened here. I slept most of the day. I think I've finally gotten over my insomnia. Back to Winchester tomorrow. There's nothing for me here.'

'Probably for the best. Besides, I'll join you soon.'

'Have you learned anything new about the case?' she asked. 'About the attack on the oil rig? Today, they saw the boat again, circling off the coast of Scotland.'

'I heard. We'll need to act fast,' he interrupted. 'I talked to Ida, our Norwegian counterpart, I told you about. She's discovered something disturbing about the Captain and Dr Stromm.'

Zara frowned. 'What is it?'

'Apparently, Captain Engel was transferred to Bergen from Hamburg in the winter of 1943. Ida couldn't find anything in particular about his service prior to 1943, but she discovered the order of his appointment to take command of U-713 as a Kapitänleutnant. It was his one and only patrol aboard the boat. She went missing in February 1944.'

'Went missing? Under what circumstances?'

'The record claimed she was sunk by depth charges from a British destroyer north-west of Narvik. But our cross-references contradicted that claim.' Stefan shrugged. 'In fact, there're so many gaps in the story. The previous commander of U-713, Oberleutnant Henry Erlich, suddenly had fallen ill a couple of days before the journey. He died a week later from severe food poisoning. Other personnel had no food-related health issues. They immediately appointed Captain Engel, although the First Watch Officer had been waiting for a promotion for a while. There were a few other suitable candidates on the base, too. I couldn't find anything about Captain Julius Engel in the German archives. It's unlikely that they would transfer a newly promoted captain somewhere else straight away. He would have had to serve as a Kommandantenshüler aboard a training U-boat before being promoted from first watch officer.'

'A Captain without a boat? Why would the High Command send him to Norway?' Zara mused aloud. 'To replace Henry Erlich? Why would they replace an experienced commander with a rookie? It makes no sense.'

'Captain Erlich was quite open about his political views on the war, the party, and even the Führer. The captain criticised the regime and didn't hide his thoughts from his crew. As much as Admiral Dönitz loved and respected his submariners, he could only cover Erlich for so long. In the case of Erlich's arrest, the rest of his crew could've risen as well. At the end of the war, officers were tired of the party and the Führer. The High Command could bury an "inconvenient" Captain or prosecute the entire fifty-man crew.

'If my theory is right, Captain Engel was a man of many talents: the High Command's assassin and a trained U-boat commander.' Stefan couldn't hold a chuckle.

Zara shook her head. 'I don't believe the admiral would've approved such methods. Yes, Dönitz was in the Nazi Party, but being an ex-submariner, he wouldn't have done that to his men. He wasn't the type to stab others in the back. Erlich would've been submitted to a fair trial or as fair as a Nazi trial could be.'

'Thanks for the history lesson on Admiral Dönitz's controversial personality.' Stefan rolled his eyes in false annoyance. 'As for my theory, I'm just trying to make some sense out of Engel's sudden appointment. Ida agreed with this theory. However, without hard evidence, any theory of what happened on the base is nothing more but speculation.' He waved a pile of printouts in front of the screen.

'What're those?'

'The pages of a medical officer's diary. He described his brief encounter with Captain Engel when he came to the infirmary for a prescription. The officer was very detailed about his feelings towards everything happening on the base. According to this, Engel was quite the character. He wasn't popular amongst his fellow submariners, but favoured by the Hafenkapitän Josef Landau-Stromm, the base commander and... the younger brother of Dr Gerhard Stromm.'

'What? Dr Stromm was in Norway together with Engel?'

'I think so,' Stefan said. 'Or at least, he visited Bergen often. Ida told me that both brothers worked in Norway. Josef's appointment in Bergen didn't last long, though. He returned to Germany at the end of 1944.'

'Did Josef know about his brother's discovery? Did the two work together on the device?' Zara asked. 'It doesn't matter now. Engel knows Dr Stromm.'

'The brothers covered their tracks well,' Stefan continued. 'Josef preferred to be known by the first part of his surname, Landau. Maybe he wanted to distance himself from his high-ranking SS brother? The Kriegsmarine officers despised the SS, as you know.'

'True. Or maybe there's something more to this story.'

'I'll email you the documents,' he said.

Zara kept silent for a few seconds.

'Dr Gerhard Stromm, the creator of Die Fledermaus. His name's emerged again.' She broke the pause. 'I'm sure there's a connection between the two U-boats and Stromm or, better to say, his creation. In my vision, he called himself Der Meister. The master. The maestro. The lord. What does it mean?'

'What if Dr Stromm tested DF before they built the new, XXIII-type U-boats?' Stefan mused aloud. 'What if U-713 was a "pre-pilot" version to test the device before revealing their discovery to Admiral Dönitz?'

Zara frowned. 'If so, do you think Dr Stromm persuaded his

brother to use the device aboard U-713? Captain Engel was an agent, recruited by the SS?'

'I know it sounds more bizarre than science fiction. Yet, before going big in front of the Kriegsmarine's officials, Dr Stromm might've tested the device in Norway, far away from the High Command. His brother helped Gerhard find a captain who was willing to take such a risk.' Zara shook her head. 'Type VIIC? They were large vessels with up to fifty sailors aboard.'

'Well, they used what they had to hand.'

'I do think there's more to it than that.' Zara bit her lip. 'We're missing something.'

'Whatever it is, you need to be extremely careful now. Captain Engel, or whoever talked to you in your vision, is a dangerous being. I'm sure he lied to you when he said he didn't kill Milne and Ivor Kazinski. And worse, he might've been behind the death of Commander Henry Erlich.'

'I promise to do my best. Scout's honour.' She released a deep sigh. 'Although he'll find me if he wants to. He appears and disappears as he wishes. I don't know why I'm the only one who can see him. If he's a part of the phenomena, why can the witnesses see the U-boat, but not the Captain?'

'I can't answer that at the moment.' Stefan shook his head. 'The only thing I know is that I want to be there to protect you.'

'If only you could.'

Chapter Thirty-Six

Zara

The diary of Klaus Fischer
Bergen, 10th January 1944

Today, I had the "pleasure" of meeting the newcomer, Commander Engel, in person. He's made an appointment to get a prescription for some gastric issues. What an unpleasant, weird individual. I try not to listen to the gossip the men spread, bored while ashore. Yet, I'm starting to believe them now.

He didn't talk much, only "yes" or "no" as if he was doing me the greatest favour. His face expressed nothing but boredom and superiority above others.

I asked some standard questions: how many units of alcohol he consumed a week while ashore? He became deeply offended and snapped that he didn't drink at all. I tried to make a joke, saying that a nice glass of Trollinger with a good meal never hurt anybody, but he retorted he had none of that.

Indeed, nobody ever saw him in a bar with a drink or partying with other officers. The men say the Captain is full of himself, despises locals, and treats ensigns and petty officers with low regard. Nobody had seen him around women either. Although, according to his record, he was single. Maybe, apart from the problems with digestion, there're other serious health issues? Or maybe the rumours about his close friendship with the Hafenkapitän's wife are true. Then, it explains a lot.

Frau Landau looks like a working horse, which had a long, hard life on a farm. She's some twenty-five years older than Captain Engel, but everybody has different taste, I suppose.

And Hafenkapitän? I've heard he invited Engel for dinner to his house on numerous occasions. The two seem to get along well. What is it? A ménage à trois, as French call it? Perhaps. Or perhaps Becker is right, saying we can exclude Frau Landau from this equation. She's just a cover for the two men. I'd rather stop listening to vulgar rumour. This Becker. He's a filthy swine, full of sick fantasies.

The one thing is crystal clear – I feel sorry for Captain Engel's crewmates. It must be torture serving under his command.

'God.' Zara finished reading and reclined in her chair.

The wind seemed to have calmed outside. The cold plate of the full moon shone in the clear sky. It was too late to go for a walk, but she needed fresh air.

She'd not eaten the entire day. But the hotel pub would still be open.

She dressed and went downstairs. Despite the late hour, the pub was still busy. Zara ordered a light meal and relaxed in the corner with a glass of Muscadet. A waiter brought her order, and after the meal and a drink, Zara felt positive about a stroll along the beach. She left the hotel and continued her way down almost empty streets to the shore.

The dark mass of the sea was glowing under the watch of the full moon. The strong winds had now faded to a chilly breeze. A lonely female figure walked her dog in a distance. Zara inhaled the salty air and smiled to herself. The sea always eased her anxiety, giving her new hope and strength. Wrapped up in a trench coat and scarf, she came closer to the approaching waves when she noticed a black shadow in the corner of her eye. Silent apart from the monotonous rustling of the waves. No headache or nausea came, but she knew he was close.

'Good evening, Zara,' a familiar male voice sounded behind her.

'You again?' She turned, irritated rather than scared or shocked to see Captain Engel.

A half-smile ran across his pale lips. 'Our conversation was unfinished.'

Dressed in a long coat over a white shirt and wide black trousers, Captain Engel looked more like the Golden Age Hollywood star than a German officer.

'You've changed your Kriegsmarine's uniform to a more glamorous style.' Zara snorted.

'I've done it for you. Do you like it?'

'You disgrace and dishonour your uniform,' Zara continued. 'A murderer and a liar. You don't deserve to wear it.'

He frowned. 'What makes you say that? I've explained I had nothing to do with the professor and diver's deaths.'

'You've poisoned Captain Erlich, haven't you? You've taken over his U-boat. The Stromm brothers? What did you plot together?'

He took a step closer. Her heart skipped a beat. He was almost as tall as Stefan, but slimmer built and towered a good few inches above her.

'You and your boyfriend have progressed far with your research.' He chuckled. 'I'm aware of your every step. See what you see; feel what you feel. I'm in your thoughts if I want to be.' He made a warning gesture, predicting her reaction. 'What proof do you have, apart from the forged diary and some rumours? How can you be sure the records weren't created after the U-boat went missing? Erlich was the star of the base, a respected captain, a real ace – or at least, he wished to be. Everybody liked him. I wasn't so popular. That's true. But it doesn't mean I killed him, nor did I commit any of the disgusting things this idiot, Medical Officer Fischer, and his fellows accused me of.'

She squinted. 'And of course, you've nothing to do with the Stromms and the device?'

'As you already know, Dr Gerhard Stromm was in the SS. The

Kriegsmarine had nothing to do with those maniacs. However, Josef Landau-Stromm took his brother's side. I'm sure Captain Erlich knew too much and wanted no part in the dirty games of the SS. Either way, Josef helped his brother to get rid of the problematic captain. I knew nothing about their plan. I could only suspect and speculate, I couldn't disobey my order, and the order was to take command of U-713.'

'So, what was the plan? I assume it didn't work well.' Zara squinted. 'What's happened aboard U-713? How to send her back to 1944? And how am I connected to all this mess?'

Engel shook his head. 'So many questions, Zara. So many questions. If you want answers, you need to come with me.'

'Come where?' She backed down into the icy waves. 'To the Chamber?'

'To my lifeline.' He stretched out a pale hand to her. 'I can show you the Chamber if you wish.'

Zara shot a look at his outstretched hand, then around – nobody was on the beach.

'Oh, come on!' Engel grinned. 'There're more than twenty souls aboard. Technically, these men are still at war with your country. They're confused, angry, and scared. The vessel carries about fifteen torpedoes and two anti-aircraft guns. I wonder how nobody has been killed yet. The longer we're talking and wasting time, the messier the situation becomes. Besides,' he paused. 'You don't want the device to end up in American or Russian hands, do you?'

'I don't.' Zara choked. Stefan. He could kill both him and Ethan. 'Okay.' She exhaled. 'I'll go with you wherever you're taking me.'

She touched his smooth, cold palm. Their eyes met before a dazzling light swallowed her.

Chapter Thirty-Seven

Zara

By the time her vision returned, the light had completely extinguished and she floated in a milky mist. Sounds muted and body weightless, a similar sensation to what she'd experienced aboard U-4713/A. A blink, another one, and the full picture came into focus.

She sat at a small round table in a spacious restaurant with black and gold walls. Crystal candelabras and mirrors in elaborate Art déco-style frames decorated the room. The quiet music, jazz, or something similar from the thirties, sounded from somewhere above. The place was busy. Smartly dressed guests occupied all tables. Waiters in tuxedos moved soundlessly and disappeared behind the stained-glass screen.

The picture still looked blurry, especially in the farthest corners of the room. Zara tried hard to focus even on a single guest, but the figure seemed almost colourless, reminiscent of an old-fashioned photograph. The entire room radiated a similar hue. The colours, even the bright gold and silver, seemed faded. She could only guess what they might look like in reality. Although she didn't know what could be reliably called "reality" anymore.

Engel slowly materialised before her. 'Welcome to Germania!'

Unlike the other guests and staff, his colours appeared natural and bright. He sat in front of her and enjoyed a cigarette. He had exchanged his long coat for a smart jacket and black tie.

'What is this place?' Her jaw dropped as Engel pointed out a wide window.

Below, a colossal city lived an otherworldly life. Long,

straight streets and wide avenues busy with traffic. Elegant classic cars from the thirties and forties stretched far into the low horizon. Some vehicles drove on the road, others hovered twenty or thirty feet above the ground. Art déco and Romanesque buildings adorned with frowning eagles on their gables, swastikas and Gothic German writing towered along the strassers as far as she could see.

Towering above the urban sprawl, an enormous dome dominated the skyline. A concrete eagle spread its golden wings at its summit. Despite its gargantuan size, the dome floated weightlessly in the air. The building made St. Paul's Cathedral, St. Peter's Basilica, and Hagia Sophia look like tiny chapels in comparison. But this wasn't a religious monument.

'The Volkshalle,' Zara spoke aloud. 'The People's Hall. Hitler's never-built architectural fantasy. Germania? Hitler's capital of the Third Reich? The supposed-to-be city of the world?'

'Not Hitler's.' Engel beamed. 'Mine.'

'What? Sorry. Are we lost in translation?' She turned to him and only then noticed that her clothes had changed.

Instead of her cosy trench coat, straight blue jeans, and her favourite woollen jumper, she wore a black cocktail dress and high heels. She shot a glance in a wall mirror – her untidy ponytail had turned into cascading glossy ringlets.

'What's this masquerade for?' she yelled.

'Sorry, darling, I shouldn't say it to a lady.' Engel lowered his voice. 'You couldn't come here dressed like... well, like you were. You needed something appropriate for the occasion. Fashion in your lifeline is horrendous.'

'At least I felt comfortable and-'

'Well, I feel comfortable in my pyjamas, but I don't wear them out,' he snapped.

'You've not only kidnapped me; you've also stolen my clothes.'

Engel waved. 'You'll be returned to them soon. I don't need this trash in my city.'

'Your city? So, what is this place?'

Engel beamed again. 'You wouldn't have believed me if I told you. Now, you understand why I needed to bring you here.'

'I still can't believe I'm not dreaming. I'm completely lost now. I can't distinguish dreams from reality anymore,' she almost shouted.

'You're not dreaming. Although, what is our reality if not just another heavy dream?' He waved. 'I'm not sure what the original plan of the Stromm brothers was, but it didn't work well. I believe Dr Gerhard Stromm wanted to defect to the Americans, so he promised to deliver them Die Fledermaus by U-boat. The First Watch Officer and the Chief Engineer were involved. They turned the crew against me. A mutiny was inevitable. Unafraid of court-martial, they planned to do similar to what Ulrich Schultz did a year later.' He nodded. 'Yes, I know about him and U-4713/A as well-'

'And you?' she interrupted. 'Did you try to stop them?'

'They didn't listen to my command and took over the boat, changing her course. They took me hostage in my quarters and were heading to meet an American destroyer. What deal were they going to make? What did the Stromms and the Americans promise them? Who knew? The First Watch Officer tried to stab me, but I shot him and escaped, sabotaging the device. I ended up here, and the U-boat "jumped" to your lifeline. Seconds for them became eternity for me.'

'If Dr Gerhard Stromm wanted to buy his way to America, using Die Fledermaus, why did he build another to use aboard U-4713/A? It doesn't make sense.'

'His plan was unsuccessful, but his SS superiors demanded results.' Engel shrugged. 'He might've changed his mind. He didn't repeat the fate of many other Nazi scientists like von Braun or Debus, who received cushy jobs in the American Space Program years later.'

'He escaped, didn't he?' Zara squinted. 'To another lifeline or something. Last time we met, it seemed to me you were afraid of him.'

'I'm not afraid of anybody.' Engel grimaced. 'Dr Stromm, or Der Meister, as he calls himself now, decided he was above everything and everyone. Blinded by his excessive pride, he thought he could trick black matter or bend it to his will. At the end of the war, he tried to escape prosecution, using his latest prototype of Die Fledermaus, but failed. Black matter sent him so far beyond the frontiers of any known reality, turning him into something… extremely powerful and evil.'

'How did I meet him? Did I "travel" to this place too?'

'Most likely, Der Meister "travelled" far to meet you. That's what bothers me.'

Zara frowned. 'I saw my father there. He ran from me. I tried to catch him, but-'

'Are you sure it was your father?'

'Well, he looked much younger and different somehow-'

Engel waved her off. 'It wasn't your father. These places, these "transition zones", as I call them. They're able to create doubles or doppelgangers and other bizarre beings.'

Zara swallowed her anxiety back, but asked, 'What does Dr Stromm want from me?'

'He doesn't need you. He wants to get close to me and Germania.'

'Sorry, I don't understand,' she shook her head.

'Of course.' Engel grinned. 'Human logic is too primitive to explain everything in the known universe, let alone black matter.'

'What about you? How did you appear in Bergen, for example?' she asked. Engel didn't leave her much room for an argument. 'Stefan couldn't find anything about you in the German archives. You're as elusive as Dr Stromm, it seems.'

'I'd been promoted from the First Watch Officer. My boat sank in 1943, and I was re-appointed in Norway.'

'What boat was it? Where did she sink and under what circumstances?' Zara stared at him, unblinking.

His eyes caught her in their icy cage again; a sad smile stretching his lips. 'You already know the answers. You saw it. You've been there.'

'God! I saw it in one of those vivid nightmares,' Zara mumbled. 'She was depth charged by two destroyers. It wasn't a dream, after all.' The room spun around her, but she pulled herself together.

'See, I told you how close we're connected.' Engel bowed his head.

She wanted to ask something, but a waiter approached their table.

'Guten Abend! Kann ich dir-' the man started with a wide smile.

'A glass of 1944 Domaine Romanée-Conti, please,' Engel interrupted him and winked at Zara. 'Try it. It's French and costs a fortune in your lifeline.'

'Und für das Fräulein?' the waiter understood Engel's demand in English but continued in German.

'The same.' Zara waved, and the waiter disappeared behind the stained-glass screen. 'Is Stefan right? Did the SS recruit you?' she continued, turning to Engel.

He grimaced. 'I've told you already I had nothing to do with the SS.'

Perhaps not with the SS, but he was lying through his teeth about the Stromms. She composed herself and said, 'You repeated the "great escape" of Radio Officer Walter Dix or, better to say, he repeated yours.'

'Yes, but he was lucky.' Engel chuckled with a bitter smile. 'I've ended up here, in this lifeline, as I call it, or a time bubble, as your boyfriend deduced. Either way, unlike Walter Dix, I'm trapped here forever until the lifeline collapses.'

'Why's that?'

'Using the device, a human body accrues a certain amount of black matter, which gradually replaces normal matter. The more you use it, the higher the concentration of black matter resides in you. As for me, I've had too much of it. I don't have a body made from "normal" matter, as we know it. Everything you see around you, including me, is black matter.'

'It's impossible!' Zara blurted. 'Black matter is highly unstable. It moves quicker than the speed of light. If you know what I know, then you're aware of Karl Milne and the explosion. Even a tiny amount of it is too much for our lifeline.'

Engel snorted. 'Oh, yes! I know about that idiot. The blast of the explosion unbalanced my lifeline to the point of near collapse.' He composed himself and continued seriously, 'I'm not a scientist, but I've learned something about black matter, sitting here for so long. It's all about balance and density. If I'm wrong, how can you explain your visions, your vivid dreams, nightmares, sensations that seem so real?'

'Wait a minute.' Zara made a warning gesture. 'Are you saying I've accrued too much black matter as well? That's why I can see you, but other people can't? That's why I met Dr Stromm. That's why he needs me to get to you and Germania. We're all connected in a way.'

The waiter appeared from behind the screen, placing their order on the table and pouring wine into the glasses.

Engel put his hand on hers when the man left them alone. 'Moreover, you and I have exchanged a large amount of matter when DF malfunctioned aboard U-4713/A.'

'What?' Zara jumped from her chair, but sat back, noticing the guests' curious looks.

'Do you remember what you saw that day?' Engel asked, lowering his voice, and moving his chair closer.

'Of course, but I thought it was U-4713/A. I thought the device threw me back into her past.'

'Oh, I wouldn't use words like "past" or "future", speaking of black matter and the device. They're all equal and ever-present in the fabric of the continuum, making it a patchwork of lifelines with large or small doses of black matter in them.' Engel shook his head. 'Let's put it this way: the device threw you aboard my vessel. You thought you saw crewmembers of U-4713/A, but actually, you saw my crew and me. As did Ivor Kazinski during his unlucky dive. Or better to say, simultaneously, I sabotaged the device before being re-materialised here. My U-boat "jumped" to your lifeline a few weeks ahead.'

Zara took a large sip of her wine and stared at him. 'Does it mean I'll also die?'

'No. At least, not now.' Engel smiled his crooked half-smile. 'It means you're lucky to exist in both lifelines, whereas I can only visit yours from time to time. Black matter moves too fast. It pulls me back, and I require a lot of energy to resist it. It's exhausting and I require a long time to recharge.

'As I've told you already, everything you see here.' He made a wide gesture around the room. 'It's just a well-balanced black matter, or as I call it, a solidified matter. When I re-materialised in this lifeline, cold and bare nothingness surrounded me. I floated in the milky mist, surrounded by the fragments of black matter. I didn't know whether I was dead or alive. There was no earth, no air, no water, only pure, primordial nothingness.

'I used my knowledge, my imagination, but the main thing, my intention to build this world from scratch. My cosy little world. I've created everything you see around you. Everything and everyone in Germania is a product of my creation, imagination, and taste, after all.'

Zara rolled her eyes. 'Apart from swastikas and other Nazi symbols, I must admit you have a good taste. An impressive creation.'

'I've taken the best from both regimes.' For the first time since their meeting, his porcelain-white cheeks blushed. 'Do you like the Art déco theme?'

'Very bourgeois for a Nazi officer. The Führer wouldn't have approved-'

'I'm not a Nazi.' Engel snapped. His eyes scrutinised her. 'Although National Socialism gave me and my family a lot. Without it, my father would've been unemployed, unable to feed our family. I would've never graduated from marine school and become an officer. As for the Führer, forget him. He and his crazy ideas died long ago.'

'Oh, really? What happened to him and the other Nazi Party leaders in Germania?' Zara grimaced. 'Just historical curiosity.'

'Germany won the war. The Führer died soon after. Germania is the most prosperous place in the world. This backstory is enough for my lifeline.'

'You've dispensed of the Nazi leaders. Are you in charge of this place now?'

'Of course, no. I'm an officer, a respected veteran, not a politician. The government pays me a good pension. I keep myself occupied in the Kriegsmarine's Headquarters and live a simple life of a bourgeois in a big city.'

'And who's in charge of the government now?' Zara continued.

'Admiral Dönitz is the Reich Chancellor and Albert Speer is his second in command. It may be over soon if Dr Stromm finds his way to Germania. But that's enough politics for now.' Engel clapped his hands. 'I'm starving. Let's have something to eat.' Before he had finished the phrase, a large plate with a steak, salad, and other accompaniments appeared in front of him. 'I just don't want to wait for food to be cooked. It's the quickest way.' He winked. 'You can also do that. Have a look at the menu and imagine whatever you fancy. You can do it.' He passed her a thick journal.

Intrigued, Zara followed his advice and opened the menu on the first page with starters. 'Traditional Russian crepes with black caviar,' she read the first line.

'Great choice.'

She tried to focus on what the dish might look like. She even closed her eyes, but instead of the Russian delicacy, she saw Stefan's worried face, her hotel room in Portsmouth, and her mother, smiling at her.

'You're not trying to escape, are you?' Engel's mocking voice made her jump. 'You can't do it without my help. You have enough black matter, but you're still not in control of it. It requires lots of patience and practice.'

She jumped from her chair. 'Enough games! What do you want from me? I'm still waiting for an answer.'

He rose from the table, coming so close to her she could feel his frigid breath.

'I told you I need your help.' He stretched his palm, and his long, thin fingers touched her cheek. 'I need my U-boat and crew, but I can't go there myself. In your lifeline, I don't have a body to do it.'

An icy chill ran through Zara's back. She gritted her teeth. 'Don't touch me.'

'I don't mean you any harm. I'll never hurt you.' The ice of arrogance melted in his eyes. 'Remember, we're linked. Hurting you, would hurt myself. It's torture to be attracted to you, being a part of you at the same time.'

'Attracted?' Zara snorted, pushing him back. 'I'm six, seven years older than you. Go back to your nannies and toy soldiers, you nasty little boy!'

'What does age matter?' Engel shrugged. 'I always preferred more mature women.'

'So, the story of your affair with Frau Landau-Stromm was true?'

'Damn you!' He came closer again. 'Why do you keep repeating these foul rumours? It's nothing but gossip and slander,' he whispered, and the light dimmed in the room.

The guests, the staff, even the furniture turned into a dark mist. Engel continued whispering in her ear, 'It's such a strange feeling to be a part, being unable to possess you. To be a part, being apart.' His lips were an inch from hers. A slight glowing of his marble skin, his half-closed eyes. 'I haven't kissed a girl in over seventy years.' His long, black eyelashes fluttered like a pair of dark butterflies. 'No. Longer than that. Eternity has passed since.'

'Oh, I'm sure you can create a whole whorehouse here. Don't be such a dramatist. You can have as many girls as you wish to satisfy your wildest fantasies,' Zara hissed.

Engel's lips pursed. 'I know what you think about me, but I'm not like my fellow sailors. Submissive girls and paid sex never appealed to me. Besides, you're a part of me. How can I ignore you?'

Zara clenched her firsts, ready to push him back. The next moment, she felt something cold and solid in her right hand. A dagger?

'Sorry, darling. I'm not interested in a date, especially a date with the worst part of myself.' She drew her hand forward. The thin blade pierced the man's stomach.

'Oh!' Engel backed down, pressing his hand to the belly, shock in his eyes.

God! What've I done?!

'Zara, Zara...' Engel pulled the dagger out of his body, chuckling. 'Do you know how many times I tried to do it?' He shook the pristine, steel blade in front of her. 'About a hundred, using different methods.' He threw the dagger to the floor, then came to her, taking her hands in his and kissing them gently. 'Please, don't hate me.'

He went to his knees, embracing her legs and looking into her eyes. 'I'm not a monster, not a murderer or an evil Nazi. I'm not sure what I am now, but none of that. Please, tell me you don't hate me.'

She looked into his eyes but didn't find the eternal coldness they had reflected before. What if Stefan was wrong, and the man was innocent? Doomed for eternity in a strange, surreal world, in the far corner of the universe. Trapped in his bizarre fantasies, alone and forgotten. Unable to predict when it would all end. Now, Engel was a part of her, aware of every step and thought. Could he read them right now? Did he expect the dagger?

'I don't hate you,' she said finally. 'Tell me how I can help, exactly, then we're done here.'

'Let's go. I'll show you the Chamber and around the city. It may clarify many things.' Engel nodded with a sweet smile.

Chapter Thirty-Eight

Zara

Zara stood unblinking outside the restaurant. The multi-coloured snake of traffic almost crawled, with cars both driving and hovering above the wide road.

'Surprised?' The captain grinned, following her look. 'I have plenty of time for reading. German engineering has turned science fiction into reality. There's nothing impossible in Germania.'

Zara didn't reply, following him, perplexed by the size and scale of the place. Dark shadows of people passed by in silence, some paid no attention to them, and others shot Zara anxious looks.

'The locals aren't overly friendly here,' she mused aloud.

'You're an alien entity, an intruder.' Engel shrugged. 'Black matter tries to protect itself.'

'Are you saying they have consciousness? Is black matter self-aware?'

'Some are more self-aware than others. However, their consciousness isn't the same as in your lifeline, not as you understand it there. Do you wish to take a short stroll, or should we catch a taxi? It's not too far.'

She nodded. 'Let's walk.'

The air was still and neither warm nor cold, perfect for a short evening stroll. The captain turned around the corner, leaving the busy avenue behind, and made his way to one of the narrower streets, which opened to the darkish alley of a park.

'It's much quieter here,' he explained, and they continued on their way in silence for a few minutes.

Zara gazed around. 'What's outside Germania?' she broke the pause first.

Engel shrugged. 'Nothing, I guess.'

'You've never been outside the city?'

'If I want to, I can create the place I want to go: a seaside resort, a chalet in mountains, another lifeline, so to speak.' He grinned. 'You still can't get it right, can you? I am Germania, and where I go is Germania.'

'What's there? In other lifelines? Are they similar to this one?' Zara continued.

'Some of them are empty. Others are full of weird beings, the debris of memories, dreams which never came true, unfulfilled desires, random snippets, or streams of consciousness – nothing exciting. They are the transition zones I've told you about. I guess Dr Stromm is stuck in one of them. They're dark, dangerous places full of evil, decay, and pain. It requires a lot of energy and black matter to retrieve a person from there.'

Zara stopped. 'Does that mean I've enough black matter to return?'

'It would seem so.'

'Pete, the second diver? He must've ended up in a similar place, and so did First Watch Officer Hermann Thiel. What about Ethan? He must've travelled there too. He saw his sister.'

'The diver wasn't as lucky as Ethan Milne.' Engel snorted. 'I'm not surprised by his behaviour towards you, though. What did you expect? Like father, like son.'

'What about his father? What exactly happened when Professor Milne was thrown into your lifeline?'

'All around the universe, black matter is connected and balanced. Your lifeline counterbalances places like Germania, for example.' Engel slowed down and lit a cigarette. 'When one lifeline collapses, another replaces it. The amount of black matter should stay more or less the same. Any sudden shifts create anomalies in your lifeline where the amount of it is minimal. If they're powerful enough, they can also destabilise my lifeline. Transition zones are different. They follow different laws. There're too many kinds of matter conglomerates there. I'm not a physicist, I can't explain.' He paused before resuming his walk. 'When Professor Milne arrived, it felt like the most powerful disturbance in black matter I've ever experienced. Sometimes, when other beings sneak here from other lifelines, black matter either ejects them or they become a part of it, assimilating as I did. With Milne, it was different, though.'

'Did you talk to him? How did he know about the second U-boat?'

He shrugged. 'First of all, I was polite and introduced myself. It wasn't difficult to derive a conclusion. Remember, for black matter, time has no meaning. Before or after, later or earlier, was or will – it always just is.'

'And…' she faltered. 'What happened to Die Fledermaus?'

Engel eyes shot her daggers. 'The device has gone. Dense black matter from the cylinder breached the core, and… I thought it was the end. However…' His eyes smiled again. 'I'm still alive.'

Zara wanted to ask something, but Engel grabbed her sleeve and pulled behind him. A few steps away, something tall and dark lurked behind trees.

The dagger, the same weapon Zara tried to stab him with, shone in Engel's hand. He aimed it at the dark figure. An ear-splitting scream ripped through the tranquil park. Zara saw it straight in front of them. A creature, cloaked in a blackish mist, emerged from the shadows of the trees, screaming, and spitting a dark, viscous liquid. Hairless, its slimy grey skin shone in the pale light, reflecting a spine that protruded through the skin like barbed wire. Strange reticulated eyes positioned at the sides of the head; its wide maw gaped with several rows of fangs.

The dagger struck its shoulder, and the creature wailed, enraged by its injury.

'Spy!' Engel barked. 'Did Der Meister send you here?'

Zara screamed, covering her mouth.

'Run, demon!' Engel hissed, stepping closer, but the creature outstretched its arm with its long, thin fingers, pointing towards Zara.

She instinctively grasped Engel's shoulder. But he had changed, too, into something equally disturbing and frightening. His features distorted, mouth stretched into a long snout, pupilless eyes dissolved into massive black holes.

He inhaled loudly.

The creature yelled. This time, it sounded more like a scream of pure horror.

Engel continued to inhale. His snout became thinner and thinner, and Zara saw the glimmering black shreds stretched from the creature's chest to Engel. The monster attempted to break free, to run, but its whole body, turned into endless shreds, were just disappearing inside Engel's snout. It looked like a cocoon of glimmering yarn now. No head, no legs, no arms – just tendril-like shreds, floating in the surrounding air.

Engel exhaled a dark cloud of shiny orbs.

The orbs morphed into something familiar.

'It's a…' Zara mumbled in shock.

'A tree peony. I know they are your favourite.' Engel picked a flower. 'Black peonies. A rare variety in your lifeline.'

Zara shifted her gaze from the man to the flower and back. Engel's face looked normal now. He smiled his ideal smile. The black peony reflected in his blue eyes.

Zara took the flower with shaking hands. 'What was all that? I… Whatever it was, I want to unsee it.'

'Some kind of interdimensional parasite,' Engel said. 'They try to break through the city's frontiers from time to time from transition zones and other lifelines, but the defence systems of the city kick them out. This one…' He gestured to the peony. 'Managed to break through somehow. Black matter didn't assimilate it too. It makes me think that it was sent here by Dr Stromm.' He paused. 'To spy on me. If so, we need to hurry.' He turned around, ready to go, but Zara pulled him back.

'What happened? What did you do to it?'

He shrugged. 'I've eaten it.'

'You…' She faltered. 'What?'

'Oh!' Engel rolled his eyes. 'I've dematerialised it if you prefer a more scientific explanation.' With that said, he turned to the park's exit, lurking in front of them. 'Ah, we're almost there.'

She raised her head and saw it. The Volkshalle's enormous dome, illuminated by thousands of lights, dominated the dark evening sky. It looked even more powerful now, taking over almost the whole space around. It rested on a heavily set square structure with endless rows of columns in front, which made the illusion of the dome floating in the air even more spectacular. With a minimal amount of decoration on the facades, nothing distracted the view, making a visitor feel all the grandeur of the place. The closer they came to the building, the smaller Zara felt, swallowed by its size and proportions designed for giants, not common people.

Engel beamed with pride. They made a half-circle around, as he insisted on approaching it from the main entrance.

The endless set of marble stairs led them to the columns, hiding the mega double doors adorned with swastikas and ancient Germanic runes. Despite their enormous size, the doors swung open soundlessly as if they had been waiting for the two to come.

'Please, after you.' Engel gestured to the entrance and took a step back, although it wasn't required. A space large enough to fly a helicopter.

Zara wandered in and held her breath. Semi-circular rows with thousands of seats reminded her of an ancient Roman amphitheatre. A speaker's platform rose high above them. A metal eagle spread its wings on the marble wall behind it. The dimmed light of the extinguished evening flooded the hall from long, narrow windows in the dome's turret – the only source of natural light in the building.

They were the only visitors, and Zara's every step echoed throughout the hall, dispersing somewhere far above in its dome. Statues of Germanic knights, heroes, and ancient gods in the niches along the walls represented the megalomania of their creator. She raised her head to the dome's ceiling. She expected a painting or a mosaic, glorifying the German people and their victorious past, a massive fancy swastika at least, but what she saw there made her knees go weak and her jaw drop. It was something terrifying and mesmerising at the same time – a massive, black, pulsating blob, a beehive-shaped mass. Its glossy surface reflected Zara, Engel, and the entire hall. Its pulsating, nervous vibration made her head spin.

'What is this?' She exhaled, unable to look away from the mass.

'We're in the Chamber. This is the core, the centre of this lifeline.'

'Such an amount of black matter can send the whole universe to hell.'

'Well, if I have another visitor like Karl Milne, it definitely will.' Engel grimaced. 'At the moment, it's stable enough. I'm afraid not for long, though.'

'Is it the reason you kidnapped and brought me here?' Zara took a step back. 'Sorry, I can't imagine how my presence could help stabilise this situation.' She pointed to the pulsating mass.

'It can.' Engel nodded. 'My boat and crew. They still possess Die Fledermaus with the amount of black matter needed to stabilise it here. Your lifeline doesn't require it. At least, not in such quantities. The crew can't go back to 1944, nor can they stay in your lifeline. Bringing them here is the only way to save them. Unfortunately, I can't do that.'

'What?' Zara interrupted him. 'You want... what? Do you want me to go aboard U-713 and kindly ask your crewmen to travel to your lifeline?'

'Not exactly. First of all, I won't leave you alone in such a dangerous situation. I'm going with you,' he said. 'I've made a promise. I swore I would come back in any form, and they would have no choice but to accept me. The power of black matter and my knowledge will protect you from violence.'

'If it was a mutiny, if they rebelled against you, why do you need them here? Or is it your revenge?' She bit her lips. 'Even eternity couldn't make you forgive.'

'It's nothing about revenge.' Engel waved, annoyance in his voice. 'I need black matter to stabilise the core, but most of all,' he paused, 'most of all, I need my men here. The First Watch Officer and the Chief Engineer turned them against me, spreading dirty rumours and accusing me of God knows what crimes. Besides, now Dr Stromm is hunting for Die Fledermaus and me. I can't allow him to get to the U-boat first.'

'Why does he need you? Why does he need Germania and Die Fledermaus?'

'He's seeking revenge, believing the failure of his plan was my fault. He blames me for the death of his brother, Josef.' His lips quivered in an eerie half-smile. 'Josef Stromm was very fond of me, you know. Dr Stromm blames me in his death. He believes Josef killed himself because I failed him and the mission. That's not quite true. Josef Stromm committed suicide when he was called back to Berlin, and all his evil deeds were investigated and exposed, including the murder of Captain Erlich.' Engel chuckled bitterly. 'Dr Stromm is stuck in a miserable shit hole of a transition zone. He wants Germania for himself; wants it to be his. Craves unlimited control over black matter.'

'If he needs me to get to you and Germania, why does he let me go?'

'I don't have an answer to it.' Engel shook his head. 'Maybe you're much stronger than he thinks. You escaped from him somehow. I'm sure he intended to get to your lifeline using Ivor

Kazinski. He drowned, right?'

Zara snapped, 'Yes. And up to now, I've had no doubts you killed him.'

'I've told you before, I have nothing to do with it.' Engel grimaced. 'Your boyfriend claimed he saw Ivor's body floating in a bath. I have no doubts that Dr Stromm got rid of him when he realised the diver was useless for his plan. Now, he's after you. You're his key to Germania and me. That's why we need to team up and bring here my crew. We need to save not only ourselves but them as well.

'As for them, it's the only way out. What waits for my men in your lifeline, even if they're not killed in action? Germany lost the war, castrated by the allies. Their relatives and loved ones are long dead. Children, if they have any, would be old or dead. Nobody waits for them ashore other than detainment in labs where they'd be studied to death like rats. They don't deserve it. Here, we'll build greater Germania. Here, we'll restore our Fatherland, as we, common German people, wanted it to be. Dr Stromm won't dare to mess up with us.'

A suffocating pause filled the air. Engel's shoulders dropped, his blond head bowed lower, and he stared at the marble floor without movement.

Zara sighed. What if he was telling the truth? He'd lived an eternity here, surrounded by his fantasies to the point that he'd started to believe in them. He was so young. What had he seen in his life, apart from his struggling Fatherland, the war, death, deception, and betrayal of his crewmates? He'd known fear, anger, hatred, solitude, war, and pain, nothing else. His crew? He was right. There was no redemption for them in her lifeline.

She came closer and put her hand on his shoulder. 'What if… what if I say "no"? Will you kill me?'

He raised his eyes to her. 'Even if I could, I'd never hurt you.'

'What about Stefan?'

'I'm not a murderer, whatever you think about me.' He smiled his crooked smile. 'You love him. I know it, I feel it. I'm jealous not only because of you, but because of your love. He loves you, too. Even more than you can imagine, even more than he can imagine. I'll never harm him, because of all the love he feels towards you. Love is one of the most powerful feelings in any universe. It feeds me; it gives me strength regardless of its source.'

'Bullshit!' She shook her head. 'Don't you think your words contradict your actions? You're kidnapping and threatening people while musing about eternal love.'

'Damn it!' Engel exploded. 'Okay then. You can refuse to help me, return to your lifeline, and try to forget about everything that happened. In this case, my U-boat and her crew will remain in your lifeline forever, bringing your country to the brink of an international scandal. Eventually, the core will collapse, destroying Germania and killing me, or even worse, will become a playground for Dr Stromm and his maniac experiments. A part of you will die together with me. You can die too, but even if you'll survive, a part of your psyche will be lost forever. Poor Stefan! It will be hard for him. Believe me or not-'

'I don't want to believe, I want to know the truth,' she yelled, and her voice reverberated all around the Chamber.

Engel's fists clenched. 'Please, stop it! I've told you everything I know, and that's all you need to know now.'

'I think I deserve to know more,' she snapped. 'You said you didn't have a choice. I bet you did. You could've chosen Ivor Kazinski, but you chose me instead. Why is that? I don't believe it's because of the amount of black matter or because you want to torture your men. There's more to it.'

'Unfortunately, Ivor is dead,' Engel hissed. 'Der Meister killed him, predicting my next move. Or maybe he saw it in trillions of possible futures.'

'Even if I agree to help, nothing will stop you from killing me when my mission is complete.'

'It's not true.' He shook his head, coming closer. 'The choice is yours, and you need to trust my word. So…' He outstretched his hand. 'Have we made a deal?'

Zara gritted her teeth. He was right. There was only one way to solve this, even if he was lying. 'I have conditions,' she squeezed out a reply.

'Go ahead.'

'When we're done, you'll disappear from my lifeline forever. No visits, no visions, no nightmares, no hallucinations, or any other weird stuff. I want my life back. You'll keep your shit under control. No leaks of black matter and no "accidental" travels from your lifeline to mine. No harassment of Stefan, Ethan, or anybody else somehow evolved in this case.'

Engel nodded. A satisfied smile illuminated his face. 'I can't promise you the side effects of black matter will vanish completely, but I can reassure you that you'll become immune to them, as Walter Dix and Ulrich Schultz did. As for me, you have my word, the word of a Kriegsmarine's officer. I will never bother you again.'

He stretched his hand for the second time.

Zara stared into his eyes for a second. 'I hope the word of the Kriegsmarine's officer still means a lot to you.' She touched his hand and plunged into a heavy, milky mist.

Chapter Thirty-Nine

Stefan

London, U. K.
Present day

Stefan had just entered the airport lounge when he noticed the tall, familiar figure of Agent Cartwright. Where was Zara? He sighed, searching for an inhaler in his jacket's pocket. Something had happened.

'Good morning, Doctor. I hope you had a quick and pleasant flight.' Cartwright approached; her face remained serious, without a hint of a smile.

'Zara? Where is she?'

'I wanted to ask you the same question.' Cartwright shrugged. 'She should've checked out of her hotel in Portsmouth this morning, but it never happened. I tried to call her several times. No answer. That's why I'm here.'

'You know she hasn't been well for the last few weeks. I was worried when she didn't confirm our meeting here this morning, so I decided to hire a car and drive from Heathrow straight to Winchester in case-'

'Let's discuss it on the way to the office.' Cartwright touched his sleeve, gesturing to follow her.

The two headed to the car park.

'The hotel's room service tried to get in touch with her, but found her mobile phone in her room,' Cartwright started again as they left the airport and headed to the city centre. 'Witnesses claim the last time they saw Zara was yesterday in the hotel bar.

She left about eight thirty PM and never returned. The hotel's CCTV records have confirmed that. Her car was still in the car park, so she didn't go far. The staff were worried and called the local police.'

Stefan closed his eyes and exhaled. 'Damn it!'

'Doctor? Are you okay?'

He gritted his teeth in helpless anger. 'Someone has kidnapped her.'

'What? How?'

'I know it's hard to believe, but I'm pretty sure now it is the Captain.'

Cartwright chuckled. 'Even if so, why does he need her? Kidnappers make demands. This individual, whoever they are, had enough time from yesterday evening to make a claim, but they've made no demands yet.'

'Any news about the U-boat?' Stefan didn't listen to her.

'She's just vanished.' Cartwright slammed full-on at the pedestrian crossing. 'What about the Captain? Have you got a lead?'

'I have.' Stefan sighed. 'He's an extremely dangerous individual. He's directly involved in the murder of Ivor Kazinski, amongst other crimes. I have no doubts.' With that said, he told the agent everything he learned from Ida and Zara.

Meanwhile, their car finally squeezed through the shocking morning traffic and turned onto a narrow street. Cartwright nodded to a Georgian-style building with white columns and exposed brick walls. 'Here we go.'

She stopped the car, opening the door to make a "follow me" gesture into the NCA Headquarters.

'If your assumption is correct, and Julius Engel has kidnapped Zara, the only place he could bring her was the U-boat,' she said, passing by the spacious reception area and nodding to the security guards. 'This entire operation will be classed as a terror attack. MI5 will be on it straight away. I doubt they'll allow us to carry on with this case.'

'I understand.' Stefan nodded. 'That's why we can't waste our time. We need to intercept the U-boat and try to negotiate.'

Cartwright snorted. 'And how do you think we intercept something we don't even know the whereabouts of?'

They passed the long, dark corridor and stopped at an office door. She opened the frosted-glass door, ready to come in, but a husky male voice stopped her.

'Morning, Patricia.' A tall man in his late forties, dressed in a short black leather jacket and black jeans, approached them. 'Dr Krause, I suppose.' He greeted Stefan with a nod.

Cartwright rolled her eyes. 'Oh, no.'

'Yes, yes, it is I.' The man's thin lips curved into a mocking smile. 'Ian Lenard of MI5.' He stretched his hand to Stefan for a handshake, and he touched it absently.

'Please, let's get straight to business,' Cartwright snapped.

'Our bosses have finally agreed to transfer this operation to MI5. From now on, you're working with me.' Ian shrugged and turned to Stefan. 'An attempted terror attack has happened in British waters, so…' He nodded towards Stefan's suitcase. 'Doctor, I'm afraid Agent Cartwright dragged you from Germany for nothing.'

'You read the report. You should know how much Dr Krause has helped us with this case,' Cartwright said. 'As for the submarine, the crew has made no demands yet. Nobody has claimed responsibility for both attacks on the container ship or the oil rig, either. On what grounds have they transferred the case?'

'You specialise in…' Agent Lenard opened a paper file he brought with him, paying no attention to Cartwright's words, and addressing Stefan. 'The Second World War German naval history, in particular, in the Kriegsmarine's underwater technologies before and during the war,' he read aloud from the file.

Stefan nodded. 'That's correct.'

'So, you have nothing to do with hazardous substances, weapons of mass destruction or counter-terror measures? That's what we're now dealing with here,' Agent Lenard continued with a half-smile. 'Sorry, Doctor, but I don't think your expertise applies to this case.'

'It seems like you didn't read my report in full,' Cartwright interrupted him, impatience in her voice. 'What we're dealing with here is a seventy-five-year-old German U-boat full of aggressive, confused men in possession of a hazardous device we know very little about. They're not terrorists, and yet, they're dangerous. I believe Dr Krause can resolve this situation carefully and without violence. All we need to do is to intercept the U-boat, disarm the device, and see the vessel off to German waters, leaving Germany to deal with its citizens.'

Agent Lenard's thin lips twitched. 'I've read enough of your report. You had a chance to retrieve the device, yet you lost it. I can't afford for that to happen again. As for the U-boat's crew, I can lead the negotiations. Don't forget, I was born and lived in West Berlin. I speak German well enough to-'

Stefan took a step closer. 'Perhaps you lived in Germany, but not in Germany in the thirties and forties. Their way of thinking and their mind-set differ from ours. I bet you've never been on a World War Two U-boat. These guys carry fifteen to twenty torpedoes and they're not afraid to die.'

The agent's eyes scrutinised Stefan for a couple of seconds. He had just opened his mouth to object, but his mobile phone's loud vibration interrupted him. 'Yes?' he barked, picking up the phone and taking a step back from the two.

'God! Couldn't MI5 send somebody less bitchy and more serious than this douchebag?' Cartwright mumbled when her counterpart turned away to the window.

Nobody can beat you in that, Patricia. Stefan chuckled to himself, but said instead, 'I think it's unwise to tell Agent

Lenard about Zara's disappearance right now. Especially if we don't know where exactly she is.'

Cartwright nodded. 'I agree. If he knows about Zara, he'll have even more reasons to call it a terror attack. Then not only you, but the NCA and I will be out of action too.'

Agent Lenard hung up the phone and returned to them.

'Some news about the U-boat, I guess.' Cartwright smirked.

The agent squeezed through his teeth. 'We've traced the vessel to the coast of Inverness. Looks adrift.'

Cartwright shot an inquiring glance at Stefan.

'Most likely, they ran out of fuel. The batteries might be flat.' He shrugged. 'Remember how much power DF requires?'

'Whatever technical difficulties they may have, it may be our only chance,' Agent Lenard said. 'HMS Aurora is on her way to intercept. We need to join the party before she'll meet the U-boat.'

'I'll tell my guys to send a helicopter for us.' Cartwright nodded. 'I believe Dr Krause requires full clearance from your team before boarding our submarine.' She raised her eyes to the agent.

'Hah.' Agent Lenard folded his arms on his chest. 'You act as if you're still in charge of this mission.'

'Do you want to take the risk?' she snapped. 'I can't object to my superiors. If they're happy to transfer the case to MI5, I can't do anything, apart from stepping back and leaving you in charge, tête-à-tête with this pain in the arse.'

Agent Lenard eyed the two with contempt, his eyes cold and virulent. 'May I have your ID for a few minutes?' he asked Stefan after an oppressive pause. 'I need a copy for my operatives.'

'Thanks. We'll wait for you in my office,' Cartwright replied instead when Stefan handed him his passport.

'I hope my choice won't disappoint me.' Agent Lenard nodded; his eyes still fixed on Stefan.

'Thank you,' he mumbled, and hurried to Cartwright's office.

A traditionally dull office room, which Agent Cartwright

shared with her team, met him with curious looks from her operatives and the potent smell of coffee.

'Morning, all. Dr Stefan Krause.' She gestured at him, and a few people nodded and waved absently, distracted from their computer screens.

'Can I offer you coffee while we're waiting?' Cartwright asked after taking off her jacket and making a request to her assistant to call a helicopter.

Stefan left his suitcase and his coat in a built-in wardrobe in the corner and followed her to a station with tea and coffee facilities. 'That was close. With Agent Lenard, I mean,' he started. 'My heart skipped a beat when you offered to drop the case.'

Cartwright smirked and pressed a button on a giant coffee machine. 'I've known Ian long enough to use this special tactic. He's not sure he's able to do it on his own. If we fail, he'll be the first to blame us in front of the NCA and MI5 bosses.'

'Don't even tell me about the failure.' Stefan took a seat on a couch next to the coffee-brewing noisy monster. 'I pray I'm wrong, and Zara isn't aboard this sub. Surrounded by a few dozens of rough men who still think they're at war…' He sighed.

Cartwright sat next to him, holding two mugs with a steaming drink. 'I can imagine your despair, but we need you to stay focused. Judging by your story, Captain Engel needs Zara for a reason, for a far more complicated and dangerous purpose than just abuse. Maybe he's a conspirator, but he's not a thug.'

Stefan took a mug from her hand. The freshly brewed espresso energised him. The caffeine kicked in after a couple of sips. 'Thanks.' He nodded. 'I hope we can stop him, whatever he's plotting now.'

'Zara is a clever woman. She'll protect herself.' Cartwright's eyes reflected a shadow of a smile. 'I worry about her as much as you do, Doctor. She reminds me of my twins.' She chuckled, looking away from the window. 'They're just a few years younger, but as stubborn and cheeky as she is.'

'You? Have children?' Stefan asked but bit his tongue.

'You can't believe a woman like me can have kids?'

'Of course not. I didn't mean that,' he mumbled.

Cartwright patted his shoulder. 'Oh, come on, Doctor. I know it's hard to believe, but I'm not the same person. I'm not the same young, naïve girl left by her boyfriend with two newborns. Looking back, it felt like my darkest hour, but I didn't let it swallow me. This is your darkest hour. Don't allow it to prevail. I was alone. While you have me and many others to support you.' With that said, she left him alone on the couch and headed to her working desk.

Stefan had just finished his espresso when the office door swung open, and Agent Lenard entered.

'We're good to go.' He nodded to Stefan, without greeting other operatives, and proceeded straight to Cartwright's desk.

'Ma'am, the helicopter is ready and waiting for you,' one of Cartwright's aides said.

'Wonderful.' She nodded and disappeared into another room with a code lock by the entrance.

It must be the weapons' lockers, Stefan mused.

'Has anybody briefed the Aurora's captain?' she asked, back in the office. 'No hostilities at any cost.'

'My people informed him about his mission and our arrival.' Agent Lenard grimaced. 'Hurry! We don't want to be late.'

The trio exited the office and made their way to the lift, which took them to a landing pad on the rooftop. As promised, the helicopter had already been waiting for them.

'One last thing, Doctor.' Agent Lenard turned to Stefan when they settled down in the spacious cabin. 'No improvisation when aboard. I read about your stunts in the Mouritz Hotel. You're partial to a risky extravaganza, but we can't lose the device again.'

Stefan didn't reply, just bowed his head.

Chapter Forty

Stefan

The endless expanse of the North Sea spread far beyond the lead-grey horizon. Calm for the time of the year, the waves had creased slightly. Stefan's heart skipped a beat when he noticed an elongated black body of HMS Aurora down below. The helicopter descended, and the pilots asked them to get ready. Unable to land, the craft hovered over the black hull as low as possible so, dressed in waterproof suits, the company could get out using a ladder and ropes.

A tall uniformed woman accompanied by two sailors awaited them on the conning tower.

'Welcome aboard! I'm Chief Officer Janette O'Neil.' The woman approached them as the helicopter's humming dispersed in the distance and the wind calmed down. 'Nice to meet you.'

'Morning, Officer. I'm Ian Lenard, MI5,' the agent replied, nodding to the rest of the company. 'My colleague, Agent Patricia Cartwright, the NCA, and our German specialist, Dr Stefan Krause.'

'Please, follow me.' The chief officer smiled, but her eyes remained hollow. 'The captain is expecting you.'

They followed their hostess through the hatch and into the bowels of the giant aquatic beast. They took off their protective gear, leaving it to a petty officer.

Stefan admired how much larger and more spacious this vessel looked compared to her Second World War sisters. This creature provided more crew comforts, but critically, more space for her arsenal. They followed Chief Officer O'Neil and passed the first floor with the control room and the officer's quarters, descending to the second level where the commanding officers' cabin and living spaces were located.

'How much time do we have before their systems intercept us?' Agent Lenard asked.

'At our current speed, about twenty minutes.' Janette shrugged. 'Maybe a bit more, although I doubt their sonar is so advanced.'

'I wouldn't be so sure,' Stefan mumbled, but asked instead, 'Can we also have the chief engineer and the weapons engineer with us?'

The woman nodded and opened a door leading to the captain's quarters.

'Morning and welcome aboard HMS Aurora.' A heavy-set man in his mid-forties rose from his working desk, spreading his wide hand for a handshake. 'Captain George Barrows.' Not a hint of a smile on his clean-shaven face. His pale eyes behind thin spectacles reflected nothing but contempt.

Stefan shook the captain's hand. What else could MI5 bring him, apart from a pain in the arse?

He glanced around. A large working desk, a few shelves with books and journals, a Union Jack, and a portrait of Her Majesty the Queen in the far corner of the room. In another corner, a partition with a bunk behind it – the routine reality of a submarine's officer.

Meanwhile, Agent Lenard introduced the team again, and Captain Barrows offered him a seat while Chief Officer O'Neil summoned the rest of the officers. The trio settled down around the desk, and within a couple of minutes, a man and a woman appeared on the doorstep.

'My Chief Engineer and Weapons' Engineer.' The captain nodded to the newcomers, and another round of handshakes and introductions followed.

'Let's start.' Agent Lenard grimaced, glancing at his watch. 'Chief Officer O'Neil doesn't think we have much time left.'

The captain only nodded, and the agent took the initiative.

'As you can see, this is a complicated and delicate case,' Cartwright added when her colleague finished the short briefing. 'We insist on the non-aggressive response at any cost.'

Stefan observed the reaction to their words. Mocking half-smiles, frowned eyebrows, shaking heads. They didn't believe them.

Captain Barrows interrupted the lengthy pause first. 'You claim this vessel carries a weapon that is far superior to ours and that allows travelling at the speed of light? I can't imagine how we can withstand it. Besides, what makes you think they'll give us this weapon? It seems like they're holding all the cards.'

'We need to negotiate,' Cartwright started, but the captain didn't let her finish.

'Negotiate what? As I understand, they haven't made claims yet. They've just invaded our waters and harassed our shipping. They appear and disappear as they wish.' He shrugged. 'How are we supposed to stop them, apart from torpedoing the U-boat and collecting survivors from the surface?'

'No.' Agent Lenard rose from his chair. 'It'll destroy the device, the U-boat, and may affect us as well. We still don't know how the device's content can influence a nuclear reactor of your vessel.'

Stefan joined him. 'We need to know what these people want. Why they're here, in British waters?'

An alarm howled from the corridor.

Agent Lenard frowned. 'What's that?'

'Torpedo attack,' the weapons officer yelled.

The captain nodded, and she made her way to the door, the other officers following her.

The captain picked up the communicator fixed on the wall. 'Report immediately!' He listened for a few seconds and then hung up. 'We've tried to come as close as possible, but our German guests didn't hesitate to fire a torpedo. Luckily, they missed. On purpose or otherwise, it doesn't matter.' He rose from the table, ready to follow his officers.

'Wait. What are you going to do?' Cartwright touched his sleeve.

'We need to stop them before they fire again. I'm not challenging their luck this time.'

Stefan jumped in front. 'No. You can't do that.'

'Pardon?' The captain's eyes scrutinised him.

Out of breath, Stefan squeezed an inhaler in his pocket and replied, shouting out the alarm's howl, 'We believe they have a female hostage aboard! A British citizen.'

'What?' Agent Lenard hissed, turning to his colleague. 'Damn you, Cartwright!'

'You believe, Doctor?' Captain Barrows snorted. 'Should I risk more than a hundred lives, my vessel, and the threat of radiation exposure just because of your belief?'

Cartwright stood between the two men. 'Gentlemen, please, compose yourselves.'

'Let me guess the name of the hostage,' Agent Lenard interrupted them. 'Miss Zara Rose. Am I right?' He grinned.

'Yes.' Stefan nodded, turning away from the submariner. 'I believe this U-boat is under the command of Captain Julius Engel. He's an extremely dangerous, mentally unstable individual who might've been involved in the murder of his fellow captain and the kidnapping of Miss Rose. I also believe this torpedo attack was just a warning. They're testing us.'

'At least now we know who we're dealing with,' Captain Barrows replied, opening the door, and inviting the trio to follow him.

The emerged HMS Aurora towered above her older diesel-electric sister like a whale above a whitebait fish.

Stefan, surrounded by agents and officers, watched the hatch fly open, and a group of sailors dressed in the Kriegsmarine's uniform appeared on the bridge.

No captain. Stefan's knees weakened. *Where the fuck is he, and where's Zara?*

'Captain George Barrows of Her Majesty's Royal Navy,' the

captain barked over the loudspeaker. 'You've entered British waters without permission and attacked us. I demand to speak with your commander immediately to clarify your hostile actions.'

The sailors remained silent.

'Perhaps they don't understand me?' Captain Barrows mumbled, turning to Stefan, who took the loudspeaker to translate, but the next moment, Stefan's jaw dropped.

A slim, familiar silhouette appeared from the hatch. Dressed in a short leather Kriegsmarine's jacket and a white officer's cap, Zara raised her hand in greeting from the bridge.

'Morning, Captain Barrows. Morning, agents.' Her voice sounded lower and with an accent. 'I am Captain Julius Engel of the Kriegsmarine's 11th Flotilla, the commander of this vessel. Please, don't allow my look to confuse you.'

Chapter Forty-One

Zara

The North Sea off the coast of Inverness
A few hours earlier

The milky mist dispersed enough for Zara to see the life raft she was standing in, adrift in the middle of the sea. The sunrise approached, colouring the low horizon in shades of pink and orange, but the thin, grey veil of fog persisted around her.

She glanced at her clothes; the glamorous dress and high heels had vanished, submitted for a short leather jacket with Kriegsmarine's insignia, khaki trousers, and a white captain's cap. Her vision and hearing grew sharper, but struggled to focus on a single thought, as if some unknown force pulled them away. Her body ached, a stony discomfort, where every muscle and joint stretched and stiffened. She touched her face; even her skin felt overstretched.

She closed her eyes. The faces of people she'd never met emerged in her mind's eye. She knew their names now. Gory snippets of the past flashed into view. The dimly lit gangway of a U-boat, a revolver in her hand, the body of an officer on the floor, a bloody silhouette framed him.

Her tiny raft rocked, captured by upcoming waves, and she needed to sit down to keep her balance. An enormous grey mass had been crawling through the waves, and Zara recognised the familiar silhouette of U-713. They were adrift, out of fuel, and couldn't charge the batteries. She didn't control her thoughts. They controlled her and her actions now.

On the bottom of the raft, she discovered a torch and a loaded revolver. Using the torch to attract the attention of the three officers on the conning tower, she holstered the revolver on her belt.

Within a couple of minutes, the vessel was in proximity, allowing Zara's raft to approach her.

'What the hell?'

'A woman?'

'Here? In the middle of the sea? Dressed as an officer?'

'Am I dreaming, Chief? Or can you see her as well?'

'A mirage?'

'Nothing surprises me now.'

She could hear men's anxious whispers in German. There was no language barrier for her. She raised her head. The familiar faces of her crewmembers, all familiar faces: Chief Engineer Günter Hoff, Navigator Otto Brühler, and Second Watch Officer Max Richter.

The trio peered at her as if they saw a ghost.

Those bastards! He'd teach them a bitter lesson. These thoughts, coming from nowhere, made her smile to herself.

'Hey, Chief. Will you continue to stare at me or will you help your commander to get aboard?' Zara broke the weird silence first.

Her words, in perfect German, dropped from her mouth, heavy as stone. Her voice sounded lower. Not all these changes scared Zara. Instead, she enjoyed the growing power in her muscles and the depth of her voice.

'What? Who the fuck are you, lady? What're you doing, dressed like this in the middle of the sea?' Günter Hoff shouted.

'It must be a trick. Some kind of bizarre mirage of this reality,' Max Richter whispered in his ear, but Zara could hear it as if he whispered it in hers.

'No tricks, no mirages, no other realities, Second Watch Officer,' she replied instead of the Chief, coming closer and starting to climb the thick rope attached to the starboard.

The officer pulled a gun out of his holster. 'She knows me.'

'Oh, you've always been so fucking dramatic. I know my current look is a bit confusing, but it doesn't mean you shouldn't salute your captain.' With that said, she reached the deck and waved to the men to come closer. 'Oh, come on! I know you're well-known cowards who stab their captain in the back, but now-'

'What? Whoever you are, woman, I'll make you regret your words.' Brühler slid down the rail, his gun pointing at Zara's head. 'We've seen enough weird shit here, now you-'

She didn't let him finish. A powerful hit between his legs made the officer kneel. His gun bounced off the deck and disappeared in the waves.

'Oh!' He growled. His peers rushed down the ladder, but it was too late.

Zara grabbed him from the floor like a rag doll. Squeezing the man's throat, she slammed him into the conning tower.

'Another step and I'll neck him like a chicken,' she hissed to the Chief, gun pointed at her head.

The man stepped back. His neatly trimmed beard hid his grimace, but his deep eyes fired anger.

'How quickly you forgot me,' she continued, pressing her victim harder. 'When you attacked me, trying to kill me, I promised you I'd return. Any time, in any form, I would return. Even after thousands of years, I wouldn't forget what you've done to me. So here I am. And you? You're stuck here, in this lifeline, some seventy years away from our Fatherland. What choice do you have now?'

'Don't listen to her, Chief. She's not real. It must be some kind of hallucination,' Richter mumbled. 'The batteries are leaking too much gas. It can affect-'

Zara smirked and squeezed her captive's throat tighter. The man's lips turned bluish and his eyes rolled. 'I'm sure the pain I'm causing him is very real.'

'Whoever you are, drop him.' The Chief raised his gun at her head.

All his movements seemed slow, delayed for a few fractions of a second. Zara banged Brühler's head off the metal, releasing him from her deadly grip, and jumped in front of the slow-moving officers. She grabbed both guns by their barrels, turned them around in her grip, and pointed them at the officers' heads. 'Now, we're talking.'

The two stood speechless while their comrade fainted on the deck with his head bleeding.

The Chief said, staring at his wounded crewmember, 'I need to remind you of a few things, whether you're our commander or not. We didn't attack or try to kill you. You betrayed us, disobeyed orders, and wanted to defect to the Americans. First Watch Officer attempted to stop you, but you shot him, sabotaged Die Fledermaus machine, and escaped, leaving us…' He made a wide gesture to his peers, 'to deal with all this mess. Now, we have no idea what's happened to us. The machine went out of control. During our chaotic "jumps" we've lost more than half of the crew.'

Zara gritted her teeth and squeezed the guns tighter. 'You're a fucking liar. Tell these fairy tales to your ugly kids, although they're long dead.' She smirked. 'As for the boat and the crew, you're trapped here in this lifeline.'

She wanted to say something else, but her vision blurred.

Engel stood in the middle of the control room. He recognised the long face of his First Watch Officer Fritz Mayer, red with fervent anger. Almost all, the officers gathered around them. The maddening heat, stench of fuel and hot metal were unbearable, but he didn't pay attention.

'This is treason, Commander, and I'm not a part of it. Neither is the crew,' Mayer shouted in his face. 'Chief, Richter, place him under arrest in his quarters. We need to report it to the base immediately.'

'Do you want to face a firing squad, men?' Engel turned

around but met no support. 'Follow the orders of this lunatic, and I can guarantee none of you will escape a court-martial.'

'A court-martial for what?' Mayer exploded. 'For following the orders and continuing our patrol? You read the latest order, and so did I. We must stay on our current course to join the "pack" to attack this convoy together. Your random decision to change the course… where did it come from? As your First Watch Officer, I have all rights to know and challenge it.'

'This is a mutiny!' he hissed, taking a step closer to the officer. Hand on his holster, the Chief's heavy hand stopped him.

'Don't make it any harder, Captain.'

Zara's vision cleared. Loud thuds and distant voices sounded from the tower. A motorist and an electrician appeared at the top, attracted by the noises.

'Stay back!' the Chief commanded the newcomers.

Zara didn't see their faces, but they were likely as surprised as their peers.

'Come on! Kill us as you killed the First Watch Officer.' The Chief nodded to the gun, pointing at him. 'What will you get out of it?'

'I don't need to kill you.' She grinned. 'We need each other to get out. Without my knowledge and fuel, you won't be able to move. A British nuclear U-boat, about five, ten times bigger than ours, sent to intercept us a few hours ago, will arrive at any minute. So, how much time do I need to waste to persuade you of who I am before she'll torpedo us?'

'A nuclear U-boat, eh?' Richter chuckled. 'What else nonsense are you going to tell us? You've always been a liar, a traitor, and a bitch. Now, you're just showing us your true colours, your true nature – a pretty face but a rotten soul, full of shit.'

Instead of an answer, Zara smacked his face with the barrel of the gun. Richter groaned, squeezing his bleeding nose. 'Shit!'

The Chef took a step closer but froze on the spot.

Zara raised her eyes to him. 'Do you need more persuasion, Chief, or can we finally talk like officers, not like thugs?'

He frowned, but his voice remained calm. 'What do you want?'

'I want my crew and my boat back.' She shrugged, paying no attention to the injured officers. 'You know you can't operate the machine now. The manual is useless.'

'What happened to us? What is this place? Can we return?'

She gave him a mocking smile and put the gun down. 'I've told you already, you "jumped" to another lifeline from 1944 to some seventy years later. There's no way back. Maybe for the better.'

The Chief's hazel eyes studied her face for a few seconds. There was no aggression or violence in them. These deep, sad eyes reminded her of somebody, somebody important in her life, another life.

'It's impossible.' He exhaled. 'It means… it means what? The base? Our families? We'll never see them again? What about Germany? What's happened to the country? We've lost the war, no doubt about it.'

'Yes, we've lost. There's no Fatherland anymore. At least, not as you all know it.' She nodded. 'The Allies and the Soviets have won. They pretend to be friends now. It doesn't work well, though.' The wave of pain from a headache squeezed her temples, her vision blurred again, and her legs weakened. Reality slid away from her. 'Call the rest of the crew. I'm sure I'll be able to explain in all details what has happened, and what we're going to do right now,' she continued, scrambling to keep the rest of her consciousness.

The motorist and his peer helped the Chief to assist the injured officers, and Richter rushed to gather the crew – some twenty men who were left after the Chief's fruitless attempts to return them to 1944. All young, the oldest in their early twenties, the men appeared from the hatch one by one. The

Chief Petty Officer brought a medical kit to help the wounded.

Zara squinted, observing the crew. Apart from the Chief, these men were all kids. Knights of the sea, eh? They looked more like an unruly kindergarten. Admiral Dönitz had scrambled everything he could to keep the underwater fleet going. No doubt, Tommies and Yanks were laughing at them.

Curiosity and confusion in every look, anxious whispers, vulgar jokes and comments.

The Chief barked, 'Men, your commander is back. Eyes left! Hail your captain.' He turned to Zara. 'Twenty hands are present and accounted.'

She could hear every whisper now.

'Eh? What?'

'What the fuck is going on?'

'Chief? Is he blind?'

'What a pleasant turn! I'm starting to like this place.'

'Whoever she is, she looks great.'

'Have you lost your mind, Chief?'

She raised both guns and fired in the air. 'Shut up, you thick bastards, and listen to me and your officers! I won't tolerate the second mutiny. Eyes front! At ease!'

'Oh, this voice. I recognise it. A higher pitch, but the voice is the same.'

'We're all going mad.'

'Has she done it to Richter and Brühler?'

'Who else? She's got their guns as well.'

'She's talking about the mutiny as if-'

Zara wished she could close her ears and not hear all these voices. 'I've promised you to come back. I always keep my promises. Here I am, Commander Julius Engel,' she said. 'Despite your disgraceful mutiny, your disobedience, I've returned not to prosecute you. I'm here to help.'

The whispers intensified.

'Oh, this place is much worse than I thought.'

'Will we all turn into women?'

'Don't be silly!'

'A woman is aboard. That's it, guys. We're cursed. This boat is cursed.'

'Cursed, eh? We're doomed now like the Flying Dutchman or something.'

She continued to talk about their "jump", the faulted machine, and their inability to return to 1944.

'Looks like she… eh, he… whoever the fuck it is knows everything about us.'

'I don't want to stay here and be friendly with Yankees, Tommies, and Soviets. I don't want to be torpedoed by this Tommies' nuclear boat or whatever she's going on about.'

'The Chief has tried to return a few times. Each time, we lose more and more men. Do you want to disappear as well?'

'Tommies have a nuclear U-boat? How's that? A nuclear-powered U-boat. I'd like to see-'

'I'm sure they'll be happy to organise you a guided tour, you moron.'

'She's a demon. Some kind of witchcraft is going on here. She's enchanted the Chief and Richter already.'

'Witchcraft doesn't exist. Another month aboard, and any woman will enchant me, demon or not.'

'Damn! You filthy swine! You can't be that desperate.'

'It's supposed to be a joke.'

'Shut your traps, you two, or I'll fuck you both.'

'Ha-ha! I always suspected you fancied me.'

'What a freak!'

'Now, it's your choice, men: glorious Germania where you could build your world from scratch, to meet your loved ones again, or this miserable, backward lifeline. Here, you'll be nothing but guinea pigs for inhumane experiments, which I'm sure the Tommies will put you through if we survive the meeting with their nuclear boat. The men who came from the past. They'll interrogate and study you to death. The Tommies won't let you go.' She finished her speech and observed the crew, but only hostile silence answered her. 'Help me transport Die Fledermaus to Germania, and I'll forgive your treason.'

'And how do you wish to be addressed?' The Chief Petty Officer broke the oppressive pause first. A couple of smirks and giggles supported him.

'How did you always address me?'

'Eh… Ugh… Herr Kapitänleutnant,' he faltered. 'Herr Kaleun for short.'

'I can't see why this should change,' she snapped.

'Dismissed!' The Chief barked, and the crewmen went back to their stations, queuing at the hatch.

Only two watchmen remained on the bridge.

'The discipline aboard is horrible, Chief. I see the bad influence of you and the First Watch Officer is starting to show.' Zara turned to the Chief. 'I'm going to fix it. Now, show me what's going on with the batteries and Die Fledermaus.'

Chapter Forty-Two

Zara

The dark interior of the U-boat swallowed her with its dim, red light, and unbearable stench of fumes, fuel, damp food, filthy clothes, and men's sweat. She followed the Chief and one of the motorists through the control room, the officers' mess and to the engine room.

'Report. I need a full report.' She nodded to the Chief when they stopped at the room's hatch.

'We ran out of diesel. The engines are dead,' he started, opening the hatch, and pointing to two ten feet long blocks. 'The batteries are leaking. Twenty cells have run dry.'

She nodded. 'I can smell that. The stench is infernal.'

'The sulphuric acid from the batteries is mixing with seawater, forming chlorine-'

'Please skip the chemistry lesson.' She waved him off. 'I'm well aware of the batteries' construction.'

'Luckily, we've surfaced. The ventilation system is still intact.'

'What exactly happened to the batteries? Can you identify the leaks?'

'They've been damaged during our "jumps". I need to run the diagnostics to see where the damage is and bridge it over.' He shrugged. 'It requires time, materials, and people. There're only a motorist, an electrician, and I remaining who can do this job. It'll take us forever. As you can imagine, the concentration of chlorine and hydrogen in the room is far beyond normal. If something goes wrong…'

She didn't listen, staring at the lifted floor plates and the dark abyss in the floor, where the leaking batteries rested. Lengths of cables and tools surrounded the opening.

The Chief handed her the rescue gear with the oxygen cartridge. 'The air down there is unbearable.'

'And we need diesel to fill in the engine and power Die Fledermaus for the final "jump",' she mused aloud.

'Yes.'

She grinned. 'This Tommies' U-boat can help us, you know.'

The Chief and the motorist exchanged anxious looks.

'They need the machine and me. This body will buy us time and fuel.'

'Sorry, I'm not sure I'm following.' The Chief frowned.

'This pretty shell belongs to a British woman. The Tommies are so soft nowadays. Most people are in this lifeline. They won't bargain on the lives of their citizens. So, it's in your interest to keep me safe, unharmed, and happy,' she continued. 'They may save men's lives as well, but... I wouldn't rely on British honour.'

'It seems like you've got a plan in place already, Herr Kaleun,' the motorist commented with a careful half-smile.

'Of course. I'm not leaving my men in trouble, even though they followed the advice of a traitor and conspirator.' Zara nodded. 'I'm ready to discuss my plan with the senior officers, but first, I need to fix the machine.'

The motorist opened one of the special cupboards on the ceiling and pulled out a tool kit. 'Aye, Herr Kaleun.'

Zara took the heavy box as if it was a feather and opened the plate, covering Die Fledermaus, connected to the broken batteries.

'Get out!' She barked, and the motorist rushed to leave the room.

The Chief didn't move. 'Do you wish me to assist you?'

'Only I can fix it.' She shook her head. 'You have no choice but to trust me. Leave me now, Chief. I'll talk to you later.'

The officer hesitated for a moment, but Zara grabbed his shoulder and pushed him to the hatch. 'Don't force me to repeat my orders twice.'

Chapter Forty-Three

Chief Engineer Hoff

'Chief, please don't tell me you believe this creature.' Richter circled the cabin, his grey eyes fixed on the Chief Engineer. 'You're the oldest and the most experienced amongst us. Tell me it's not real.'

'Your nose is still bleeding.' The Chief raised his head from the journal he'd been writing in. 'How's Brühler?'

'Ah, came back to life all right. A few bruises and a headache, nothing serious.' He waved, squeezing a handkerchief to his still swollen nose. 'We have more serious problems to think about right now. Who is she? What is she doing here? How does she know so much about us, about the captain, and the British U-boat? We need to get rid of her as soon as possible and find the way back home.'

'Damn!' The Chief banged his fist on the folding desk he occupied. 'Haven't you got it yet? There's no way back to the past. At least, to our past as we know it. The creature has confirmed it. I tried several times. I thought I'd fixed the machine, but the more I tried the worse and worse it became. The manual? It's useless. I don't want to lose more of our men. I've told you already they didn't allow me anywhere near the machine when the boat was docked. This is my tenth patrol, but I've never been so bloody helpless.'

'I wouldn't leave her alone in the engine room if I were you.' Richter stopped in the middle of the compartment. 'Do you want to go to this place? This Germania, if only it exists? It's too fucking good to be true.'

The Chief shook his head. 'No, I don't believe her. However, if she had intended to kill us, she would've done it already. She held a gun to our heads, remember? She knows something about this place we don't. It may help us to get out of here. I don't want to go to Germania, but I don't want to stay here either.' He paused, covering his face with his palm.

All conversations about home had become taboo since the boat appeared in this hostile lifeline, but the Chief couldn't get rid of the thoughts about his family. He promised his girls to take leave for Elsa's sixteenth birthday. Now what? Some seventy years later, she was dead. Both his girls were dead. His grandchildren? Did he have any? God! They were a few decades older than he was. 'Nobody's waiting for us here. Nobody needs us anymore,' he said finally.

Richter sat on a tool chest next to him. 'Even if we can't go back home, we need to get rid of this creature.' He lowered his voice. 'You saw what she was capable of. This was only the beginning. She's here for the machine, not to save the crew. We must get rid of the bitch before she gets us, one by one.'

A thick pause filled the heavy air.

The Chief gritted his teeth, annoyed. 'It seems like you forgot you're still wearing this uniform. We're officers, not murderers who kill women. Shame on you!'

'No. Shame on you, Chief!' Richter jumped from his seat. 'She's not even a human. I'm not going to participate in this circus. If you don't have the guts to finish this mess, just put her in a raft and let her go back to wherever she came from.'

The Chief shook his head. 'Don't you dare command me!'

Richter squinted. 'You saw her, didn't you? Saw her there… in the dark, evil places between realities. You recognised her.'

'I'm not sure. Somewhere, somehow, between the worlds we've met. I wasn't there, and neither was she. Yet, a part of me remembers her well.'

The Chief wanted to say something else, but the next moment, Brühler appeared from the hatch. With his head bandaged, he mumbled a short greeting to the Chief and Richter.

'Discussing Herr Kaleun, I guess?' His dry lips stretched in a mocking smile.

The Chief didn't reply, just nodded to another seat next to him.

'She's a Soviet spy, no doubt about it,' Brühler continued, taking a seat at the desk. 'The Allies don't just spy on us. They don't trust each other. Where do you think the information about the British U-boat came from? Soviet intelligence-'

'If only this boat exists at all,' Richter chuckled.

'We'll know in a couple of hours.'

'Even the Soviets aren't mad enough to send a woman here.' Richter shook his head. 'It's bizarre, illogical. Her voice, her strength...'

Brühler waved. 'She's stuffed with hormones. I read an article a few weeks before the patrol about Russian experiments. They want to create a super soldier. Here she is. Besides, it's such a joke to send a woman here. Russians are laughing at us, I'm sure.'

'The Soviets have a weird sense of humour.'

'No. Perhaps she lies to us about Germania and the Tommies' U-boat,' the Chief said. 'Yet, she's a tool for Engel's evil deeds. She's hosting his corrupted psyche.'

Brühler giggled. 'It's a random choice of a host.'

'Let's be honest, Herr Kaleun has always been fucked up,' Richter replied. 'He, well, she… they believe in their innocence, but there's so much blood on their hands. Captain Erlich, First Watch Officer Mayer. Who's next?'

'You may try to kill her, but nothing guarantees Engel won't find another host.' The Chief shrugged. 'It could be one of us.'

Richter wanted to say something, but a blood-stopping scream ripped the thick air. 'What's the hell is it now?' He jumped from his seat and followed Brühler to the door.

The Chief rose as well, but the buzz of the communication system made him stop.

'I need you in the engine room. Immediately!' Zara's voice barked from the receiver.

Chapter Forty-Four

Zara

Alone in the engine room, Zara stared at Die Fledermaus. The device looked twice the size of the one aboard U-4713/A. A tiny black dot fluctuated in the middle of the glass cylinder. The glowing liquid seemed thicker than she remembered it, and all the disks with the scales looked intact. This time, there was no auxiliary engine involved. The conventional U-713 relied on her batteries when submerged. The batteries were positioned below the engine room, and Die Fledermaus connected directly to them.

The Chief had done an impressive job fixing it. But there wasn't much time. Die Fledermaus needed charging. She bit her lip in annoyance. The toxic gases were burning her face, making her eyes water. She closed them and…

The icy blasts of wind and grey waves smashed against the concrete pier. Engel raised his head. Seagulls struggled to keep their course, unable to find rest in the raging sea, either.

'Remember, you're doing it for all of us. We're all in this together: me, you, Gerhard – all of us. You're doing it for Germany, a new, better Germany,' Josef Landau-Stromm's voice pulled him out of his reverie. 'We risked everything to get it right.' His grey eyes challenged him. 'Especially Gerhard.'

Engel couldn't hide a smirk. 'Your brother is in the SS. He'll be fine, even in the worst-case scenario. The SS is for the SS only.'

'I've told you already why he chose it: more funds for the project, more freedom for him as a scientist. Gerhard has high-ranking patrons and supporters in Berlin who believe in his work, who believe a new Germany is still possible.'

'The crew? What will happen to the men?' Engel asked, making his way along the beach, away from the roaring waves.

'They will be captured and treated as prisoners of war.' Josef shrugged. His thin face with sharp features reflected no emotions. 'The best outcome for the men in the current situation, I suppose.'

'What if the Yankees test the device before we reach their coast?'

'It's a gamble, but you know how to get back. Gerhard is going to provide you with all the instructions.' Josef stopped and put his hands on his shoulder, making Engel turn to him. 'He won't leave you unprepared. We're together in this, remember?'

'Yet, I'm the one who will need to deal with the Yankees and the machine.' He chuckled, turning back to the raging sea. 'While Gerhard enjoys his life ashore.'

'Let me remember you again that he's saved your life.' Josef grabbed his shoulder and turned him around. His eyes scrutinised him. 'His people found you in a hospital, dying. You spent a couple of hours in the icy waters with almost all the organs being damaged. Your frost-bitten skin had become a massive open wound.' A mocking smile ran across his thin lips. 'But you... you didn't give up. You clutched onto life so desperately, so determined to live. That's exactly what we required for this mission – a man full of determination. Gerhard has given you a new life. Look at you now. Your body, your skin... it's smoother than Italian marble.' Josef's gloved hand touched his cheek slightly, making him cringe, but he shook it off.

'A new life as a guinea pig for Gerhard's crazy experiments?' Engel smirked, taking a step back. His lips quivered in disgust. 'The SS has got millions of slaves in concentration camps for such an occasion, but your brother has chosen me.'

'Slaves? We don't need slaves for this mission. We need you.' Josef came closer. 'Black matter is more than just a weapon of mass destruction. It is the weapon, but the fundament as well. All these massive tanks, ships, cannons, and rockets our Führer is so obsessed with are just primitive toys compared with black matter. Who possesses it, possesses time. And time is the deadliest weapon of all.

'It's too dangerous to be tested in Germany's territories. That's why we need the Yankees to believe that we want to bring our technology to them on a golden plate. With America out of the game, the Allies will be too exhausted to continue the war. Until that time, we'll progress with Die Fledermaus and smash what remains of them.' Josef's hands patted his back. 'The world will shatter to its core to be rebuilt again, and we'll be the ones who'll do it. Everything relies on you now.'

Engel did not reply. The oppressive pause hung in the air. 'What if Gerhard's calculations are incorrect, and Die Fledermaus doesn't work as we expect?' He asked finally.

The shadow of a sad smile crossed Josef's lips. 'Your sacrifice for the Fatherland and its people will never be forgotten.'

Zara sat on the floor of the engine room with a wrench and the escape gear's snorkel still in her hands. Her normal vision returned to her, and her head cleared up. Her psyche ebbed in. She stood up and stared at the device. Engel didn't sabotage the machine. Did he realise what it was capable of? The fabric of reality has been torn apart and buried Engel under its weight. The desert in her throat and a returning headache made her take a seat again. She needed to find the way. Needed to break free from him. The crew. There was no salvation, but at least they deserved a choice.

The moment of the blackout aboard U-4713/A surfaced from the abyss of her memory. Straight after that, another memory emerged: the British submarine heading to intercept them. Travel to the past wasn't possible. If the past was as far from them as them as every single possible future, the future where Stella was still alive, where she and Stefan lived happily together, then moving objects with the speed of light where just one tiny fraction of the black matter's purpose. The superimposition of lifelines, scattered fragments of reality, torn apart or stitched together from debris like Germania... What else it was capable of?

Voices behind the hatch pulled her out of her contemplation. The entire picture came back into focus. The strength she enjoyed so much filled her body again. She recognised the voices behind the hatch. The Chief Petty Officer, the radio officer, and the stocker whispered in the next compartment, but she could hear them as if they stood in front of her.

'I'm not sure it's the right thing to do. You saw what she's done to Richter and Brühler.'

'Stop being such a pussy! Finish the bitch and that's it. Tough.'

'Yes, but the Chief-'

'He's an old fool. He inhaled too much gas while working in the engine room. His brain doesn't function properly anymore.'

'Let's not finish straight away. Let's have some fun first.'

'Oh, you're a fucking perverted freak!'

'Why not use a chance?'

'Don't forget to clean cobwebs first. This lady is a good ten years older than you, idiot.'

'So, what? She looks great for her age.'

'Look at Brühler. He's had some serious "fun" already. She almost cracked his skull like an eggshell. She's a demon.'

'Will you help me or stay here and keep yakking?'

The voices muted, and the heavy hatch swung open. Zara rose from the floor, noticing a large galley knife in the Chief Petty Officer's hand. His eyes reflected nothing but aggression and hatred.

The world slowed down, and she attacked first, grabbing his wrist. The bone cracked, and the yell of the unbearable pain ripped the air. The man dropped his knife. She plunged her forehead into his nose. Another bone crashed, and the sailor's body fell into the arms of his peers behind him.

'How about this kind of fun?' She grinned at the agonised body.

The two backed down, grimaces of horror on their faces.

She stepped over the body and picked up the receiver of the communication system.

Chapter Forty-Five

Zara

'What's happened here?' the Chief asked, observing his dead crewman. His voice remained calm.

Zara stared at him without a word. Her head was ready to explode. Her vision blurred again, and she didn't know whether it happened due to her fight with the crewmate or because of Engel. She wanted to push him out of her psyche, but it would leave her body vulnerable.

The Chief frowned. 'Commander? Can you hear me?'

She slid to the floor. The superimposition of personalities. That was it. But she needed to be alone. Needed to tell the truth.

'Are you injured?' the Chief's voice sounded muted.

His deeply set eyes. They reminded her of her father. Even his beard looked similar.

She stood on the balcony of their summer house in Alsace. Climbing roses and wisterias shaded the balcony from the intense midday sun. Her father smiled his warm smile. His eyes were sad, though.

'Father.' She took a step closer. 'Is it really you? Was it you in the tunnel? Why did you run from me?'

'A part of me is always with you, Zara.' He continued to smile. 'I always try to protect you. You know that.'

'What will happen if Germania is destroyed?'

He shrugged. 'Another patch of reality will vanish, but what's the reality after all?'

'What about Engel?'

He turned away from her, staring into space. 'Engel lied to

you. Almost everything he said was a lie. Yet, you feel sorry for him. He believes in his lies. He made you believe in them too. He's manipulating you.'

'He's a part of me now.'

'At least, this is true.' He released a deep sigh. 'After all, he was used as well.'

'What about him? What about the crew?'

'They'll either vanish together with their reality or they'll figure out a way to stitch a new one.'

'Der Meister? What if he finds his way to Germania?' she asked again.

'He possesses lots of power, destructive power. It's worrying.'

'And...' she faltered. Her voice trembled. 'Stefan and I? If Engel vanishes, will I die? Will I lose my mind?'

Her father rose from his chair and headed to the balcony's door.

'Please, don't leave. Tell me. Will we survive? Am I dead already?'

He turned to her, a smile in his eyes. 'There're unlimited variants of possible futures. I'm sure you'll make a wise choice.'

'Herr Kaleun?' the Chief's frowned face emerged in front of her. 'Your eyes are watering? Are you... what?'

'My eyes are watering because of the gas.'

The alarm's loud howl made her jump.

'We've got company,' the Chief mumbled.

'Let's show the Tommies a warm welcome.' She grinned. 'First, tell the men to clean up this mess.' She gestured to the motionless body in the puddle of dark blood.

'What about the others?' The Chief frowned. 'I've heard a few voices when-'

'Forget about these two cowards.' She waved. 'I'll deal with them when we reach Germania. They were given another chance to redeem themselves, but they fucked it up. Punishment is inevitable. Remember it, Chief.'

Chapter Forty-Six

Zara

'Flood tube one!' Zara commanded from the bridge, and Richter repeated it to a man in the conning tower.

Their opponent, the British submarine, crawled through the waves. The U-boat held her bow right up against the target. The water smashed dully against the buoyancy tanks.

'They don't even try to-' Richter mumbled, but noticing Zara's frown, he bit his dry lip.

'Stop your pointless musing, Second Watch Officer. The Tommies weren't born yesterday,' she hissed. 'Tube one stand by for a shot.'

A few unbearable seconds passed, the grey waves boomed against the hull, seagulls screaming in a distance.

Zara drew a deep sigh. 'Fire!'

A powerful jolt ran through the boat as the torpedo left its tube.

'Tube one discharged,' the report came from below the hatch.

Richter and the Chief set down their binoculars, both faces as pale as the approaching waves.

'We've missed the target,' the Chief returned. 'As expected, though.'

'Good. Now, they know that we're happy to see them.' She grinned.

'What about your plan, Herr Kaleun?'

'I'll ask our British counterparts to provide us fuel and necessary assistance with the batteries' repair. In return, I'll give them what they want. When you start the engine, the machine

255

will be charged and you'll go to Germania.' Zara clapped her hands.

The Chief frowned. 'What about you? How are you going to get back?'

'Oh, don't worry. I'll take care of myself.' She turned to Richter. 'Now, we'll go and say hello to our big British "friend."'

The Second Watch Officer climbed down the ladder, gathering the others.

'The machine's set.' Zara lowered her voice, moving closer to the Chief. 'When the engine's on, all you need to do is start it.'

'What if the Tommies don't agree with your conditions?'

'I need two people to go with me as guarantors of our clear intentions.'

'What if they don't have time to return?'

'It's a gamble. They'll remain in this lifeline.' Zara shrugged, turning to the men who appeared from the hatch one by one. 'That's why my men have the freedom to decide their fate.' She raised her voice again. 'I need two volunteers to come with me aboard their boat. Who has the guts and understands English well enough for this challenge?'

After a few seconds, a couple of shy hands rose in the air.

'Good.' Zara nodded to the volunteers and turned back to the Chief.

His eyes challenged her for a few seconds. 'There's no Germania, is there? We're trapped between many worlds. You're leaving us again, Herr Kaleun.'

'I've set the machine for the final "jump."' She said, making her way to the hatch.

Chapter Forty-Seven

Stefan

'A female hostage, you say?' Captain Barrows turned to Stefan, gesturing to Zara's silhouette on the U-boat's conning tower. 'She doesn't look like a hostage to me.'

'Can we talk to Miss Rose, please?' Cartwright asked, addressing the U-boat's crew but ignoring Zara's presence. 'Zara? Is she here?'

Zara smirked, taking a loudspeaker to her lips. 'Yes and no. It's complicated. You'll be able to talk to her if you agree to our conditions.'

'What conditions? You torpedoed us in our waters minutes ago,' Captain Barrows barked. 'You're not in a position to set any conditions.'

'Trust me, I am.'

Whoever it was, it wasn't Zara anymore. Stefan stared at her in shock, unblinking.

'What are your conditions, Captain?' Agent Lenard asked. 'We're ready to negotiate to find a peaceful solution to this… ehm, delicate situation.'

'I'm sure we will.' Zara nodded. 'We need fuel to start the engine and our batteries are leaking. We need men, time, and equipment to identify the damage to fix it. As soon as we're good to go, we'll disappear, and you'll never hear about us again. You have my word. Your vessel is far superior to my U-boat. You've nothing to fear.'

Agent Lenard frowned. 'What will we receive in return?'

'I'll return Zara, happy and unharmed.'

The agent grimaced. 'Captain, it seems you know us well.' He gestured to Cartwright and Stefan. 'Then you should know what we're after. How about we don't blow up your ancient piece of scrap metal, give you some diesel, and let you go to German waters in exchange for Miss Rose and Die Fledermaus?'

Zara shook her head. 'Typical Tommies, eh? They want to have their cake and eat it.' Without warning, Zara pulled a gun from the holster and pressed it to her temple.

'No! Please, no!' Stefan yelled, his chest burning.

Cartwright pulled him back. 'Please, Doctor, compose yourself.'

Zara pushed the gun against her head again. 'I know your people well, Agent. That's why I'm giving you a chance to choose: Zara or Die Fledermaus. I know you'll make a wise choice.' She put the gun down and addressed her Chief Engineer, but neither Stefan nor his companions could hear what the two were discussing.

'Damn! We'll never get the device,' Agent Lenard whispered.

'Zara and our crew's safety are the key priorities now,' Cartwright snapped.

'I hope you understand, Captain. I need some guarantees before I'll send my engineers aboard your vessel to help you with the batteries,' Captain Barrows said to Zara.

'Of course. You'll send us fuel and people who can assist my Chief Engineer. In return, my crewmen and I will come aboard your submarine. When everything is ready, we'll exchange our men, and I'll leave Miss Rose with you.'

Captain Barrows gritted his teeth. 'Deal.'

'I'm looking forward to meeting you, Captain.' Zara beamed, staring at Stefan, and he could feel mockery in her gaze.

Captain Barrows turned to his Chief Engineer. 'I need two people from engineering, familiar with such "antiquities". Start refuelling when they're ready.' Turning back to Cartwright and Agent Lenard, he said, 'I hope you know what you're doing, agents. If something happened to my crew aboard this thing-'

'I'm going with them,' Stefan said. 'They may need an interpreter.'

'No.' Agent Lenard shook his head. 'I'll go and try to get the device.'

Cartwright touched Stefan's sleeve. 'Ian is right. We need you here. You're the only one who can talk Zara out of this shit. The situation has turned sour, Doctor. We thought Ian could extract Zara from the sub. He's a specialist in these types of operations. Now, it looks like we need to extract Zara from Zara. I still can't fully understand what's going on. You know her better than all of us. If she opens to somebody, it'll be you.'

The company headed back to the captain's quarters. A light-headed Stefan followed his peers. Captain Barrows continued his way to the engine room.

'I understand why Captain Engel needed Zara's help.' Stefan sighed, entering the captain's compartment, and closing the metal door. 'He needs his boat and Die Fledermaus.'

'Why can't he do it himself? How did he occupy her body?' Cartwright asked. 'The device is on his U-boat, so-'

'I don't have all the answers, not yet.'

'No matter how he conjures these tricks, we need to get the device first,' Agent Lenard interrupted them. 'We can't afford to lose it now.'

Cartwright shrugged. 'Even if you succeed, what'll happen to the crew? What are we supposed to do with them? They've made it crystal clear they're not going to surrender.'

'Technically, they've been dead for over seventy years.'

'Technically, they can torpedo us. They've already done it once.'

The captain appeared from behind the door, and addressed Agent Lenard, 'Are you ready? We set off immediately.' He nodded at two technicians behind his back, carrying metal cases with tools and packs with the protective gear.

Agent Lenard waved to Cartwright and Stefan. 'Wish me luck. Time to improvise.'

'Don't improvise too much.' Cartwright snorted. 'Your improvisation may cost us all dearly.'

Agent Lenard nodded Stefan goodbye and followed the technicians with the captain.

Chapter Forty-Eight

Zara

Zara knew he should be there. Yet, when she saw Stefan, surrounded by the officers and agents, an invisible band squeezed her heart. His eyes were full of sorrow, fear, and pain. All colour drained from his face. For a second, it seemed to her she was herself again, but she kept on saying what Engel wanted her to say. She kept on feeling aggression, the condemnation, the suspicion, and anxiety he felt.

She pushed the gun harder against her head. 'I know your people well, Agent. That's why I give you a chance to choose. Zara or Die Fledermaus. I know you'll make a wise choice.' She put the gun down. A thick mist blurred her vision for a moment. She knew they'd make a wise choice. Why did she say that? She'd heard them somewhere already, words not her own.

Her father's face appeared from the milky mist around her. 'There're unlimited variants of possible futures. I know you'll make a wise choice.'

'I am Germania, and where I go is Germania.' Engel's words vibrated in her ears.

'Germania must be destroyed at any cost. It's the only way to redemption for all of us.' She raised her eyes and, instead of Engel, the Chief's face appeared in front of her. 'Germania and Engel, they're parts of black matter. Engel is the consciousness of black matter. Another reason why Der Meister wants to get to Engel.'

'Herr Kaleun?' The Chief stared at her, perplexed. 'I didn't really catch-'

'Germania, Chief. It's a trap. A trap for me, for you, for the crew, for all of us.' Her lips trembled. Her eyes were burning with tears. 'Germania is a prison. The only redemption is destruction.'

'So, there's no hope for us? No home, no life, nothing?' the Chief faltered.

'You and the crew can remain here in this lifeline. Sooner or later, Engel will find a way to get to you. Germania or twenty-first century Germany? Engel will find you and take his revenge.'

'This lifeline isn't an option.' He shook his head. 'At least, not for me. Judging by the number of volunteers ready to go aboard the British boat, it's not an option for the rest of the crew either.'

'There're unlimited variants of possible futures. Fight Germania and destroy it, Chief. You have the weapon to do it. The amount of black matter aboard is enough to create another lifeline and to shift black matter from Germania. We still have some time before the British arrive to help you with the engine. It should be enough for me to reset the machine. You…' She squeezed his shoulder. 'I know you'll figure out the rest. You'll know what to do when you see the chamber and the core.'

He stared at her for a second. 'Aye, Herr Kaleun.' Then he added quietly, 'I have no choice but to trust you. Whoever you are, I hope you're right.'

Zara exhaled. 'It was you there, in the tunnel. Right? Why did you run from me?'

He bowed his head. 'Yes, I remember you there. A part of me remembers you. I didn't know what was going on. I was confused. So I ran.'

'Then I can trust you, Chief.' She nodded.

'I hope you understand, Captain. I need some guarantees before I'll send my engineers aboard your vessel to help you with the batteries,' Captain Barrows's voice interrupted them.

'Of course.' She turned away from the Chief.

Chapter Forty-Nine

Stefan

Half an hour later, Zara climbed aboard HMS Aurora, accompanied by the cook and one of the petty officers. Captain Barrows, Cartwright, Stefan, and two armed security guards had been awaiting them.

'Captain Barrows? Nice to meet you.' Zara beamed, stretching her gloved hand for a handshake.

The man only nodded, touching her hand slightly, but Zara squeezed it so hard that his face went pale. He bit his thin lips but said nothing.

'Ah, Cartwright.' Zara turned to the agent. 'What an unexpected place to meet you!'

'Morning, Captain,' Cartwright replied, her voice cold and official.

'Please, take care of my men.' Zara nodded to her two crewmembers. 'They're unarmed and well-behaved.'

'Do you speak English?' one of the security officers asked the cook.

'Yes, sir. A bit.'

'Come with us, lads.' The older officer made an inviting gesture, opening the hatch and descending the ladder first.

Zara glanced at Stefan, but he avoided eye contact. His chest was burning with the aching pain.

'Please, follow me.' Captain Barrows broke the pause first. He gestured to the hatch, and one by one, the company disappeared inside. 'I insist on you staying in my quarters until I receive a message from my crewmen and Agent Lenard,

263

confirming they're ready to set off,' the captain continued when they reached the second level and he opened the door to let the company in.

'I wish to have a word with Dr Krause tête-à-tête,' Zara replied.

Stefan nodded. 'Please, Captain, excuse us for a few minutes.'

Captain Barrows shifted his gaze from Zara to Stefan and back. 'The room is yours.'

The heavy door shut behind the two, leaving Stefan and Zara alone.

She made a wide circle around the compartment. All her movements looked abrupt and neurotic.

Whoever it was, it wasn't Zara anymore.

'Finally. We're alone. No Zara between us,' she started. Her voice sounded deep and alien. 'Finally, I see you clearly. Zara's perception doesn't overshadow mine. Her psyche is so strong. She's almost kicked me out a couple of times when we were aboard the U-boat. Just a few seconds of a complete blackout. Oh, she is much stronger than I imagined.' She grinned, coming closer and touching his shoulder.

This grin, this voice, these icy hands. He could feel their coldness even through his thick coat.

'I hope I didn't disappoint you.' He smirked, taking a step back. 'Where's Zara? Can I talk to her? How are you going to return her?'

'I've told you already. It's complicated. I've taken her to Germania.' She squinted.

'Germania?' Stefan chuckled. 'You can't be more pathetic, can you? So, what exactly is your interpretation of Hitler's city of the world?'

'It's my place. Nice and cosy. It has nothing to do with the Führer. It's all mine. Zara enjoyed her visit there.' She shrugged.

'How do you travel to and from this place, this so-called Germania, without Die Fledermaus? Why do you need Zara's body? You have your boat and the device now. Why not take them and leave Zara and us alone?'

'It's far more complicated than you believe. Do you think a few pages of the U-4713/A manual and the memoirs of some demented old sailor explain black matter in all its details?'

Stefan didn't reply. The unbearable pain in his chest was growing every second.

'I don't need Die Fledermaus to travel to or from Germania. Black matter is Germania, and I am a part of it,' she continued with a broad smile.

'Are you saying…?' He struggled to speak. A dry cough scratched his throat. 'Black matter is-'

She approached him again and didn't let him finish. 'What does she see in you? I can't get it.' Her hand squeezed his head. 'She's ready to die for you, you know.'

'Leave her and take me instead. I'm ready to-'

'No, no, no.' She interrupted him, pressing her long finger to his lips. 'The correct question should be: are you ready to live for her?'

Her eyes filled with tears, and he could feel her warm breath on his face.

'Zara? Are you back?' he whispered, trying to catch a familiar expression on her face.

'It's not that simple.' A mocking grin distorted her soft features again.

Stefan pushed her away. 'Then stop touching me, you freak.' The room was spinning around him, and he grabbed the back of a chair to keep his balance. 'Play your sick games with Josef Landau-Stromm or his brother, Gerhard, or any other insane bastard, but don't touch me.' He released a heavy sigh and continued, 'Tell the truth. Fire it out! You poisoned Captain Erlich to take over his place, to get to the U-boat and the device. What else? You betrayed your crew, sending the men directly to an American destroyer. Your perverted, corrupted mind is fucked up. You should've faced a firing squad together with your best friends, the Stromms.' He stopped out of breath, the unbearable burning pain squeezing his lungs.

'Bullshit!' Zara screamed. 'It was Josef who poisoned Captain Erlich, not me. Everything else, including my close friendship with the Stromms, is nothing but rumour.' She fell silent, staring at him, before coming close again. 'I wish I could kill you, but it will kill Zara, and we'll die together.'

'So, why are you torturing her? Why are you torturing both of us?'

She grabbed his shoulders, body shivering in fever, lips trembling. Her hand ran up to his neck, then face, messing his hair, caressing it on the back of his neck. 'Prove to me why I shouldn't kill you. Let me know how much you love her, and how much you want to live for her. Her feelings towards you, her emotions – they're out of my way. It's only between me and you now.'

Stefan jerked, but couldn't get rid of her deadly grip.

Her hands squeezed his head. He yelled, but her body squashed him to the wall.

'Just a kiss. You can't resist her kiss, can you?' Her lips were almost touching his. 'Just a kiss. Is it too much?'

The pain was ripping Stefan's chest apart. His watering eyes made his spectacles slide. His breath wheezed, and his knees gave up, but Zara didn't lose her grip.

Their lips finally met, and time froze. The entire world stopped. Her delicate lips, just as he remembered them, poured into him all sorrow, solitude, pain, fear, despair – the whole universe, unbearable and alien.

'That's it.' She let him go. 'That's all that matters. Now, I know it all. All emotions, all feelings, everything.' Her arms dropped. She took a step back and stared into space without movement.

He swayed on his weak legs but kept his balance. He reached into his pocket for an inhaler.

The next moment, the whole submarine vibrated, and dull thuds from the outside ripped the silence. The voices of the chief officer, Cartwright, and Captain Barrows sounded from the corridor. The loud howl of a siren sounded all over the submarine. The communicator on the captain's desk buzzed, and the light dimmed in the compartment.

'What's going on?' Stefan mumbled under his breath.

'Ah, the nuclear reactor is overheating.' Zara grinned. 'It seems like it can't bear my presence aboard.'

'What the hell is-?' Stefan dropped his inhaler.

Zara didn't reply. The mocking grin vanished from her face. She looked terrified.

She squeezed her head with her hands. Her mouth produced a long, infernal scream. 'Germania. It's destroyed,' she yelled. Her face expressed nothing but fear and pain. 'They've tricked me. Zara has tricked me. Germania is dying.' She kept on howling and roaring, circling the room.

The door swung open. Cartwright and a soaking wet Agent Lenard stood on the doorstep. Agent Lenard's gun pointed at Zara's head.

'Your crew has escaped together with the device. Now, stop messing with the reactor and give us back Miss Rose as promised,' he shouted.

'Nobody promised you the device,' Zara groaned. 'As for the crew, they've tricked both of us. Now, Germania and I, we're dying.'

'What? Germania? What is it all about?' Agent Lenard frowned. 'I don't have time for this shit. I just managed to escape minutes before your bloody U-boat vanished into thin air, taking our engineers with her. Hands up! You're under arrest.'

Zara turned to Stefan. 'I can't live without Germania and Zara. Zara can't live without me. We're all connected. Nothing can't break this link.'

A lightning-fast strike…

'Ah!' A shot of sharp pain pierced Stefan's stomach.

A thin naval dagger stuck out of his belly. His visions blurred. Cartwright's scream echoed in his ears. Three gunshots made his ears ring. Through the thick veil of his fading consciousness, he saw Zara sliding to the floor. An ominous stain turned her white uniform jumper into a mess.

'Zara, no…' He reached out his hand to her, but only the deaf darkness replied.

Chapter Fifty

Agent Cartwright

'Are you mad?' Cartwright yelled as the heavy door of the captain's quarters slammed closed behind her back.

Agent Lenard sat at the captain's desk in front of her. His head was squeezed between his hands, his eyes hollow, his wet clothes still dripping water.

'Ian, Zara is in critical condition,' she continued. 'What have you done?'

'It was necessary to stop her. She's stabbed Dr Krause. You and I would've been next. Then she would've gone for Captain Barrows, his crew, and the reactor. It's a miracle the engineers managed to stabilise it. From a victim, she's turned into a criminal. I needed to stop her.' Agent Lenard shook his head. His eyes fixed on the bloody stains on the room's wall and the floor – the gory reminder of what had happened half an hour ago.

The next moment, the heavy door swung open, and Captain Barrows appeared on the doorstep.

'My men. Where are they?' He banged his fist on the desk. 'Damn! The U-boat? She's gone. What happened there?'

Agent Lenard shot an anxious look at the captain, then Cartwright. 'This information is classified.'

'Classified my ass, Agent!' Captain Barrows exploded. 'My engineers have vanished. You've shot a civilian aboard my sub. The reactor and communication system went out of control. I think I'm entitled to some explanation.'

'We arrived and met the Chief Engineer and two other crewmembers. The Chief was in charge. Our two technicians went with his men to examine the batteries. I wanted to follow, but he protested, saying they understand English well enough to communicate,' Agent started through gritted teeth.

'He didn't want you to be around.' Cartwright nodded.

'Everything happened so quickly.' The agent's eyes stared into space without a blink. 'As soon as the engine's tanks were filled up, the Chief ordered me out. He took my gun. I had no choice. I saw it. I saw Die Fledermaus. It was there, in the engine room, connected to the batteries. It looked similar to the one you described in your report, but twice as large. I couldn't detach it from the batteries quickly enough. I didn't have time, and the compartment was full of Germans. Then, the Chief took me outside, returned my empty gun, and pushed me overboard. He had so many chances to shoot me, but he didn't. He spared me. Why? I have no idea. The U-boat vanished, dazzling me in bright white light. I battled the icy waves. You saw it from the conning tower.'

'Their crewmen. They're still here. Didn't they intend to return for them?' Captain Barrows frowned.

'The Chief said it was their choice. They've volunteered to stay with us.' Agent Lenard shrugged. 'In a way, he saved their lives.'

'I need to talk to these little Nazis.' The Captain turned to the door, ready to leave. 'They may shed some light on the U-boat's location.'

Cartwright rolled her eyes. 'Please, Captain, leave the kids alone. Don't make them the scapegoats. I tried to talk to them. Shock and confusion made them forget not only English but their mother tongue, too. They just sat there in stubborn silence. I don't think they know more about the device than we do.'

'Well, if your charm didn't work...' Agent Lenard smirked. 'We'll send them to Germany and let German intelligence deal with it.'

Captain Barrows wanted to say something, but the door opened and Chief Officer O'Neal entered the compartment. 'The air ambulance has arrived, Sir.'

'I'm going with Zara and Stefan.' Cartwright nodded to Agent Lenard.

He leaned back in his chair and closed his eyes.

Chapter Fifty-One

Agent Cartwright

Inverness, Scotland
Two weeks later

Cartwright sat at the table in the café across the road from Inverness train station, watching people walk past. Her gaze travelled across the street to where a crowd of passengers left the station's main exit, dispersing in all directions. She sipped her lukewarm coffee slowly and glanced at her watch: half-past eleven. He'd be there any minute.

The message from Agent Lenard, expressing his wish to join her in Inverness, had taken her by surprise. They hadn't seen each other since their failed mission. He'd remained aboard with the two German crewmembers before receiving a lift to Inverness by a military helicopter. Cartwright had accompanied a badly wounded Stefan and Zara in the air ambulance. Shortly after, she'd urgently returned to London and hadn't had a chance to talk to him in private.

Maybe he wanted to apologise. She smirked. Perhaps it was a new MI5 trick. She owed apologies to Zara and Stefan for dragging them into the investigation.

'Good morning,' his familiar voice made her turn around.

'Morning, morning,' she mumbled, gesturing Agent Lenard to the seat in front of her. 'A cup of tea or coffee? I bet it was a long way from London by train,' she continued. 'I wonder why you wanted to join me. I thought you'd prefer to fly here and-'

He waved, taking off his jacket and gloves, making himself

comfortable. 'I've been demoted. I have more free time now.'

'I heard.'

'On my request.' He sighed. 'You were right. I lost my patience and self-control. Three bullets. God! I fired three bullets when it wasn't necessary. A quiet office position is the only option for me now. Perhaps I'm too old for field operations.'

Cartwright poured more coffee into her mug from a glass jug. 'So… what exactly happened aboard the U-boat?' She squinted. His cold eyes remained hollow. 'I've known you long enough. You've been in far more dangerous places, yet…' she continued. 'The story you told aboard Aurora can be sufficient for Captain Barrows or even your MI5 bosses, but not for me.'

'My missions took me from the Middle East to Africa, but I've never experienced anything like that.' He exhaled. 'Time… It seemed to fluctuate. Everything happened too quickly. Time aboard the U-boat passed differently. I don't know how to explain it-'

'Time fluctuated? Time doesn't exist. At least, according to Stefan, it's as elusive as reality.'

'Stefan? How is he?'

'I haven't seen him yet. We talked over the phone, but he's doing exceptionally well, although still weak. He was only released from the hospital yesterday, but he wanted to wait for Zara and accompany her to Winchester.'

'Do you believe in his theory?'

'I don't know.' Cartwright shrugged. 'I'm even starting to doubt that I'm real now. Captain Engel is the key figure here, not Die Fledermaus. He's corrupted time somehow.'

'Who was he? Was he human? Was he real at all? Where did he come from? Where did he go? Did he die together with this so-called Germania? Did the U-boat "jump" there?'

'Whoever or whatever he is, the only person who can shed light on his identity is Zara. She should know what was going on in his mind and his motivation.' She rose from the table, taking her jacket off the hanger. 'Let's try to get at least some ideas about what's happened to him and all of us.'

They left the café, heading to Cartwright's car, parked around the corner.

'What about the two crewmen? The boys from the U-boat?' she asked.

'We've sent them to Germany.' She shrugged. 'They'll receive new identities with corrected dates of birth, "legends" about their lives, help from psychologists, and have a fresh start in new Germany.'

'I feel sorry for them. How old are they? Eighteen and twenty? God! Just kids, smashed by the war.' He pointed at the fancy bag Cartwright was holding. 'What's that?'

'Ah, some goodies for Zara to cheer her up.'

'Ha! Since when did you become Ms Nicey-Nicey?' He chuckled. Cartwright ignored his comment.

They left the busy city centre and drove to Raigmore Hospital. The reception desk was empty and the often too busy waiting area was deserted. Cartwright pressed a buzzer on the desk.

A minute later, the receptionist appeared from behind the "Staff Only" door. His soggy face squeezed into a polite smile. 'Good afternoon. How can I help you?'

'Afternoon. We'd like to see one of your patients, Miss Zara Rose.' Cartwright waved her ID in front of the man. 'She was transferred here yesterday from the intensive care unit.'

'Zara Rose?' The receptionist frowned. 'I'm sorry, Officer, it must be a mistake. We don't have anybody called Zara Rose.'

'Are you sure? Can you double-check your database?' Agent Lenard broke into the conversation.

'I'm pretty sure. It was my shift yesterday.' The man nodded. 'I'll double-check for you, of course, but…' He unlocked the computer screen and input the details. 'The database reads, Miss Rose was discharged from our ward yesterday at… erm…

seven twenty in the evening.' The receptionist frowned. Blood drained from his face. 'It's impossible…' he faltered.

Agent Lenard frowned. 'Why?'

'I… I don't understand.' Deep shock reflected in the receptionist's eyes. 'It was my shift, but I don't remember recording this patient on the database. I don't remember discharging Miss Rose. She wasn't… she didn't-'

'Okay, okay.' Cartwright made a calming gesture. 'Are there any comments about Miss Rose's condition? Why was she discharged so quickly?'

'The discharge is requested by the NCA. Authorised: Head of Security,' he read aloud.

Cartwright's legs weakened. 'What?'

Agent Lenard shifted his gaze from Cartwright to the receptionist and back. 'Do you have access to the CCTV cameras on these premises?' he asked.

'Yes, of course,' the receptionist mumbled, voice trembling. 'I don't understand. I was here the entire shift…'

Agent Lenard clenched his fists, waiting for the CCTV camera's feed to load.

Cartwright put her hand on his shoulder.

'Do you want to come here and have a look?' The receptionist rose from his desk, gesturing them to come closer.

'What's the hell is going on?' Agent Lenard stared at the screen.

Nineteen minutes past seven. The camera feed showed an empty reception. Twenty minutes past seven. The screen went dark.

'Damn!' Agent Lenard turned from the monitor.

'I don't understand,' the receptionist whispered. 'The camera went offline. It errored out or something… but it worked fine yesterday. I don't-'

'Thank you for your assistance.' Cartwright smiled politely. 'I hope you understand the nature of our conversation. I ask you not to disclose our visit to anybody, including your superiors. We'll contact them directly if required.' She turned to a still shocked Agent Lenard, gesturing to a pair of empty chairs in the corner. 'Let's take a seat.'

'Don't you want to talk to the head of security?' He followed her to the corner.

She sunk into the soft chair. 'He's outplayed us. Can't you see?'

Agent Lenard didn't say a word. Cartwright pulled her phone out of her pocket and dialled a number.

'What are you doing?'

'Calling our last hope.' She put the phone on the loudspeaker.

A robotic voice replied with a recorded phrase in German.

'The number you're calling does not exist,' Agent Lenard repeated in English.

Cartwright squeezed his shoulder. 'There're no Zara and Stefan here anymore.'

Chapter Fifty-Two

Captain Engel

A burning pain was rising from his punctured abdomen and the bullet wound. He was unused to a physical pain, a long-forgotten sensation. Now, it drove him mad. He shot a glance at his shaking hands. His every step and breath caused him more pain. Legs weak and entire body fragile, he knew he couldn't stop. Not now.

His world, Germania, was collapsing on itself. Black matter was devouring its creations, plunging the city into chaos, its citizens decomposing into black, lifeless shadows. The city's straight, wide avenues, its elaborate buildings, its heavy traffic, all turned into meaningless, primordial non-existence. A larger, much stronger, more stable lifeline morphed into existence next to it. Like a newborn star in a galaxy, it was absorbing Germania and all smaller lifelines around it. The enormous scale of fresh black matter was splitting his world apart, pulling Germania's debris into its churning core.

He raised his head, watching the dome of the crumbling Volkshalle collapse in on its raw carcass.

As he entered the hall, black orbs of dark matter the size of tennis balls surrounded him. The core was collapsing. He shook his head, scared to glance at the ceiling.

In the middle of the hall, amongst the wreckage, shattered glass, and destroyed statues, the enormous eagle from the dome's top laid lopsided, but still undefeated. Engel took a few steps closer. The eagle's wide wings spread in an awkward refusal of death, as if the giant bird sought to protect something.

Two hospital beds with Stefan and Zara's motionless bodies.

Engel took a seat on the bed's edge, staring at Stefan. 'Sorry, I stabbed you, but it was the only way to trick your psyche and bring you here.' He sighed after a reflective pause. 'Die Fledermaus has destroyed Germania, but nothing can destroy us. There's still hope. As long as my consciousness is alive, we're alive, and so is black matter.'

He touched his lips and pressed his fingers to Stefan's. 'Just returned your kiss, but please, don't judge me. I know what you'd say, but it's not what you think. It's not that everybody thinks. We're connected now, all three of us: you, Zara, and I. I'll be reborn again. Through eternal pain to rebirth. I've done it once and I'll do it again.'

He rose and circled the second bed, shaking his head. 'Zara, Zara. She's beaten me at my own game. She and this fucking Chief Engineer Hoff. I was wrong, saying she wasn't strong enough to control black matter. Oh, no! She's much stronger than I am. I don't hate her, though. How can I hate her if she's a part of me now? I'll find her, wherever she is.'

Coming close again, he took Stefan's hands in his. The giant eagle swayed, and one of its wings cracked, dissipating into thousands of black orbs.

'Our time is up here.' Engel smiled to himself, pulling a glass cylinder from a hidden pocket.

A tiny black dot fluctuated in a glowing liquid inside.

'Professor Milne wasn't a useless fool, after all.' Engel squinted and turned the device on.

Chapter Fifty-Three

Zara

Zara didn't recognise her surroundings. She had awoken in a lifeless, sorrowful valley, devoid of trees and vegetation. The dull-grey plateau stretched in all directions, joining an ancient cloudless sky on the low horizon.

There was no wind in the unmoving atmosphere, and Zara felt neither warm nor cold. Only a whitish veil of thick fog crawled over the rocks where she perched, indicated the environment wasn't in a vacuum.

What was this place? She thought, attempted to rise on her elbow, but a sharp pain in her stomach stopped her. She still wore the same white uniform jumper she had aboard the submarine. Agent Lenard's gunshots. She stared at her bandaged belly in disbelief. After another attempt, she managed to take a seat, leaning back on the rock.

How had she ended up here? Another lifeline or a transition zone? Her eyes scanned the unfamiliar horizon. There were no movements or signs of life whatsoever. Just an empty, desolate universe. It reminded her of surrealism of Dali or De Chirico paintings. A lonely, unsettling, and deeply disturbing world.

A loud humming sounded from behind the rocks, interrupting the calm air. A creature emerged, no more than four or five feet tall. moving on long sinuous legs, its sharp spine and a gaunt ribcage protruding through the pale grey skin. It darted about, leaving a long black trail of fog in its wake.

Zara flattened to the rock, trying not to make a sound, but the creature's huge black eyes studied her. As it probed, the humming intensified. The creature's pale, hairless body reminded Zara of figures in the pods from one of her visions.

The creature sniffed the air, taking a step closer to her. Its flat nose released a high-pitched whistle.

Another much smaller yet identical creature appeared from behind the nearest rock, leaving a similar black trail as it ambled along. The creatures grew uninterested in Zara, instead circling the nearby stones, to scrap and eat brownish fungus from the rough surface.

Despite their enormous eyes, she realised they must be blind. They relied on their sense of smell, taste, and hearing. The pair continued to hum, whistle, and quack before losing their interest in her.

Overcoming the gnawing pain in her stomach, Zara pulled herself to her feet to better observe her surroundings. Her rocky shelter occupied a low hill, and below she could see the foggy valley stretching as far as her eyes could see.

'Beeil dich! Schneller! Schneller!' A booming male voice sounded from behind the rocks, followed by a group of helmeted soldiers in SS uniform. They scrambled up the hill, leaving dark trails behind them. As the first soldier reached the top, they opened fire on the creatures.

The larger of the two creatures galloped past Zara, carrying the smaller on its back, screaming in horror. Bullets whistled all around them, kicking up dust and debris, until the adult creature rolled down the hill, dragging the already dead body of its child with it.

'Hey, hey! Stop! Please…' Zara ran towards the soldiers. They all looked the same. Not only their uniform and guns, their height, their pale faces, their eyes shining from under the helmets and reflecting nothing. Each an uncanny double of the last, identical to the averaged World War Two-era German soldier.

'Miss Rose.' One soldier bowed, greeting her in English. 'We mean you no harm. We were sent here to protect you. How do you feel? Can you walk?'

'Well, yes. I guess I can walk, but where?' Zara instinctively pressed her hand to her stomach. 'Why did you kill the creatures? They didn't-'

'We have strict orders, Miss Rose. Please, come with us. You can lean on my arm. You're still too weak.' He stretched out a gloved hand.

Zara frowned, glancing at the soldiers. 'Where're you taking me?'

'To Der Meister. He's waiting for you.'

With a blink, the ground slipped from under her feet and she grasped at the soldier's sleeve. As she opened her eyes, the desert, the rocks, and hills lay far behind them. They stood on a sheer cliff, jetting out over the black primordial mass of an ancient ocean. Its thick and oily waves attacked the cliff but produced no sound.

A dozen feet above the cliff, a long polyhedral structure hung suspended in the air. Its gleaming black sides and sharp corners reminded Zara of an obsidian shard.

Was it some kind of craft?

Before she could ask her guard, the side of the structure melted, revealing a void-like entrance. An invisible force swallowed the group and her along with it.

Zara stood in the silent darkness, her eyes adjusting to distinguish shadows around her.

She stood in a long hall, absent of pods, wires, and pipes. There was no machinery this time. The hall seemed empty, except for a sinister light, radiated from underfoot. Zara squinted through the dim, unable to see in the dark corners or the very end of the hall. Carvings covered the walls, reminiscent of Germanic runes and ancient symbols. As she walked, they moved imperceptibly, expanding, and shrinking as if the hall themselves breathed. Were these carvings or veins and blood vessels of some slumbering giant?

'Finally, Zara. We've met again.' A familiarly accented voice echoed around her. 'Welcome, my darling. Now, it all makes sense to you, doesn't it?'

A few paces behind her, leaning back in his massive wooden chair, sat Der Meister. He had changed his SS tunic and cap for a more traditional three-piece suit. Zara squinted through the haze, without blinking, able to distinguish his features.

Stromm looked more like an office clerk than a ghost from another dimension. He was about Zara's height, with stubborn features with short, tidy grey hair. Yet, something in his look was unsettling, something deeply horrifying. The figure in the chair looked flat somehow, as if unable to reflect the light. He rather absorbed it, as if his body was unbound to three dimensions.

'Dr Stromm? Why am I here? What happened to me? Where's Stefan?' she asked, surprised at how her voice trailed off all along the hall.

'The fall of Germania and your injury made your psyche more vulnerable. I've traced it and brought you here before Engel could reach you.' He grinned, a dazzling and eerie smile, just as she remembered it. 'Please, take a seat. You're still weak after such a wound and such a long journey.' He nodded to a chair, which materialised into existence behind her. 'Now, after the destruction of Germania, Engel found a new host.'

'I don't understand.' Zara slowly took a seat, the chair almost swallowing her with the softness of its cushion and armrests. 'Engel should've died together with Germania. Engel is Germania.'

Stromm shook his head. Their entire conversation had a slow, dreamlike pace. He spoke faster than his lips could move. 'Engel is black matter; the representation of its consciousness. The more he experiences, the more powerful the black matter becomes. It learns, it adapts, possesses, and grows stronger.

It feeds on emotions and feelings, and so does Engel. Your assumptions about it were correct. However…' His long finger pointed somewhere to the ceiling. 'You didn't take one thing into consideration, Zara.'

'And what is it?'

'Engel is a liar. He lied to you about Professor Milne and Die Fledermaus. Now, Engel has his new body and the salvaged device. The only thing missing is you.'

'You wanted me to bring Engel here. Why do you need him when Germania is destroyed?'

He rose from his chair; a long black trail following his abrupt movements.

'Engel is a traitor. He failed our mission.' Stromm paused, shoulders dropping as if distressed by her words. 'He's my creation, so to speak. A creation, who outplayed and ultimately turned against me. The boy needs to learn a bitter lesson.'

'Why do you need him in your lifeline or transition zone?' Zara asked.

He stopped in front of the wall where a high, narrow void opened. 'Transition zone? Hmm… You could name this place as such, I suppose.' He gestured to the void. 'Please, come closer.'

Zara took a couple of steps closer before realising that it was a window. She could see the dark ocean of black matter below, carrying its glossy waves far beyond the low horizon.

'All lifelines are different. Each has a different lifespan.' Stromm broke a prolonged pause. 'Some are more or less static, others are constantly changing. Some live longer and die slower; others simply explode, giving birth to new ones. This place is devolving, decomposing, degenerating in its slow, agonising death.'

'Devolving?' Zara shifted her eyes from Stromm to the ocean and back. 'The creatures I saw in the desert? The creatures in the pods? Were they similar to us?'

He shrugged. 'In a way.'

'Your guards killed it and its baby,' Zara snapped. 'Maybe the creatures are devolving, but they mean no harm.'

'Please, don't tell my guards the truth. It would be rather distressing.' He made a warning gesture, voice mocking. 'They've witnessed enough upsetting events here.'

'Distressing? Your guards aren't even real.'

Stromm turned away from the window and approached Zara. The black mist trailing him almost engulfed her.

'I thought you might've excluded words like "time" and "reality" from your vocabulary by now,' he said. 'Are you sure we're real? Are we real to each other?'

Zara stared outside, voiceless. The pulsating black mass of the ocean mesmerising her. She was unable to take her eyes off it. The vibrating waves made her head spin. She swallowed a bout of nausea.

'This is… Oh, God! The entire ocean of black matter. Right here.' She exhaled. 'Wild, primordial black matter without a core. I wonder how many lifelines it's able to destroy or create.'

'Countless. However, I'm uninterested in the destruction of other lifelines,' Stromm said. 'Engel will help me restructure this place and stop it from dying. Together, we'll create another, bigger, greater Germania.'

'Hah! Tell me at least one reason I should help you.' Zara smirked. 'You're a Nazi, an SS officer who killed dozens of people, experimenting with black matter during the war. Even now, your inventions continue to kill people. Why should I help a man like you?'

'Zara, Zara…' Stromm shook his head. 'I'm a scientist. Nothing more. A scientist who sacrificed everything for science, even myself. Significant discoveries require great sacrifices. Something you're intimately familiar with.'

'Am I?'

'The two divers, Ivor and Pete. Don't you remember how easily you put them in danger attempting to reach the U-boat?' The oceanic voids of his eyes captivated her, the pain in her wounded stomach intensifying. 'What about your colleague, Professor Milne? He was ready to sacrifice everything, including you and his son, for the sake of science.'

How could he know all of that? She recalled her encounter with Stromm's interdimensional spy, killed by Engel. They were everywhere.

'I didn't know I put the divers in danger. As for Milne, he wanted to see his daughter,' she snapped.

'To sacrifice his living son for a chance to reincarnate his dead daughter? Hm…' Dr Stromm rubbed his narrow chin. 'And you're saying that my actions make no sense to you?'

Zara remained silent; her nausea growing along with the pain in her belly, sapped her strength to protest.

'Anyway.' Dr Stromm waved. 'You and I are similar in our desire to know the truth about things, whether they belong to history or physics. We share the same goal. I need to find Engel and bring him here. You need to find him to recover Dr Krause.'

A bright beam of light emerged from the ceiling, illuminating a transparent cube in the centre of the hall. There, suspended in the air, Stefan's body materialised.

'Stefan?' Zara cried, shifting her eyes from the cube to Dr Stromm and back.

Stefan's pale body looked like a broken doll dressed in a hospital gown, his eyes closed.

Zara turned to Dr Stromm. 'What does it mean? Where is he?'

'If only I knew.' He shrugged. 'He's hosting Engel's psyche now. And as we both know; Engel is a madman. Having the device and Stefan's body, he can travel in and out of your lifeline. You're linked to him. You can track him down. Bring him here, and I'll release you and Dr Krause from Engel. You know the coordinates of this place. They're stored in your subconsciousness.'

'How are you going to do it without killing all three of us?'

'Oh, you underestimate me, dear.' Dr Stromm smiled, lips stretching in a monstrous grin. 'Die Fledermaus isn't my only invention.'

Stefan's body disappeared, the cube flickering empty, but the ceiling began to move. A long, thin tentacle stretched from the ceiling to the cube, slithering across the top and sides, as if attempting to swallow it. The air inside turned to a greyish fog. A black excrescence bulged from the cube's ceiling, forming into a pulsating sack.

'I call it the black matter infuser.' Dr Stromm gestured to the cube. 'I started my work on it at the same time as the first Die Fledermaus, but I needed to abandon it, following orders from the High Command. Project Der Obsidianturm: Obsidian Tower. Sounds good, doesn't it?'

Zara smirked. 'The Nazi scientists were masters of poetic names. What does it do?'

'Originally, it could infuse black matter. But now, it can extract black matter as well.' He gestured out the window. 'How do you think I gathered so much black matter in one place without ripping it to pieces? I've harvested it all over the universe.'

Zara pressed a hand to her burning belly. She grabbed the back of the chair, head spinning, trying to keep her balance.

'This is it. That's what happened to Ivor Kazinski. Then, you drown him. Right?'

'I couldn't afford to let Engel reach him first. I acted fast, but not fast enough. Engel got you and now Dr Krause.'

Zara closed her eyes for a second, overcoming another powerful spasm. The vision of the tunnel emerged in front of her closed eyes.

'Pain and rebirth.' Dr Stromm's words reverberated in her ears, and again she saw the body slipping out of the sack on the concrete floor.

Then another, even more powerful, vision returned. The control room of the U-boat. The loud explosions of depth charges and shouting of the surrounding men.

'Of course. Superimposition of time and reality. Again. Engel had died long before he reached Bergen.' She exhaled. 'He'd been infused with black matter before U-713 made her last journey. I saw it in the tunnel. Then, Die Fledermaus ripped the two layers of his reality apart, sending him to Germania.'

'Engel was almost dead. My discovery was his only option for survival. I saved him, superimposed him on himself. Yes, the process of infusion can be controlled. However, something went terribly wrong after his second exposure to black matter. I didn't predict him to be so powerful after he left the lifeline completely in 1944. I wish I had more time to work on the Obsidian Tower, to understand better its influence on the human body and psyche, but all these morons in the High Command, the Führer and his cohort of idiots and parasites… They didn't see it this way.'

Zara backed down to the window. 'You were superimposed too. That's why the witnesses gave different testimonies about your death. The driver took you to an airdrome. The housekeeper saw you taking a cyanide pill. None of that has ever happened.'

The man's hand squeezed her shoulder. 'Your mind knows where to go. Find him and bring him here, and you'll be free.' Dr Stromm's eyes grew larger, turning into two consuming black vortices. 'Hurry, Zara, hurry. Normal matter in your body isn't able to withstand the speed of this place any longer. I have eternity to wait, but you don't have such luxury. Your wound. It can't wait too.'

The hall started to spin around her. The pain became unbearable.

'First, Professor Milne, and then Cartwright, after her, Engel.

Now you. I had enough of serving other people's needs. Why does everybody think that they can use me?' Zara mumbled.

'Maybe because you were too naïve, too trustful, and too scared, after all.' He shrugged. 'I'm not going to use you. I offer you a fair deal. Bring me Engel and return to your lifeline, free of him and black matter.'

She gritted her teeth through the tears burning her eyes.

'There're unlimited variants of possible futures. Remember it, Zara.' Her father's voice sounded in her ears. 'The only way out is to trust your psyche and black matter. The only way out is a fall.'

Zara took a few steps back to the window.

'Black matter is neither good nor evil. It is what you want it to be," the voice continued. 'Engel tamed it, made it his. So can you.'

Dr Stromm yelled, his voice reflected from the walls and ceiling, 'Don't even try to escape from me.'

Zara continued to back away.

'Zara!' He stretched out his arm.

Zara stepped on the edge of the low windowsill and turned to the black ocean below. Her only way out was to trust black matter.

Chapter Fifty-Four

Zara

No pain, no dazzling white light, no sound. Just bleak non-existence.

Zara found herself in an unfamiliar bedroom.

Beige curtains covered wide windows from the midday sun. A stained-glass chandelier gazed at her from the high ceiling. The pain in her belly reminded her of recent events. She rolled up her pyjama top to see if gunshot wound was still there.

'Oh, you're awake. Please, be careful, don't move too much.' Stefan appeared from another room. Warm eyes shining through a worried face. 'You're still too weak. I wonder why they allowed you to leave the hospital.' He took a seat on the bed next to her. 'How do you feel?'

She stared at him, studying his face.

'Are you okay?' He took her hands in his.

'Eh… I don't remember much. Everything happened like a nightmare,' she mumbled. 'I was in a desert with these bizarre-looking creatures, then… I don't remember when I was released from the hospital.'

'It was yesterday. I brought you here, to the hotel when they discharged me. Don't worry if you can't remember things. When Agent Lenard shot you, you hit your head on the metal floor. The doctors believe you might have a minor concussion that led to a short-term memory loss.' He adjusted pillows for her to sit. 'It's a temporary condition; your memory will return. It's a miracle you survived, but it looks like your wounds are healing well, and that's the main thing.'

'I stabbed you with a dagger. Where did I find it? I remember Cartwright and Captain Barrows took all my weapons away. Yet, the dagger appeared from nowhere. Like in Germania, I just imagined it and… Oh, I killed a boy on the U-boat. Jesus! What have I done?' She closed her eyes and covered her face with her hands.

'It wasn't you. Captain Engel did it.' He embraced her shoulders. 'I almost went insane worrying about you. You were kidnapped and put amongst those terrifying men. God! I can't imagine what you've been through.'

'I lost control over my body. I wasn't myself.' She rubbed her forehead in a fruitless attempt to pull her thoughts together. 'All I remember are just feelings. These men. I felt their fear, pain, confusion, hate, desperation. All those destructive thoughts and emotions.'

She grimaced as a blunt ache jabbed her stomach and she reclined back on her pillows. 'I can't imagine how huge the scars on my belly will be after they take off the bandages.'

'That's the last thing you need to worry about right now.' Stefan kissed her forehead. 'Please, try to relax. We can talk about it later when we return home.'

'Home? My home or yours?' She chuckled. 'Your home is too far in my current condition.'

'Our home, angel.' He smiled with warmth.

'You're such a dreamer.' She bowed. 'There was another man there. He was different,' she started again. 'Chief Engineer Günter Hoff. He reminded me of my father when he was younger. His sad eyes and furrowed brows. His appearance and mannerism brought me back to my dad.' She smiled. 'He pulled me out of Engel's grip. Trusted me and helped destroy Germania.'

'Germania? The place you told me about on the Aurora?'

Zara nodded. 'Engel and black matter, they're connected in some strange way. Black matter has a consciousness of some sort, his consciousness. Engel is black matter. The representation of its consciousness. The more he experienced, the more powerful the black matter became. It learns, adapts, possesses things and people, and grows stronger. It feeds on our emotions and feelings and so does Engel.' She stopped. 'Why am I saying it? Those aren't my words. It was… It was Der Meister. He told me that.' She squeezed his arm in panic. 'He was there. He brought me from the desert and showed-'

'Okay, angel. We can talk about all these things later. Now, you need to relax.' Stefan rose from the bed. 'Please, take your pills, and I leave you to rest.'

'No. No. Wait.' Zara didn't let him go, pressing him to sit back. 'He told me that…' She broke off again. 'Is it you?' Tears filled her eyes. 'Stefan, is it really you? Are we free of him? Are we finally free from Engel and black matter?'

'You told me that Germania was destroyed.' He shrugged. 'Engel died together with it.' He touched her cheek. 'After the air ambulance picked you up from HMS Aurora, you spent some time in the hospital. Everything else happened in your dreams. You've been kept unconscious for too long. It influenced your perception.'

She leaned back on her pillows and kept silent. Dreams. So vivid and yet so real? But what was "real"? She didn't even know what it meant now. She shot a look around. No desert, no deformed creatures, no foggy trails. Stefan's voice sounded natural. Had she returned to her lifeline?

'You look different.' She turned to Stefan.

'What do you mean? Is it because I'm wearing lenses today?' He chuckled.

'You look younger, perhaps. Your skin's glowing. It feels so smooth. Your stab wound? You recovered so quickly…'

'Ah, an old man like me should take it as a compliment.' He kissed her hand. 'Try to sleep. These pills they prescribed you in the hospital… They should help you to have a good, undisturbed sleep without dreams. I'm here with you if you need me.'

Zara took a pill from a tray on her bedside table, and Stefan poured water into her glass. She swallowed it in one gulp, closing her eyes. Stefan had kept his promise. There was only one viable future for her; a future with him. A thick slumber wrapped around her; all sounds muted, all thoughts slowing. Everything else was just a dream, a grotesque nightmare, which perished at the first light of a sunrise.

Chapter Fifty-Five

Stefan

Watching Zara doze in bed, Stefan left her alone, heading to the bathroom. He disrobed and stepped into the shower cubicle, peaceful under the hot water jets. The shower relaxed and rejuvenated his tired muscles. Taking care to avoiding the massive scar on his stomach as he gently cleaned his bruised body. Zara was right, he thought, glancing at the steamed-up mirror. His skin felt renewed in the dim glow of the bathroom light; he noticed the crow's feet in the corners of his eyes had disappeared. He no longer needed spectacles or lenses, and his body was slimmer as if he'd lost weight.

His lips stretched into a mocking smile. 'Not bad for an old man.' His words echoed all around his new world.

Author's Notes

–

Some of the characters, locations, and events used in this novel actually existed.

Admiral Karl Dönitz, Supreme Commander of the German Navy since 1943, played a major role in the naval history of World War II. During the Nuremberg trials in 1946, Dönitz was charged and convicted of war crimes and crimes against humanity and spent ten years in Spandau Prison. After his release, he lived near Hamburg until his death in 1980.

German submarine U-713 under command of Captain Henri Gosejacob went missing in February 1944 in the Norwegian Sea north-west of Narvik. Presumably, it must have been sunk with all hands lost by depth charges from the British destroyer HMS Keppel.

German submarine U-4713/A is a fictional creation.

Some descriptions of Germania in this book are based on the drawings and sketches of Berlin as envisioned by Hitler's favourite architect, Albert Speer.

Acknowledgements

–

I would like to thank my wonderful critique readers, whose constructive feedback made my novel shine. I also want to express my gratitude to Ted O'Connor for believing in my story and everybody at Northodox Press for working hard to make this story into a book.